D0464717

KNIFE EDGE

Books by Andrew Lane

The Young Sherlock Holmes series

Death Cloud
Red Leech
Black Ice
Fire Storm
Snake Bite
Knife Edge

www.youngsherlock.com

Lost Worlds

www.thelostworlds.co.uk

KNIFE EDGE

ANDREW LANE

MACMILLAN CHILDREN'S BOOKS

First published 2013 by Macmillan Children's Books
a division of Macmillan Publishers Limited
20 New Wharf Road, London N1 9RR
Basingstoke and Oxford
Associated companies throughout the world
www.panmacmillan.com

ISBN 978-0-230-75887-2 (HB)
ISBN 978-1-4472-4882-8 (TPB)

1 3 5 7 9 8 6 4 2

A CIP catalogue record for this book is available from
the British Library.

Printed and bound by CPI Group (UK) Ltd, Croydon CR0 4YY

*Dedicated to Gary Howell, Andrew Bird, Keith
Solder, Diana Gimber (now Diana Solder), Cliff
Shaeffer and Arlene Baxter (now Arlene Harvey),
friends in my teenage years and, thanks to Facebook,
still friends now. Where did those years go?*

*My thanks go to Polly Nolan, for yet another sensitive
but thorough editing job; to Pedro Albano, for the
(in his case unwitting) use of his wonderful name, and
to Andrew F. Gulli of the* Strand Magazine,
*for turning down one of the central ideas of the
book as a short story and thus allowing me to use
it in this novel, but then commissioning me
to write something else instead.*

CHAPTER ONE

Arms wrapped around the taut, sea-dampened ropes, the hemp fibres rough against his cheek, Sherlock Holmes watched from a position high up in the *Gloria Scott*'s rigging as the ship ploughed through the tumultuous ocean. Above him, seagulls cried like hungry babies. He could taste salt on his lips from the spray that filled the air. He'd lived with that taste for months now. He wondered what life would be like without it, without the constant pitching and tossing of the deck beneath his feet, without the regular *crack* of the sails suddenly filling with wind, without the constant shouts of the sailors and the orders barked by ship's First Mate, Mr Larchmont.

The sky above was grey and heavy with unshed rain. The sea was grey as well. For months he had been used to seeing blue skies above him during the day and black, star-splattered skies at night, of seeing jade waves sparkling like jewels all around the ship. But now everything seemed to have the vibrancy sucked out of it. The sky and the sea were both the colour of the smoke that poured out of factory chimneys in England's industrial areas.

He was nearly home.

Somewhere just over the horizon was the west coast of Ireland – the closest point to England that the ship was going to dock on this trip and the point at which he planned to get off and find his way home. He hadn't planned to leave England on the *Gloria Scott*, all that time ago. He had been ripped away from his family and friends, kidnapped and sedated and hidden away on the ship by a secretive organization known as the Paradol Chamber. He had crossed the Chamber by accident several times over the past two years, enough to make them want to get rid of him. Or perhaps they had done it because they wanted him to do some work for them in China, where the ship had been heading. Perhaps it was a bit of both. As far as he could tell, the Paradol Chamber never did anything for only one reason. They had plans nestled inside plans nestled inside yet more plans, like intricate clockwork mechanisms.

According to Mr Larchmont, the *Gloria Scott* would dock in Galway at the Spanish Arch and stay for a few days before heading to Antwerp. That was where the cargo that they had loaded in Shanghai would sell for the most money. Sherlock was going to disembark in Galway, take his pay like any regular member of the crew, and head across Ireland to Dublin. From there he could get a ferry to Liverpool, then travel down towards London on the train.

To what? That was the question he kept asking himself.

Back to Holmes Manor, in Hampshire? Back to his aunt and uncle as if he had never been away? Or maybe back to his close family, if his father had returned from India and his mother had recovered from her lingering illness. And what of his friends – would Matty still be there, or would he have set out along the canals for some other place where he could survive on his wits? Would Rufus Stone still be teaching violin and chasing girls in Farnham, or would Sherlock's brother, Mycroft, have sent him somewhere else to collect information for the British Government? What about Sherlock's teacher, Amyus Crowe? And what about Crowe's daughter Virginia?

His hand crept up to touch the outside of his shirt. Inside, in a leather pouch strung around his neck, folded up small, was the letter that Virginia had written to him, and given to brother Mycroft to pass on. He had read it on the quayside in Shanghai, and his world had caved in on him in a way that he wouldn't have believed possible.

Dear Sherlock,
This is the hardest letter that I have ever had to write, and probably the hardest letter that I ever will write. I attempted it so many times, and given up each time, but your brother is here visiting my father and he tells me that if I want this letter to get to you then this is my last

3

chance. I owe you some kind of explanation of what has happened, so here it is. I wish it were different.

You have been gone for a long time, and your brother tells me that you are likely not to return for a while — if you ever do return. I know the way your mind works, and I know that you like new and interesting things. I guess that going to China will show you lots of interesting things, and I wouldn't blame you for a moment if you decided to stay out there, in the Orient, and make a new life for yourself.

I may have been fooling myself, but I think that you and I had some kind of special connection, in that year we spent together. We certainly shared a lot of experiences. I felt about you in a way that I hadn't felt about anyone else in my life, and I could see from the way you looked at me that you felt the same way about me. The trouble is that time moves on. In your absence my father started tutoring the son of an American businessman who is living just outside Guildford. I met him one day, when he came to visit my father, and we ended up talking for hours. Since then we have been spending a lot of time together. He can ride as well, almost as well as I can. He's tall and thin, like you, but his hair is fairer and his skin tans easily. He makes me laugh. His name is Travis — Travis Stebbins.

The thing I need to tell you is that he has made it plain that he wants me to be his fiancée one day, and then later on to be his wife. For a while I just laughed it off, thinking he was infatuated with the first American girl he'd met in England and that he would soon find someone else. But that didn't happen, and I've started to realize how much I like him. I wouldn't be unhappy with him, and no, and waited for you to ome back, I might be waiting for a long time.

And what if you've met someone else while you're away? What would I do if I waited three years for you and then you arrived back with a Chinese wife?

I've asked my father what to do, but he won't give me any advice. He thinks a lot of you, and I know that he wishes you were here. I think that's one of the main reasons he stays in England — so that one day he can see you again, and take up teaching you where he left off. But he wants me to be happy, and safe, and I think that part of him yearns to be free of any responsibilities and able to ride off wherever he chooses, and camp out under the stars. He's not domesticated.

Neither are you, of course, and you never will be. That's probably the main difference between you and Travis — I can imagine him standing by a fireside, cradling a child in his arms, but I don't think that your future includes children, or domestic happiness. I hope you understand.

I still see Matty from time to time. He pops up out of nowhere, stays for a few hours, then he vanishes again. I think life in Farnham suits him — he's put on some weight since you left. Albert, his horse, died, ~~~ now — a big thing with shaggy fetlocks ~~~ one Harold. He (Matty, not Harold) keeps asking if I've heard from you.

Your brother says he will include my letter along with his, but what he will never tell you is that he misses you terribly. He is different now to the way he used to be — more restrained, more morose. Even Father has commented on it.

I wish there was more to tell you, but life continues pretty much the way it did before you left, with the major exception that you are not here. I wish you were. I wish things were different from the way they are, but life has put us on *different roads, and there's no turning around and going back.*

I have written enough. If I keep on writing then I will start to cry, and my tears will blot the words so much that you won't be able to read them. Which might be a comfort for you.

With love,

Virginia

The ink was violet, Sherlock had noticed when he first read it. The colour of her eyes. He had never seen violet ink for sale in any stationer's shop. Perhaps she had brought a supply with her to England from America. The letter wasn't postmarked, of course, because it had been included with Mycroft's letter and hand-delivered. The envelope was of a stiff card with a noticeable weave to it, so tracing the maker would present little problem, if he ever needed to. Two small stains beside Sherlock's name on the front of the envelope indicated that Virginia had, indeed, begun to cry.

Travis Stebbins. He tried to picture a face to go along with the name, but it was futile. People's names rarely said anything about their appearance, or vice versa. Sherlock couldn't help but imagine a tall, muscular boy with an open, tanned face. Handsome. Strong.

He wished Virginia well in her life. He really did.

Everything she had said had been true – he *had* been gone a long time, and he *might* not have ever come back, and even if he had come back he *might* have met someone else while he had been away. He couldn't have expected her to wait for him.

But he wished she had.

The coast of Ireland appeared as a long smudge against the horizon. Mr Larchmont stomped across the deck shouting orders to the crew to trim the sails, adjust course and, of course, look lively. When he came to the side of the ship he stared up. Sherlock expected him to inquire, with assorted curses, what exactly Sherlock thought he was doing hanging there when there was work to be done, but his faded blue eyes just regarded the boy quizzically.

'Not the way you thought it would be, I warrant,' he said gruffly.

'Not the way *what* would be, sir?'

'Your return. It never is.' He paused, still gazing up at Sherlock. 'Let me tell you the great secret of a sailor's life, son. You can never go back. The reason is that the place you think you're going back to is not the way you remember it, partly because it has changed, partly because you have changed, but mostly because you aren't remembering the truth, just a shiny memory that masquerades as the truth. That's why most sailors stay on the high seas. It's the only thing they can go back to time and time again that doesn't change.' He gazed out at the distant horizon. 'I remember when I first went to sea, I'd just got married. I was away for over a year. When I got back I didn't recognize my wife on the dockside, and she didn't recognize me as I came down the gangplank. We were strangers to each other.' He looked at Sherlock, then back at the horizon. 'If you want to stay, there's always a place for you,' he said, and then stomped away before Sherlock could respond.

Sherlock stayed in the rigging for a while longer, until a grey line appeared on the horizon. For a while it looked like a wave, bigger than usual, but gradually it resolved itself into low hills that rolled on into each other. Mr Larchmont shouted to the sailors on deck to trim the sails and change course five degrees to the south. Sherlock scrambled further up the rigging to where the spar crossed the mainmast, and set about helping to bring the sails under control. The damp wooden timbers of the ship creaked as it came gradually about, heading for where the navigator estimated Galway Bay was to be found.

The land got closer and closer: a grey-green counterpoint to the heavy grey clouds that hung over their heads. Eventually they were sailing past dark hills on the starboard side of the ship. Usually, when the *Gloria Scott* made port, the sailors were joyful, looking forward to a spell on land, but now they seemed to be morose. Maybe it was the weather, maybe it was the look of the countryside.

Far ahead Sherlock could see the quay and stone houses of Galway. He could see people moving around. Several other ships were already docked, but there were enough spaces left for the *Gloria Scott* to join them easily. Even so, it took over an hour for the ship to berth. People bustled around the quayside – dock workers, gawkers, tradesmen eager to replenish the ship's stores and men and women offering accommodation in the town. Lines were thrown from ship to land and tied to bollards and to stanchions.

And that was it. Sherlock was home – or as near to home as the *Gloria Scott* was going to carry him.

A covered carriage was waiting by the quayside. Sherlock could just about discern a figure inside wearing a top hat. Whoever it was was staring up at the ship. Maybe an official from the docks, waiting to board so that he could discuss official details with Captain Tollaway. The driver was sitting up on top and in front of the carriage, swathed in a blanket. He looked as if he might be asleep.

The next hour or so was taken up by making sure everything in the *Gloria Scott* was fastened down, tied up or covered with a tarpaulin. At some stage Sherlock caught sight of someone coming aboard via the gangplank. He glanced at the carriage but the door was still closed and the top-hatted figure was still visible inside. A shiver ran up Sherlock's back, and it took him a moment to trace the random thought that had triggered the feeling. Perhaps the occupant of the carriage was someone working for the Paradol Chamber, sent to make sure that Sherlock hadn't got back from the South China Seas alive. Well, if it was, then there was little he could do apart from dive off the starboard side of the ship and try and swim to land unobserved, and what would that achieve? He got back to his work, but the crew were finishing their tasks, obviously eager to disembark and get on with whatever it was that sailors did in a fresh port. Mr Larchmont gave the queuing crew the latest instalment of their wages, and then they were allowed to disembark. As Sherlock took his pay the ship's master said: 'I'll hold off filling your position for a day, laddie. Just in case.'

'I appreciate that,' Sherlock said. 'Thanks.' In his heart he knew that he wouldn't be coming back to the *Gloria Scott*, but Mr Larchmont had been good to him, and he didn't want to reject the man's kindness out of hand.

Sherlock walked down the gangplank, already feeling that unsteadiness that came from using legs on land that were conditioned to the swaying of a ship's deck.

As Sherlock approached the covered carriage, a hand beckoned him from the carriage's window. He crossed to it warily. Surely the Paradol Chamber had punished him enough?

It wasn't anyone from the Paradol Chamber. In the watery sunlight that filtered into the carriage from outside,

Sherlock could just about make out a plump, jowly face staring down at him from out of the darkness.

'Hello, Sherlock,' a voice said. It was deep, resonant, and very familiar.

'Hello, Mycroft,' Sherlock said, trying to contain the emotions that roiled within his chest. 'You didn't have to meet me, you know?'

Mycroft Holmes shrugged: a rippling of his corpulent frame in the darkness. 'I felt it to be my brotherly duty. Despite the fact that leaving London makes me feel like a crab that has been somehow removed from its shell and is being allowed to run around unprotected while hungry gulls circle overhead, I wanted to save you the trouble of making your own way home.'

'And you wanted to check that I actually *was* coming home,' Sherlock added. 'Rather than staying aboard the *Gloria Scott* and making a life for myself on the open ocean.'

'You have a fine mind,' Mycroft rumbled. 'Or at least, you did have before you left. Devoting it to memorizing sea shanties and the various different types of knots that sailors must master would be a waste.'

Sherlock smiled. 'Actually, you would be surprised how many things you need to know in order to be a sailor. It's not just knots and sea shanties. There's being able to predict the weather from the look of the sky or the behaviour of the birds, there are the various languages you need to be able to speak a smattering of in order to make the most of your time ashore, there's the ability to bargain over the buying and selling of your cargo, there's the medical knowledge you need to know so you can treat fungal infections, cuts, burns, digestive problems and scurvy . . .' He paused, thinking. 'But you're right – there *are* a lot of knots.'

'Could you climb inside?' Mycroft asked. 'I am getting a crick in my neck looking down at you like this.'

Sherlock walked around the front of the carriage to the other side. Sailors who were still leaving the *Gloria Scott* stared at him with undisguised curiosity, obviously wondering what made him so important that a carriage was waiting for him. The horses sniffed at him as he passed. They didn't seem over-exerted, which meant that they hadn't come far, pulling the carriage. Galway was in the West of Ireland, which meant that Mycroft had either sailed all the way around the coast from the other side or, more likely, he had taken a ferry from England to Dublin, on the east coast of the island, and travelled across via carriage. As the horses were still fresh, he obviously hadn't just arrived in Ireland. He must have been staying somewhere local. The entire thought process took less than a second. As he came to his conclusion Sherlock glanced up at the blanket-swaddled driver, but all he could see of the man's face was a pair of closed eyes. Reaching the other side, he opened the door and climbed in.

Once he got used to the relative darkness of the interior, he glanced critically at his brother. Mycroft's face was as familiar to Sherlock as his own, but his brother had put on weight. Quite a lot of weight, from the look of it. His cheeks were almost invisible beneath layers of fat, and he seemed to have developed several more chins, none of which were defined by any underlying bone. He had a walking stick of black ebony, topped with silver, upon which he rested his hands. It was thicker than most such sticks Sherlock had seen. He supposed that it would have to be, to take his brother's weight without snapping, and that told him more than he wanted to know about the changes in his brother's health over the past year.

'You're looking well,' Sherlock said eventually.

'You are being too kind. Either that or your observational facility has withered in the time you have been away. I am neither looking well nor feeling well. I fear I have the beginnings of gout in my right foot, and I may need recourse to spectacles in the near future. Or a monocle, perhaps.' He looked Sherlock up and down. 'You, however, have developed muscles in places where I had no idea that muscles could develop. Your eyes are washed out by all the sun that you have experienced, and your hair is unfashionably long. I perceive that you haven't started shaving yet, which is a small blessing I suppose, but I cannot believe that it will be long before you will be sporting an unappealing moustache and a small goatee beard.' He paused, considering. 'I see traces on you of various ports of call – Dakar, Borneo, Shanghai, of course, and, if I am not very much mistaken, Mombasa and the Seychelles as well. The rough skin on your hands indicates that the Captain has allowed you to work your passage on the *Gloria Scott*, which is what Amyus Crowe and I had assumed would happen. Your general muscular development suggests a great deal of climbing, but the change in your poise, the way you hold yourself, suggests a different form of activity.' He cocked his head to one side. 'Gymnastics? No, I think not. More likely to be an Eastern martial art along the lines of karate or judo.'

'*T'ai chi*,' Sherlock said softly.

'I have heard of it. I see from the calluses on the fingers of your left hand that you are still practising that abominable instrument, the violin, although I am unsure how, given that you left it at Holmes Manor.' He shuddered slightly, the rolls of fat around his neck shivering like a disturbed blancmange. 'I cannot tell, but I do hope that you have not picked up any tattoos on your travels. I find the idea of disfiguring one's skin with a design that can never be removed abhorrent in the extreme.'

'No, Mycroft – no tattoos. And, just to put your mind at rest, I have contracted no strange tropical diseases either.'

'I am relieved to hear it.' He suddenly reached out a hand and put it on Sherlock's knee. 'Are you . . . all right, Sherlock? Are you *well*?'

Sherlock took a moment before answering. 'What is the phrase that doctors use when conveying news to relatives? I am "as well as can be expected", I suppose.'

'You survived. That is what counts.'

'Not unchanged, Mycroft,' Sherlock said.

'If you had remained at home in England then you would have changed anyway. It is called "growing up".'

'If I had remained at home in England, then *some* things would not have changed. Or at least, they would have changed in a different way.'

'You mean Virginia, of course. Or at least, the burgeoning relationship between you and her. You obviously received at least one of the letters I sent.'

Sherlock glanced sideways, out of the window, before Mycroft could see the sudden gleam of tears in his eyes.

Instead of pressing Sherlock on the matter, Mycroft made a brief 'harrumph' sound, then said: 'Before you ask, Father is still in India with his regiment. I have received a series of letters from him, so I know that he is fit and well. Mother is . . . stable . . . but her health is still fragile. She sleeps a lot. As for our sister – well, what can one say?' He shrugged. 'She is as she always is. I am afraid to tell you, by the way, that Uncle Sherrinford has had a bad fall.

He broke an arm and several ribs. Aunt Jane is looking after him, but at his age a fall like that can accelerate the inevitable end that we all come to.'

Sherlock took a few moments to process the information. He felt a twinge of sadness. He hadn't got to know his uncle very well, but he had liked the man. Sherrinford had embodied a kindness, a Christian morality and an obsession with research that had impressed Sherlock in the time he had spent at Holmes Manor.

'What about you?' he asked eventually. 'Are you still living in Whitehall and working in the Foreign Office?'

'Sherlock, I suspect I shall be living in the one and working in the other until the day I die. When you add the Diogenes Club, where I spend most of my lunchtimes and evenings, the three locations form a triangle which defines my life.' He stared at Sherlock for a few moments in silence. 'We should have a discussion some time about your future, but I have a feeling that we will need a geometric figure with considerably more vertices than a triangle to describe it.'

'I'm not sure I like the idea of being *defined* by any shape, Mycroft. As far as I can see, my future is amorphous. Shapeless.'

'You will need to earn money somehow. You will need to live somewhere. Thought must be given to these things.'

'But not now,' Sherlock said.

'I agree. Not now.' Mycroft reached up with his walking stick and rapped it against the roof of the carriage. 'Driver! You there! Take us back to the hotel.' As the carriage lurched off he looked back to Sherlock. 'I have taken rooms at the local tavern. The beds sag but the food is acceptable. I trust you do not object to spending a night or two here before we return to England?' He paused for a second, and when he spoke again his voice was uncharacteristically hesitant. 'You *are* coming back to England, aren't you?'

Sherlock nodded. 'I am,' he confirmed. 'I have been to sea and come back. I don't want to make either a habit or a career out of it.' Just to provoke his brother a little he added: 'Maybe I'll join the circus next – for the experience.'

'There are some experiences that can be taken on trust,' Mycroft said. 'That is one of them.'

As the carriage clattered away from the harbour, and into the town, Sherlock asked: 'How exactly did you know when the *Gloria Scott* would be arriving in Galway? And if it comes to that how did you know that it *would* be arriving in Galway? There are other ports where we might have docked.'

'Ah.' Mycroft shifted uncomfortably. 'You have, as is your wont, arrived straight at the heart of the issue. There is a job here that I need to do, and I need your help to do it.'

18

CHAPTER TWO

Galway was a small town with plenty of character. As the carriage clattered along the winding cobbled streets, past shop fronts and taverns, past women in shawls and men in rough corduroy jackets and flat caps, Sherlock kept having to remind himself that he was home – well, nearly home – and not in some far-flung foreign port.

Mycroft was silent for a while after his admission. He seemed to be avoiding Sherlock's gaze, and instead stared out of the carriage window with a pensive expression on his face.

'I must confess,' he said eventually, 'that I have not told you the entire story.'

'You surprise me,' Sherlock murmured. He had already worked out that there was more to Mycroft's presence in Galway than his brother had revealed.

Mycroft glanced at him with a raised eyebrow. 'What exactly do you mean?'

'You once told me that you rarely do anything for only the one reason. You consider it lazy and wasteful of time and of resources.' Sherlock gazed at his brother, who was attempting to keep a fixed expression of supercilious

19

amusement on his face and failing. 'I know that you hate travel, and that you hate having your normal routine disturbed. I would have expected you to send someone else to meet me – perhaps Rufus Stone.' He paused, considering. 'In fact, now that I come to think of it, Galway is not a port I would normally have expected the *Gloria Scott* to visit. I recall that we were originally scheduled to make landfall in Liverpool, but the Captain's plans changed. In fact, I remember that he had a visitor, an Englishman, when we docked at Cadiz. They had a meeting in the Captain's cabin. Shortly after that he said that we would be changing our itinerary.' Sherlock felt a small bud of anger begin to unfold in his chest. 'Mycroft, did you ask the Captain to change his course and call in at Galway just because you had other business in Ireland, in this town, and it was *convenient* for you to combine your trip here with meeting me and checking that I was all right?'

Mycroft stared at Sherlock for a few moments without speaking, and then said: 'Well done. I see your mental faculties have not withered to compensate for the obvious over-development of your body. Yes, I have known for a while now that there was . . . let us say an *event* . . . in this area that I would be obliged to attend at this time. I had been tracking the course of the *Gloria Scott* homeward by means of various agents I have in ports around the world, and predicted that you would arrive in England at roughly the same time that I had to be in Ireland. I cabled one of my agents and told him to meet with the *Gloria Scott* when it broke its journey in Cadiz and talk with Captain Tollaway. He offered the Captain . . . well, let us say a small but not insignificant amount of money to change his plans slightly, to dock here, in Galway, and to try to arrange things so as to arrive here at a particular time.' He raised an eyebrow at Sherlock's expression. 'You are angry, I perceive.'

'Yes, I'm angry.' Sherlock tore his gaze away from his brother and stared out of the window. 'I thought for a little while that you had made the effort to come all this way on my behalf, because you had missed me, not because I could be moved around like a pawn on a chessboard because it suited you.'

'I confess,' Mycroft said heavily, 'that I did not take your feelings into account when I made my plans. That was a mistake. I am sorry. Please accept the fact that I am more than happy to see you, and that, had it always been a part of the Captain's plan to stop at Galway before continuing on to Southampton, I would have done my best to have been here to meet you regardless of any other plans that I had. It merely made things more . . . convenient . . . for me to combine separate events into one.'

'I'm glad that I could help,' Sherlock murmured bitterly.

The carriage pulled up in front of an ornate hotel. A doorman moved to help Mycroft and Sherlock get out.

'I have been staying here for a few days,' Mycroft said as he levered himself out of his seat. The carriage tilted alarmingly as he moved. 'Fortunately we will be relocating to Cloon Ard Castle, out along the coast road in an area known as Salthill, this afternoon.'

'For your *job*.'

'Yes, for my job.'

'And am I entitled to know what this job is, or should I just wait patiently until you have completed your work and we can go back to England?'

'I will tell you everything over lunch.' Mycroft stepped to the pavement and the carriage rocked back on its springs. 'I promise.' He glanced up at the carriage driver. 'I will not be needing you for a few hours, but please pick us up at four o'clock this afternoon, on the dot. I will have luggage. A lot of luggage.' He glanced at Sherlock. 'We will need to get you several sets of clothes, a decent pair of shoes, a carpet bag and some toiletries this afternoon. We cannot have you looking like an itinerant sailor for the rest of your life. I have taken the liberty of contacting a local tailor. He will attend us this afternoon with a range of suits in various sizes. I had considered bringing some of the clothes that you had left behind at Holmes Manor, in Farnham, but I worried that you would have grown out of them.' He stared at Sherlock as Sherlock descended from the carriage. 'I see that I was right.'

A table had been set aside for Mycroft in the restaurant area of the hotel, and the *maître d'hotel* escorted them across the nearly empty room. When they were seated Mycroft said: 'The lobster for me, I think. Sherlock, I can recommend the turbot.' When Sherlock nodded he added, 'And a bottle of Montrachet.' The *maître d'* made an apologetic motion with his hands. 'Sancerre?' Another shrug. 'Bordeaux?'

'I'll have a pint of whatever local beer you stock,' Sherlock said, surprising himself.

'And I suppose that I will have the same,' Mycroft murmured unhappily. As the *maître d'* moved away, he added, 'I wish that the climate of Ireland was more conducive to the cultivation of grapes. As it stands, the constant dampness favours only the growing of hops, potatoes and mushrooms. I understand that the enterprising locals have found a way to make a strong spirit from potatoes. It is called "*potcheen*", and I am informed that it is as much use as a fuel for lamps and a means of removing varnish from furniture as it is as a drink. So far they have failed to produce an alcoholic beverage from mushrooms, but they are an inventive people. Give them enough time and they will succeed.' He sighed heavily. 'I have often thought that the measure of a good drink

23

is how well it lends itself to being used in cookery. Just think of beef in red wine, chicken sautéed in brandy or champagne trifle. I fear that if you tried to marinate a chicken breast in *potcheen* it would dissolve in moments.' He glanced at Sherlock. 'Beer, eh? You *are* growing up, and not in a direction of which I necessarily approve. I suppose we can blame the company you have kept for the past year.'

Sherlock took a moment to look around the restaurant. 'Sailors are rough folk,' he said eventually, 'but at least they are honest in their dealings. They say what they mean and they mean what they say.'

'Unlike me?' Mycroft inquired. 'I suppose I deserve that rebuke. So, while we wait for the wonders of the kitchen to appear, tell me all about your voyage. I am agog to hear the details.'

'Didn't your agents give you a full account? I'm not sure there is anything I can add to their reports.'

'Don't get snippy, Sherlock. You have been through a life-changing experience. I want to know all about it.' He paused momentarily. 'Actually, my agents did mention something about a murderously feral child and a plot to blow up an American naval vessel, but I would rather hear the details from you. It seemed so fantastical.'

Sherlock spent lunch telling Mycroft everything that had happened to him on the *Gloria Scott*, in Shanghai and in the other ports that the ship had visited. Mycroft sat and listened, interrupting every now and then with a pertinent and focused question. As Sherlock recounted the story of his life-or-death struggle with Mr Arrhenius he could see that his brother was getting increasingly tense.

'Storms I had expected,' he murmured as Sherlock finished his story. 'Scurvy, perhaps. But this . . . this I had no idea about. You are fortunate to have survived.'

'Now it's your turn,' Sherlock prompted. 'What are you doing here, and what is it that we are expected to see when we arrive at the castle? Some kind of diplomatic meeting?'

Mycroft shook his massive head. 'What do you know about spiritualism?' he asked.

Sherlock marshalled his thoughts. 'It's the belief that when people die their spirits – their souls, if you like – live on in some immaterial form, and can be contacted by someone appropriately sensitive here on earth. I believe that these sensitive people are called "mediums". The spirits of the dead supposedly live in a place that's not exactly heaven, but is more like another plane of existence that we can't see and that they can't describe. I know there have been mediums who have claimed to contact famous dead people like Shakespeare or Mozart, and given new plays, or new musical compositions, by them at meetings called "séances". There's a lot of table tapping and the use

25

of wooden boards with letters around the edge which the spirits can supposedly use to spell out messages.'

'You sound sceptical,' Mycroft said. 'I approve.'

'It's difficult not to be. As far as I am aware there is no absolute proof that these mediums actually can contact the dead, and the kind of messages that come back from the other side are quite generic – the dead are apparently pretty happy, most of the time, and a bit vague about what they do when they're not making contact with the mediums. And, of course, the mediums take money from the people who attend the séances, which means that the entire process is vulnerable to fraud. It's a particularly unpleasant form of fraud as well – trading on the grief of the recently bereaved in order to make money.'

'Do you believe that spirits live on after death?' Mycroft asked as their main courses arrived.

'I know that I don't believe in *ghosts*,' he said finally. 'I had to think about that quite seriously in Edinburgh, over a year ago, when Gahan Macfarlane was using theatrical make-up to get people to think that reanimated corpses were committing crimes on his behalf. He wanted to frighten the locals so they would let him get on with things. I remember speaking to Matty about it.'

'I would think that young Matty believes in ghosts. I find that either the poorer or the richer a person is, the more likely it is that they will believe in the unexplained.

Those of us who are fortunate to have an adequate but not excessive amount of money tend to be more sceptical. Or perhaps either excessive bad luck or excessive good luck in life means that people seek explanations that lie outside the ordinary.'

'Matty told me that he has seen some things in his life that he hasn't been able to explain in any other way than by resorting to the idea of ghosts. As for me – I worry about the simple things, like the fact that they are supposed to be able to walk through walls but they don't fall through floors or stairs, and the way all ghosts seem to lose their minds after death. They might be great conversationalists in life, but as soon as they are dead they seem to resort to groaning and moaning and clanking chains to get their point across. Why only come out at night – why not walk about in daylight? It doesn't make any rational sense. And,' he added, 'from a personal point of view, when I die the last thing I want to happen is that I'm forced to hang around the place *where* I died with no aim other than to scare people. If anything of my character or personality lasts after death then I want to be able to move around, travel a bit, and visit some places I haven't seen before.'

'Like the centre of the earth?'

Sherlock gazed quizzically at his brother.

'If, as you logically point out, a ghost that can walk through walls as if they weren't there should fall through the floor, then it seems logical to conclude that all ghosts will end up at the centre of the earth. If, of course, they are bound by gravity. Perhaps that's why the Church teaches that hell is beneath us, and heaven above.'

Sherlock nodded decisively. 'The whole thing is based on a series of premises that make no sense.'

'So that disposes of ghosts. Very well. What about the concept that something of a person – call it their spirit or their soul – survives after the death of the body? That is, you will admit, a slightly different prospect.'

'Didn't someone once say that energy can be neither created nor destroyed, although energy can change forms, and energy can flow from one place to another? I think I read that somewhere.'

'A German physicist and physician – Hermann von Helmholtz. Very precise and methodical, the Germans. That is why they make such superb engineers. Lord help us if they ever decide to take over the world – their single-mindedness and determination would virtually guarantee their success.'

'So, if a person's consciousness is defined as a form of energy within the brain, then it makes sense that the energy isn't destroyed when the brain is destroyed. It either flows to another place or is transformed into a different type of energy.'

'An excellent point,' Mycroft conceded.

'Why so much interest in souls and the persistence of character and memory after death?' Sherlock asked, intrigued. 'And what on earth does it have to do with the reason you are here in Galway?'

'You will be aware that my job in the British Government involves collecting information from a number of agents located around the world. I trawl this information in, as a fisherman might trawl mackerel, and then I sort through it all, seeking fish hidden in the catch that are considerably rarer than mackerel, or perhaps looking for two or three mackerel whose markings by themselves appear random but which can be put together to form a bigger picture.' He frowned. 'I believe I will abandon the fishing metaphor. It isn't helping me make my point. Anyway, my job is frustrated by three things – communication, perception and death.'

'You are going to need to explain that a little more, if you don't mind. Without recourse to fishing.'

'Of course. *Communication* is a problem because it takes weeks or sometimes months for my agents to get information to me, and by the time it arrives on my desk it is often out of date, superseded by events. The man who invents a means of communication that enables someone to speak to another person on the other side of the world as though they were in the next room will, I guarantee, become a millionaire. *Perception* is a problem because I expect my agents to look at each scrap of information that comes into their possession as though they were me, but they aren't. I have a feeling that they often throw away scraps of information that they believe are unimportant but which, if I saw them, would lead me to come to important conclusions. *Death* is important because a significant number of my agents have a habit of ceasing to exist before they can give their reports to me.' Sherlock glanced at Mycroft, shocked, and his brother continued: 'I do not wish to sound callous. I know they have loved ones, and families who will miss them. The problem is that the nature of this business means that many of them work in dangerous, out-of-the-way places where accidents often happen to people or where they catch strange foreign diseases. Others have a habit of getting caught while infiltrating government buildings in various capital cities around the world and being killed either while trying to escape or, shortly afterwards, by hanging or by firing squad. It is, regrettably, a risk that the job entails. They all know that it might happen.'

Sherlock found a vision of his friend Rufus Stone flashing in front of his eyes. He knew that Rufus had been, and indeed still was, an agent of his brother. Had Rufus been sent into some of these dangerous situations that his brother was talking about? Was there a chance that he could have been, still might be, killed? He decided not to ask.

'I suppose that the problem there is that when they die, the information in their heads dies with them?'

'Indeed. It happens all too often.'

Sherlock had a sudden sense of where Mycroft was heading. 'And if there were some means of contacting them *after* their deaths, you might be able to retrieve the information they have learned and make use of it?' he asked. He was taken aback by the scale of Mycroft's vision. Was it likely that something like that could be done? Was it even conceivable?

'I understand your scepticism. Nobody has ever managed to demonstrate communication with the dead in conditions other than a badly lit room when everyone is holding hands and facing into the centre. The trouble is that the British Government has been approached by a man, a medium, who currently resides in Ireland. His name is Ambrose Albano, and he claims that he can find any recently deceased spirit and establish a two-way communication with it. *If* his claims are true, and I do appreciate the enormity of what lies behind the word "if", then the government which controls, or even first exploits, that means of communication would have an advantage over the rest of the world that would be difficult to eradicate.'

'And that is why you are here – to look into his claims?'

'Indeed. I am sceptical, and my lords and masters know

that, but when I protested about being sent all the way here they pointed out that if a sceptic such as me could be persuaded then the claim *must* be true. Sadly I could not argue with their logic.'

'Couldn't this medium have travelled to London? He could demonstrate his skills in front of a much larger audience then.'

Mycroft nodded. 'I did make that point, along with the associated point that his insistence on being examined in Ireland strongly suggested that he wanted to control the environment in which he was tested, but my arguments fell on deaf ears. He does not travel, we were told – something to do with a head injury he once received and which is connected in some strange ways with his spiritualist skills. No, despite my well-known dislike of travelling I found myself forced into planning a little jaunt across the Irish Sea.'

'How did he end up at Cloon Ard Castle?'

'I understand that Sir Shadrach Quintillan, whose castle it is, has become his protector and patron.'

'I've never heard of him.'

There is no reason why you should have – the title is not hereditary, and was awarded for services rendered to the Royal Family. He is, however, an interesting man, as you will discover when we meet him – which will be this afternoon when we travel up to the castle.'

'And what is my role in this likely to be?'

'You are an intelligent boy, and a keen observer of details. I would value your opinions as a backup to my own. In addition, there may be occasions when you see things that I am not in a position to see.'

'We are staying at the castle?'

'Indeed. I am assured that Sir Shadrach's hospitality is unrivalled – at least, in the West of Ireland.'

Sherlock stared for a moment at his brother. 'What do you want to get out of this, Mycroft? Do you want it to be true, or not, that this medium can communicate with specific and named dead people?'

'Whether or not I *want* it to be true is immaterial. I am here to establish whether or not it *is* true. Personal preferences must be ruthlessly filtered out of the consideration; otherwise they may affect the final decision.' He sighed. 'But for myself, I hope that it is not true. I am aware that a number of my agents suffered quite substantially before their deaths. There are, sadly, many regimes around the world less considerate than Britain. I would prefer to think that death was an escape from suffering, rather than just a bump in a longer road.'

'And,' Sherlock ventured gently, 'you wouldn't want to talk to them if you thought they might blame you for what happened to them.'

'Indeed. And they would. I feel sure that they would.'

That thought stopped them both from speaking for a while. There was a dessert of some kind of cream flavoured with alcohol, but Sherlock hardly tasted it. He was still thinking through the implications of what Mycroft had told him. If it was true that the spirits of the dead could be made to speak then the world would be revolutionized. The implications were immense!

After finishing their desserts, Mycroft took Sherlock up to his room. His luggage was already neatly packed. A few moments after they entered there was a knock at the door. A man entered, well-dressed but deferential, with several shirts and suits. He handed them to Sherlock, who stared in bemusement. He hadn't worn anything so formal since Shanghai, and that had been a long time ago.

'Try them on in the bathroom,' Mycroft suggested. 'I have already taken delivery of various sets of undergarments for you. I left them on a shelf in there. Please try them as well.'

When Sherlock finally emerged from the bathroom, feeling uncharacteristically constrained by the unfamiliar clothes, another man had arrived. He had a large box in his hands.

Mycroft looked Sherlock up and down. 'Yes,' he said critically, 'that will do.' Indicating the new arrival, he added: 'This gentleman has brought several pairs of shoes in different sizes. Please select the ones that fit you best while I settle up.'

A few minutes later Sherlock was fully outfitted. Or at least he thought he was. Mycroft gazed at him and said, 'A cravat, I think, will set the whole *ensemble* off. I have taken the liberty of selecting one for you.'

Back in the bathroom, Sherlock stared at himself in the mirror. It was like looking at a painting – he hardly recognized himself any more. The image in the mirror bore no relationship to the image of himself that he had in his mind.

At five to four Mycroft called for a valet to carry his bags down to the carriage. He had bought a carpet bag for Sherlock to carry his meagre possessions. Just as they were about to leave the room he suddenly raised his hand and slapped his forehead. 'Idiot! I almost forgot.' Bending down on the other side of the bed, not without some difficulty, he retrieved a strangely curved case and held it out to Sherlock. 'I thought you might find a use for this.'

Sherlock took it in wonder. It was a violin case! With unsteady fingers he opened it. Inside lay, as he knew it would, his old violin – the one he had bought from a trader in Tottenham Court Road.

'Something to connect you to your previous life,' Mycroft said. 'I retrieved it from Holmes Manor on my last visit.'

'That was . . . very thoughtful,' Sherlock said quietly.
'Thank you.'

They made their way down to where the carriage was waiting. Within a few minutes they were clattering through the cobbled streets of Galway, heading north, parallel to the coast. The road gradually began to slope upward, and Sherlock was soon looking down on the glittering grey ocean.

Sherlock couldn't be sure, but based on the size and the number of masts, he had a strong suspicion that a ship he could see at the quayside was the *Gloria Scott*. He felt a sudden and unaccustomed pang of regret. She had been hard, but she had been home. He would miss her.

He hoped he would get the opportunity to travel abroad again, at some point in his life.

It took half an hour for the carriage to make its way from the town of Galway to Cloon Ard Castle. The sky was grey with low clouds, and a fine drizzle washed the landscape. Everything that Sherlock could see from the window appeared to be coloured in various shades of green and grey.

The carriage abruptly turned left, through a stone gateway in an eight-foot-high stone wall that appeared to surround an estate of some kind.

'Say as little as you can when we arrive,' Mycroft cautioned. 'But keep your eyes and your ears open. I would be very interested to know what impression you form of the people and the situation that we are joining.'

Cloon Ard Castle, when they finally arrived, was smaller than Sherlock had imagined. It was essentially a squat, four-storey tower of grey stone in the middle of one side of a forbidding three-storey wall. There were windows in the wall – narrow slots that glowered down on to the landscape – indicating that they were thick enough to contain rooms and corridors, and were not just narrow defensive features. The corner of the wall that faced them as they approached had a similar but smaller tower built into it. Sherlock couldn't see if there was a matching tower on the other side. The whole thing was surrounded by a wide moat. A drawbridge crossed the moat to a wide arch set into the wall.

As the carriage pulled around the side of the castle to get to the drawbridge, Sherlock looked out of the other window, the one facing away from the castle. He realized that the far side of the moat was only a few yards from a cliff edge. Over the edge of the cliff, several hundred feet below, were the grey waters of the Atlantic.

The sound made by the carriage's wheels changed from wood on earth to wood on wood, as they crossed the drawbridge and entered the castle through the arch. The carriage halted and, seconds later, the driver jumped down and opened the door for them.

Sherlock emerged first, and helped his brother down. The air was fresh and cold, and smelt of the sea. The area inside the walls was paved with large slabs of moss-dappled stone. Gulls wheeled overhead.

Sherlock looked around at the inside of the castle. It was pretty much as he had imagined from outside: a square formed by the walls, with a large block in the middle of the side facing the Atlantic – presumably the main accommodation – and a smaller tower on one of the two nearest corners.

A door set into the main block opened. Sherlock and Mycroft turned to face it. Instead of a set of steps leading up to the door, Sherlock noticed that there was a stone ramp. Odd, he thought.

From the darkness of the doorway, a figure emerged – a man in a three-wheeled bath chair being pushed by a severe-faced woman wearing a black jacket, grey waistcoat and, strangely, striped trousers. Her hair was pulled back into a severe bun. For a horrible moment Sherlock thought it was Mrs Eglantine, his uncle and aunt's poisonous former housekeeper, but although this woman was similar in build and features she was not the same. The man she was pushing was in his fifties, handsome, with tightly curled grey hair, but what struck Sherlock particularly was that he was black.

He smiled down at Mycroft and Sherlock, and threw

his arms open wide. 'What a pleasure to welcome you to Cloon Ard Castle. Please, come in, come in!'

A movement in the shadows of the doorway attracted Sherlock's attention. It was only when a third person stepped forward that he could see that it was a man of about his own size and build. He was wearing a black suit and a black hat, and his unfashionably long black hair cascaded down on to his shoulders. His right eye was bright blue, and stared at Sherlock with piercing curiosity.

His left eye was a sphere of cloudy glass that seemed to glow with its own internal light.

CHAPTER THREE

'Sir Shadrach,' Mycroft boomed as he climbed the stone ramp towards the front door. 'It is a pleasure and an honour to meet you.' He stopped a little way down, so that he was not towering over the man in the bath chair. He held out a hand, and Quintillan took it, shaking twice and then relinquishing it. 'I am—'

'Mycroft Holmes, representing the British Government,' Quintillan said. 'Your fame precedes you, Mr Holmes. Welcome to my home.' He glanced at Sherlock. 'I suggest that your man takes your bags and puts them in your room.'

'I did not bring a servant,' Mycroft explained smoothly. 'This is my . . . brother, Sherlock. He has the ability to think logically, and to observe dispassionately, which I find to be rare and valuable.'

'Then your brother is welcome here,' Quintillan said. His voice was deep and warm. 'Please, come inside. We have refreshments prepared for you.' He glanced over his shoulder briefly. 'The gentleman standing in the shadows of the doorway is, as you will already have realized, Mr Ambrose Albano. Permit me to introduce you.'

Sherlock had been trying not to stare at the man, despite his striking appearance, but now that Albano had been formally introduced he felt that he could look without appearing rude.

Albano was slim and tall, with white skin and large but thin hands. His suit seemed to fit him badly: it was too large around his chest and his limbs, but the sleeves were so short on him that his bony wrists stuck out, and the hems of his trouser legs hovered far enough above his shoes that his socks were clearly visible. His milk-white face, shadowed by the wide-brimmed hat, was pocked with circular scars from some childhood disease. His front teeth were prominent, and his nostrils flared, giving him a look rather like a horse, but it was his left eye that attracted Sherlock's attention like a magnet. It was the colour of milk mixed with water, and it had no pupil or iris.

He didn't step forward to offer his hand either to Mycroft or to Sherlock. Instead, he stared at them both. 'Doth mine eye offend thee?' he said, noticing the way Sherlock was looking at him. His voice was high-pitched, and sounded strangely like someone letting the air out of a balloon.

'I'm sure that my brother doesn't wish to appear rude,' Mycroft said before Sherlock could say anything.

'I would imagine,' Sherlock said, speaking not to Mycroft but to Albano, 'that people either try to ignore your eye, or fixate on it to the exclusion of all else. I was merely trying to work out what had happened to you. An accident, I presume?'

'Sherlock . . .' Mycroft warned.

'Your brother is very direct,' Albano said. 'I appreciate that. He is right – most people either pretend that nothing is wrong, or they stare and then stutter when they try to speak.' He raised a hand to his left temple. 'The answer is simple: I was injured when I was young. I was chopping wood with an axe. A chip of wood flew up and penetrated my left eye. The eye could not be saved. For many years I wore an eyepatch, but when I was in my early twenties I journeyed to India, where I met a holy man. He told me of a stone, a special stone, that was the eye of a statue in one of the local temples. This stone, he said, was rumoured to be strong in magical qualities, and had been used in times past to see beyond the veil of this world and into other planes of existence. I became obsessed with this stone. Eventually, and through circumstances too complicated to relate now, it came into my possession. I took it to be no coincidence that the stone was just the right size to be placed into my own, vacant, eye socket. That is how I brought it home – wearing an eyepatch so that nobody would see it and comment on it.'

'And was the holy man correct?' Sherlock asked. 'Does the stone allow you to see beyond this world?'

'I believe you are here to decide that for yourselves,' Albano said, smiling a thin smile.

'Indeed so,' Mycroft rumbled. 'Now – I believe that refreshments were mentioned?'

'Silman will take you to the dining room, where a selection of cakes and sandwiches have been prepared.' Sir Shadrach indicated the severe-faced woman standing behind him. 'Silman is my butler.'

'A . . . female . . . butler,' Mycroft said, raising his eyebrows. 'How novel.'

'You will find a great many things about Cloon Ard Castle are the reverse of what you might expect. I have a woman for a butler, a woman for a gardener and women for footmen. My cook and my maids, however, are men. Why should things not be reversed, once in a while? Shaking up the established order of things can be . . . exhilarating.'

'As long as we are not expected to sleep on the ceiling and take dinner before lunch and lunch before breakfast then I am sure that we will adapt,' Mycroft said diplomatically.

'Good.' Quintillan clapped his hands together. 'You are a man of the world, Mr Holmes. I think that some of the other representatives were taken somewhat aback by my idiosyncratic arrangement of servants.'

'The . . . *other* representatives?' Mycroft raised an eyebrow questioningly. 'I was under the impression that I was the *only* representative here. Are there other departments of the British Government also represented? I can see that the Home Office might have a use for being able to communicate with the dead, given that they are in charge of the police, but I can assure you that I am negotiating on behalf of the *entire* British Government, not just the Foreign Office.'

'That is well understood, Mr Holmes. No, these are representatives of other *nations*, not other government departments.'

Mycroft was so surprised that he took a pace backwards and almost stumbled down the stone ramp. '*Other* nations?' he asked. 'Sir Shadrach, I was under the impression that this was an *exclusive* arrangement. I did not – and by "*I* did not" I mean "the *British Government* did not" – realize that we were in *competition* for Mr Albano's particular and recondite skills.' He sounded, Sherlock thought, almost outraged, although Sherlock was sure that at least some of the emotion in his brother's voice was faked for effect.

Sir Shadrach shrugged, still smiling. 'Mr Albano's talents are highly valued, and highly sought after,' he said. 'We would be foolish, would we not, to restrict ourselves to just one bidder when there is an entire world out there who could use him?'

'And who else is here?'

'The Tsar of Russia has sent a representative, and

he has brought a manservant with him. The German Empire and the Austro-Hungarian Empire have both sent representatives who have travelled alone – I will provide them with servants from my own staff. I believe the American President has dispatched a representative as well, but he is still on his way – travelling with someone else. I hope he arrives in time for the auction.'

'The *auction?*' Mycroft shuddered. 'Dear me, how plebeian.'

Sherlock glanced up at Mr Albano. It struck him that the man's pale skin probably reacted badly to sunlight, which was why he was standing in semi-darkness. 'What about you, Mr Albano?' he called. 'How do you feel about being auctioned off like a Chinese vase?'

Albano's paper-thin voice floated down the stairs: 'My gifts are intended for the greater benefit of mankind. I do not need such a vulgar thing as money. I leave that to my patron, Sir Shadrach Quintillan. I just wish to be sure that what I do is bringing benefit to the masses, and that communication with the spiritual world can enable us all to grow towards a better understanding of God's plan.'

'And I suppose that the nation offering the highest reward will, by definition, be the one that will use spiritualism to bring the greatest benefit to the masses and illuminate God's plan the best,' Mycroft rumbled.

'You understand us,' Quintillan said. 'I am glad. Now,

45

please, come inside. Sunlight fatigues Mr Albano, and we need him to be on top form for his demonstrations. I will have my footmen fetch your luggage and take it to your rooms. Silman?'

Mrs Silman, the butler – Sherlock couldn't bring himself to think of her as just *Silman* – pulled the bath chair back inside the castle. Mr Albano slipped into the shadows like a fish vanishing beneath a rock. Mycroft turned to Sherlock and shrugged. 'This is *not* what I wanted, and not what I expected,' he said quietly. 'I am sure that the resources of the British Government can outbid the Austro-Hungarians and the Germans, but the Americans and the Russians are something of an unknown quantity. We will have to tread carefully, and keep our eyes open.'

Entering the darkness of the castle behind his brother, Sherlock saw that they were in a massive stone hall. Suits of armour from various periods of history were posed around the walls, beneath hanging tapestries and the stuffed and mounted heads of horned stags. Off to the left was a stairway that led upward, spiralling around the four walls of the tower with balustrade-lined balconies on each floor; to either side and in front of them were arched entrances to other rooms. Oddly, each balustrade appeared to have a section cut out of it, a gap people could fall through if they weren't paying attention. In an attempt to prevent this from happening there were velvet ropes hanging across the gaps, attached by hooks, but Sherlock wondered about the point of it all.

In the centre of the hall was a strange contraption that appeared to be a scaffold made out of wood. Four beams, one at each corner, rose all the way up from the floor to the distant roof. Cross-beams ran horizontally and diagonally across every few feet. In the centre of the scaffolding was a box, large enough for three or four people, with a glass-fronted door that faced out into the centre of the hall. Ropes led from the roof of the box up to a set of wheels half hidden in the shadows of the roof.

'This building is the castle keep,' Quintillan announced, breaking into Sherlock's observations. 'Most of the rooms are in this section of the castle. There is another tower, however, a smaller one, where I and Mr Albano have our rooms.'

'What about the servants?' Sherlock asked.

Quintillan looked puzzled, as if it had never occurred to him that his servants had to live somewhere when they weren't waiting on him, but Mrs Silman stepped forward. 'I and the other servants have rooms in the castle walls,' she said. 'The walls link the two towers, and run around the outside of the castle grounds.'

Quintillan noticed Mycroft and Sherlock staring at the contraption. 'You are probably wondering what that is,' he said smugly. 'Allow me to explain . . .'

'No need,' Mycroft said. 'The principle is obvious by inspection. Sherlock – perhaps you would care to elaborate on the details.'

Sherlock assumed that Mycroft wanted him to demonstrate the intellectual capabilities of the British representatives to Sir Shadrach Quintillan. He cast a more careful eye over the wooden structure, noting the way the wooden box fitted snugly within the four pillars, apparently with small rollers bridging the slight gap, and the way the door opened outward, into the hall. 'It appears to be a device used for reaching the upper floors of the building without having to use the stairs. The box is large enough for several people, and I presume that it is raised by means of the rope by some outside power-source. I would suggest that steam or, more likely, compressed air or a hydraulic liquid system would be the best solution.' He turned to Quintillan. 'I presume that the rising room is used because your own rooms are on an upper floor and you cannot use the stairs.'

'Why compressed air or hydraulic liquid rather than steam?' Mycroft asked, testing him.

'Steam power would require a fire to be kept perpetually burning for the eventuality that someone wanted to use the rising room, which might only happen a few times a day. That would be a terrible waste of coal.'

Quintillan clapped his hands together. 'Very good,' he said, although his tone of voice indicated that he was slightly miffed at being denied the opportunity to explain the contraption to his guests. 'The device is known as an "ascending room". It was built especially for me by a team of American engineers – such ascending rooms are becoming more and more common in New York, I believe. The air is kept under pressure by an ingenious system which uses the local tides as a source of energy. We have strong tides at this part of the coast, and the cliff on which the castle is built is riddled with natural and man-made tunnels through which the waters rise and drain away. Now, if you will excuse me, I need to rest for a while before dinner.'

Silman indicated the room off to Sherlock and Mycroft's left. 'Please, help yourselves to refreshments in the dining room. I will return later to show you to your own rooms where you can prepare for dinner.'

Mycroft bowed slightly in Quintillan's direction. 'Of course,' he said smoothly. 'I look forward to speaking with you later, and convincing you that the British Government can best meet your requirements.'

Mrs Silman pushed Sir Shadrach Quintillan towards the ascending room. Mr Albano, still half hidden by shadows, nodded to Mycroft and Sherlock, and followed them. Mrs Silman opened the door and backed in, pulling

Quintillan with her. Mr Albano slipped in beside the bath chair. Mrs Silman closed the glass door and pulled on a lever on the side of the box. With a loud *hiss* and a shudder, the box began to rise into the air. To Sherlock it looked like some magical trick, and he had to remind himself that it was powered entirely by water under pressure. The box continued to rise in a stately and slow manner, passing the first and second balconies, and Sherlock suddenly realized the purpose of the gaps in the balustrades that he had noticed earlier. There must be an equivalent door on the far side of the box, he realized, through which the occupants could gain access to the balconies. Indeed, when the box shuddered to a halt on the third floor, Sherlock could distinctly hear the sound of a door being opened, although the one that faced out into the emptiness of the hall remained mercifully shut. Fortunately, a wooden brace between two of the pillars would have stopped anyone falling out if it had been opened.

'I can understand how proud Sir Shadrach is of his box of tricks,' Mycroft said, 'but there are several such devices already in London. I am lobbying to have one fitted in the Diogenes Club.'

'Why?' Sherlock asked. 'There are only two floors to the Diogenes.'

'Exactly,' Mycroft huffed. 'And they expect me to walk up the stairs every time I wish to take lunch or dinner.

Outrageous.' He frowned. 'And talking of food, are you hungry?'

'After the meal we had back in Galway?'

'It would be rude not to take at least *some* refreshments, given that our host has been so gracious as to point them out. I must admit that a small snack before dinner would go down very well, just at the moment. I have expended quite a lot of energy today.'

Mycroft led the way into the dining room. It proved to be twice the size of the hall, high-ceilinged, and with a massive oak table in the centre. Plates of cakes, sandwiches and other comestibles were scattered along its length.

A footman – a *female* footman in tails, trousers and a striped waistcoat, Sherlock noticed – stepped forward. 'Can I offer you some tea, gentlemen?' she asked.

'That would be most acceptable,' Mycroft rumbled.

Another man was standing on the other side of the table, staring at them with interest. He walked around the table and approached them, a hand extended towards Mycroft. 'You must be the British representatives,' he said in a strongly accented voice. 'I am Herr Doctor Holtzbrinck. Six months ago I would have been representing Prussia; now I am representing the unified German Empire.' As Mycroft delicately shook his hand, Herr Holtzbrinck stared at the two of them with his head held to one side. 'Mr Holmes, I believe?' he said to Mycroft.

'You know me?'

'I have seen your file,' Holtzbrinck said. 'It is very thick. Very comprehensive.'

'Holtzbrinck, is it?' Mycroft said dismissively. 'I do not believe we *have* a file on you.'

'That,' the German said quietly, 'is exactly as it should be.'

The footman – foot*woman*, Sherlock corrected himself – returned with a tray containing a pot of tea, cups and saucers, and a jug of milk. She placed it on the table near them and commenced pouring two cups of tea.

'And what do you make of this . . . auction?' Mycroft asked Holtzbrinck.

'The process itself is sound,' the German answered, 'but the question we must all be asking ourselves is: are we bidding on a genuine article, or on a fake?'

'Indeed,' Mycroft agreed. 'But how can we tell? We are being asked to commit a large amount of money on trust.'

'I believe that demonstrations of Herr Albano's mystical abilities have been arranged for later. Whether or not they constitute sufficient proof is another question.'

'And the other representatives? Have you met them?'

Holtzbrinck nodded: a precise little snap of the head. 'The Austro-Hungarian representative is a Louis-Adolphe von Webenau. He is very proper, very upright. A statistician, I believe. The Russian representative is a Count Pyotr Andreyevich Shuvalov. Given the chaos in

France at the moment, with the establishment of their Third Republic, there is no French representative.'

Mycroft raised an eyebrow. Sherlock opened his mouth to say 'Don't you know Count Shuvalov?' but Mycroft's right hand, hidden from Holtzbrinck behind his trouser leg, flapped to attract Sherlock's attention. It seemed that Mycroft didn't want Holtzbrinck to know that he and the Russian representative were acquainted.

'Forgive us,' Mycroft said smoothly, 'but I am beginning to feel slightly faint with hunger. If I do not fill a plate immediately then I cannot say what the consequences will be.'

'I would never stand between an Englishman and a table of food,' Holtzbrinck said. He bowed slightly. 'Later, perhaps?'

'Indeed.' Mycroft led the way over to the loaded table. 'I presume you recognized the name of Count Shuvalov?' he said quietly.

'Wasn't he the man we met in Moscow? The man that the Paradol Chamber wanted to assassinate and frame you for it?'

'The very same. I felt it might be advantageous to hide our acquaintance with Count Shuvalov from Herr Holtzbrinck. Thank you for following my lead.' Mycroft picked up a plate and moved along the table, examining each dish with interest.

'Why?'

'Why what?' Mycroft asked. He took a fork from the table and began to load his plate with slices of cold meat, chunks of marinated fish and arrangements of vegetables in various sauces.

'Why didn't you want Herr Holtzbrinck to know that you and Count Shuvalov are friends?'

'There are several reasons,' he replied, spearing some cheese with his fork and adding it to his plate. 'Partly it is because Herr Holtzbrinck would immediately suspect that we and the Russians were conspiring together against Germany, the Austro-Hungarian Empire and America, even though we are not, and he might react unpredictably. Partly, of course, it is because my acquaintance with Count Shuvalov might well *give* us the opportunity to arrange a conspiracy against Germany, the Austro-Hungarian Empire and America, and I do not want Herr Holtzbrinck to work that out before it actually happens. Mostly, however, it is because I do not know whether Count Shuvalov wishes to acknowledge our friendship in this forum or not. I need to talk to him alone first, in order to find out to what he wishes us to admit.'

'Is your whole life like this?' Sherlock asked.

'Like what?'

'Double- and triple-guessing the actions not only of everyone around you, but also of yourself?'

Mycroft considered for a moment. 'Yes,' he said finally. 'Yes, I believe it is. It is called "international diplomacy".'

Sherlock laughed quietly. 'I don't think I could do the job that you do, Mycroft. My thoughts are very direct: *A* always leads to *B* in my world. Your thoughts twist and turn in all directions, apparently depending on the time of day, the ambient temperature and the wind direction.'

Mycroft turned and gazed sympathetically at Sherlock. 'And that,' he said quietly, 'is why I envy you. My mind is already affected by what I do. I can never unwind those twists and turns. *Your* mind, by contrast, is so much simpler – and therefore so much happier.'

'I thought,' Sherlock said, before the conversation got too personal, 'that Count Shuvalov never went out in public because of the fear of assassination. I thought he travelled with bodyguards at all times.'

'That was true, when he was in charge of the Third Section – the Russian secret police. His role changed while you were in China. People come into and slip out of favour with the Tsar all the time in Russia – it is an occupational hazard. Count Shuvalov's fortunes are on the wane – he is no longer the second most important man in Russia, and therefore is no longer of interest to the Paradol Chamber, or anyone else. I am sure he sleeps a lot more soundly in his bed now. I am, however, glad to find out that he is still proving of use to the Tsar. This may not be the most important diplomatic mission he could be on, but it has the potential to *become* important.' He looked at Sherlock. 'Are you not intending to eat?'

'I'll save myself for dinner.'

'As you wish.'

A man with white hair and fluffy white mutton-chop whiskers entered the room. His clothes were very formal. He glanced from Mycroft to Sherlock and then to Herr Holtzbrinck.

'Von Webenau,' Mycroft said smoothly, moving towards the man before Herr Holtzbrinck could. 'I have heard so much about you. My name is Mycroft Holmes . . .'

Abandoned, Sherlock glanced at the food, but he was still not hungry. He thought briefly about engaging the German representative in conversation, but he was worried that he might accidentally say something of which Mycroft would disapprove, so he moved instead over to the doorway and out into the hall. There was nobody around, and he crossed over to the strange contraption of wooden pillars, wooden beams and rope. The ascending room was still up on the third floor, where Quintillan had left it.

Sherlock peered between the wooden beams, into the area that the ascending room would occupy when it returned to ground level. There was a hole in the floor, about five feet deep, and looking up at the underside of the ascending room Sherlock could see that as well as the thickness of the base there were various metal protuberances that would need to be accommodated so that the floor of the room would be level with the floor of the hall. The base of the hole looked as if it was made out of a sheet of wood, and Sherlock thought he could see hinges on one side. Maybe there was machinery beneath it.

Raising his gaze and looking around the wooden scaffolding, Sherlock noticed two slabs of metal, one on either side of the shaft. Ropes from them led upward, past the ascending room, into the roof. Thinking about it for a moment, Sherlock realized that they were counterweights for the weight of the room. Pulling the weight of the ascending room up three floors would take a lot of work, and would leave the room in a potentially dangerous situation, but if there was a similar weight on the other end of the rope then the two weights would balance each other, reducing the amount of work that needed to be done and increasing the safety of the whole thing. It was, he decided, quite clever, although he wasn't sure that he would ever want to travel in it.

A lever was set into a slot on one of the pillars. Sherlock assumed that if he pulled it then the ascending room would return to the ground. He wondered whether he ought to try it out.

'Scared?' a voice said.

He turned. Behind him stood a girl of about his own age. Judging by the darkness of her skin, she was probably related to Sir Shadrach Quintillan. His daughter, perhaps? Her eyes were brown and filled with a lively curiosity; her hair was black and curly.

'Fear is a natural reaction when confronted with something unknown or unexplained that might have the power to kill or injure you,' he said. His voice sounded like he was lecturing, and internally he cursed. 'In this case,' he went on, still sounding to himself like he was reciting a lesson, 'it's just a simple system of counterbalanced weights. There's nothing to be scared of. It's just simple mechanics.'

'Try saying that when you're in the ascending room, going upward, looking down on a hard stone floor that's getting further and further away by the second, and you hear the rope holding the room up creak.'

'Yes,' he said drily, 'I can imagine that would cause a little flutter of the heart.'

'Are you one of the representatives?'

He nodded. 'Well, I'm with one of the representatives, which probably means that, for all practical purposes, I get counted as a representative as well.'

'From England?'

'Yes.' He stared at her for a long moment. 'And you're

58

Sir Shadrach Quintillan's daughter.'

'You seem very sure of that.' She put her head to one side, gazing at him speculatively. 'You're just guessing, aren't you?'

'I never guess. Your confidence indicates that you live here, rather than being a visitor, like the representatives, or a servant. The colour of your skin and the underlying bone structure of your face are similar to those of Sir Shadrach, while your age suggests that you're either his daughter or his niece, rather than his sister or his wife. If you were his niece then that would suggest the existence of a brother or sister who haven't been mentioned yet by anyone, so it's simpler to assume that you are his daughter.'

'Like I said: a guess.'

'*Are* you his daughter?'

She gazed at him, smiling. 'Yes,' she conceded eventually, 'I'm his daughter. My name is Niamh. It's spelled N-i-a-m-h but pronounced "Neeve". Niamh Quintillan.'

'As I said: his daughter.'

'Just because you're right doesn't make it any less of a guess.'

'So, if he's a "Sir" and you're his daughter, does that make you a Lady? Or will it, in time?'

She shook her head. 'I'm certainly no lady. It's a non-hereditary title. That means it dies with father when he dies. I'm just a commoner, and always will be.'

Sherlock smiled, despite himself. 'Believe me, there's nothing common about you.'

She mock-curtsied. 'You're very charming.'

'I have to be: I'm talking to a knight of the realm's daughter. So how did your father come to *be* a "Sir" in the first place? The title must have been appointed by Queen Victoria.'

'That's what happened. We're from Barbuda. My father—'

'Barbuda?' Sherlock interrupted. He'd never heard of the place before.

'It's an island in the Caribbean, near Antigua. It's part of the British Empire. Can I go on?'

'Please.'

'The local people were treated as slaves until forty years ago. When he was freed, my father joined the Royal Navy. I don't know if he was the first former slave to join, but he was certainly in the minority. He served on a ship called HMS *Euryalus*. Queen Victoria's second son, Prince Alfred, also served on the ship. There was some kind of accident while they were at sea, and my father saved Prince Alfred's life. In recognition, and out of gratitude, the Prince persuaded Queen Victoria to give my father a knighthood.' Her face clouded over, and she looked away from Sherlock. 'That's how my father came to be

60

crippled. His back was broken in the accident. He decided he wanted to settle here in Ireland, near the country that he loved but not part of it, in a place where he could see the sea. He was gifted this castle by Prince Alfred.'

'And your mother?' Sherlock asked gently. He suspected that he already knew the answer.

'Oh, she died.' Niamh's voice was very calm, very controlled. 'Consumption. The climate here didn't suit her. She never wanted to leave Barbuda in the first place. She had dreams that something bad was going to happen if she left, and she was right.'

'I'm sorry.'

'Thank you.' She looked at him again, and Sherlock could see the unshed tears in her eyes. 'What about you? Do you have family?'

Sherlock indicated the doorway to the dining room. 'My brother is in there at the moment, filling in time between lunch and dinner by eating. Our father is in India with the British Army. Our mother is . . . ill.' He looked away from Niamh, and then back again. 'Nobody is saying what she is ill with, but I think it's consumption as well. Pulmonary tuberculosis.'

'Then *I'm* sorry.' She shrugged. 'It takes its time. It's a waiting disease.'

There was something Sherlock wanted to ask but he wasn't sure if he should. Sometimes, he had noticed, direct questions could cause people to become offended, or upset.

Niamh noticed that he was struggling to stop himself from saying something. 'What is it?' she asked. 'You're obviously bursting to ask a question.'

'Your father's interest in spiritualism – is it anything to do with the death of your mother?'

'I think so. At least, he never showed much interest in the afterlife when she was alive.' She caught herself. 'We're a Christian family, obviously, but heaven is something you don't think too much about. It's just a word you hear in sermons, or read in the Bible. But after mother died, father became . . . obsessed with the idea that he might be able to communicate with her again. He visited a lot of different psychics and mediums, but he wasn't convinced by any of them. Then he met Mr Albano . . .'

'So Mr Albano managed to establish communication between your father and the spirit of your mother?'

'So he said. So my father said.' She shrugged. 'I'm not so sure. I've taken part in séances, but the messages that Mr Albano conveys from my mother are all so . . . generic. "It's nice here, on the spirit plane." "I miss you both and I'm watching over you." That kind of thing.'

'That's one of the things that makes me hope that spiritualism isn't true,' Sherlock admitted. 'The possibility that, if it is, we're always being watched by hundreds of dead people. Everything we do is being observed. *Everything.*'

'I think,' she said, 'that the spirits aren't meant to concern themselves much with earthly things once they pass on.'

'Yet they still turn up to séances, write messages on bits of slate and move tables around?'

'Hey,' she said, raising her hands defensively, 'I'm not claiming to be an expert. I'm just relaying what I've heard.' Her face suddenly became more serious. 'Besides, if we're talking about supernatural entities, there's other things I'd worry about before I worry about the spirits of the dead.'

Sherlock was intrigued. 'And what's on top of the list?'

'How about the Dark Beast?' she said.

He smiled uncertainly. 'What's the Dark Beast?'

'It's some kind of sea creature that can come up on to the land and carry off sheep and cattle. Sometimes it even kills people. The smugglers who used to smuggle contraband up and down this coast, many years ago, were terrified of it – more terrified than they were of the revenue men.'

'Oh really?'

She just stared back at him with no trace of a smile. 'Yes,' she said simply. 'I've seen it.'

63

CHAPTER FOUR

'You are serious, aren't you?' Sherlock asked Niamh. 'About the Beast, I mean.'

It was two hours later, and they were sitting next to one another at dinner. Just after Niamh had mentioned the Dark Beast, Mrs Silman had appeared in the hall and declared that she would take Sherlock and Mycroft to their rooms. Sherlock had smiled at Niamh, and shrugged, then gone to fetch his brother.

Their rooms were on the second floor of the Castle, and they had used the ascending room to get there. As Sherlock was pressed into a corner of the ascending room by his brother's bulk he noticed that there was a wooden panel beside the door with five buttons on it. His mind quickly made connections – five buttons, but only four floors – the ground floor and three upper floors. Four of the buttons were marked 'G', '1', '2' and '3'. The fifth button was unmarked.

'What's the fifth button for?' he asked Mrs Silman, who was operating the ascending room. 'Is there an extra floor at the top of the castle?'

'No,' she said, pressing the button marked '2'. 'It's

an alarm button, in the unlikely event that there is a mechanical malfunction and anyone finds themselves trapped.'

'Wouldn't it be wiser to mark the button "Alarm"?' he asked.

'We wouldn't want anyone to be worried by the possibility of a malfunction.'

The ascending room had shuddered into life, and sedately began to raise them up the inside of the hall. Sherlock looked out and down, and saw Niamh Quintillan staring up after him. She waved, and he waved back.

Their rooms were only a little way from the hall, and there was a connecting door between them. Sherlock's luggage – only bought that afternoon – had already been unpacked, and a bath had been drawn for him. While he waited for it to cool, he walked over to the window and opened it. A warm breeze blew in. Based admittedly on a small sample of evidence, the weather in Ireland seemed very changeable, Sherlock observed. He made a mental note to keep an eye on it. The sun had gone down, but there was a nearly full moon in the sky, and by its light he could see past the edge of the cliff and out to the ocean. The breeze bore the crash of surf breaking on rocks to his ears. Moonlight glinted off the waves, turning it into a magical scene. It had been a long time since he had been able to look down on waves from this height – for the past year or two he had been much closer.

Eventually he pulled the curtain closed, undressed and slid into the bath. The water was still hot, and he found that he was disconcerted by it. Given that he had spent well over a year surrounded by water that had ranged between cold and warm, the idea of *hot* water was . . . odd.

After getting out of the bath he had dressed in his new evening wear, and had discovered to his surprise that he still remembered how to tie a bow tie. A gong had rung just as he was finishing off the bow, and he had left his room to find Mycroft standing in the corridor.

'Yes,' his brother had said, gazing critically at him. 'You will do. Come on, then.'

The dining room had been cleared of the snacks from earlier, and the table set for a formal dinner. Sir Shadrach Quintillan was at the head of the table, with Mycroft Holmes to his right and Count Shuvalov to his left. Sherlock had recognized the Count straight away – he still wore an ornate military uniform, his grey hair was still cropped close to his skull, and his moustache still turned up at the ends. He acknowledged Sherlock's presence with a slight nod. Another man in military uniform – a burly man with close-cropped hair and a dark shadow on his cheeks and chin where he needed to shave – was presumably the manservant that Sir Shadrach had referred to. He stood behind Shuvalov, staring at the far wall, ready in case his master wanted anything.

Von Webenau and Herr Holtzbrinck were seated next to Mycroft and Shuvalov respectively. Castle servants stood behind them, ready to serve as required. Sherlock was next to von Webenau, although the Austrian ignored him, spending his time turned towards Quintillan. The seat opposite Sherlock was empty, reserved presumably for the missing American delegate, and Niamh Quintillan sat at the opposite end of the table from her father.

'I'm very serious,' she replied to Sherlock's question as the footwomen served soup to everyone. 'There is a monster.'

'And you have seen it?'

'I have.'

'For real – not in a dream or in a vision?'

'For real,' she confirmed.

Sherlock took a sip of his soup. It looked and tasted like a thick, rich gravy. 'What kind of soup is this?' he asked.

'Turtle,' Niamh said simply, and took a sip herself.

'Oh. Right.' He took another sip. It was actually very pleasant. '*Real* turtle?'

'Oh yes. Snapping turtle, if you want to be precise. Father has them imported.'

'How very cosmopolitan.' He paused. 'So, tell me about the Dark Beast.'

She glanced at him. 'You're not going to think I'm stupid, are you? For believing in a monster?'

'I know you're not stupid, but I have a hard time believing in monsters.' He thought for a moment. 'Well, inhuman ones, anyway. Where did you see this thing?'

'Down by the beach. I go there a lot.'

'By yourself?'

'Of course.' She stared at him challengingly. 'Who else is there to go with?'

'I don't know. I'm a stranger here myself. Is there a path down to the beach?'

'Not one you can walk down easily. There are sections where you have to scramble down some steep areas of rock, and if you lose your footing you'll fall all the way down. There's one right by the castle. I climb like a mountain goat.' She raised an eyebrow. 'What about you?'

Sherlock remembered the endless number of times that he'd had to climb the rigging of the *Gloria Scott* to the top of one of the masts. 'I can manage,' he said.

'I was down there one evening. I'd sneaked out of the castle. I just wanted to see the sea by moonlight. I used to do that a lot back on Barbuda – sit on the sand watching the waves coming in. Anyway, I'd been there for a while when I heard something moving. I thought it might be a wild boar, or something, so I turned my head and looked behind me, towards the cliff.' She looked down at the tablecloth, but her eyes were unfocused and Sherlock knew that she was staring backwards in time, seeing again what she had seen then. 'There are a lot of caves in the cliffs, worn by the waves. The smugglers used to use them to hide things. Coming out of one of the caves I saw . . . a *thing*. It was as big as a bear, but . . .' Her gaze flicked up at Sherlock for a moment, gauging his reaction, and then back to the tablecloth again. 'But it had more arms and legs than a bear.'

'How many arms and legs did it have?' Sherlock asked in a low voice.

'It was difficult to tell in the darkness. The moon was low in the sky, behind the cliffs, and the monster was walking in shadows.'

'Where did it go?'

'It lumbered along the beach for a while, and then went into another cave. I just sat there, motionless, hoping that it thought I was just a piece of driftwood or something.'

'Very wise.' He paused for a moment. 'You know how that story sounds, don't you?'

'It sounds like a dream, but I wasn't dreaming. Look, I can prove it!'

'How?'

'Because the people in the town talk about the Beast as well. The fishermen all know about it. Any time one of their nets gets ripped, they say that it's the Dark Beast.

I talked to one of the servants here in the castle who said she saw it once, at night, walking around the outside of the moat.'

'That's hardly proof,' Sherlock pointed out.

'But it means I'm not the only person who has seen it.'

'How far back do these stories go?'

She thought for a moment. 'Apparently there have been stories of the Dark Beast for hundreds of years, but there have been a lot more sightings recently. Maybe it's been asleep for a while. Or maybe something happened to make it leave its natural habitat.'

'Or maybe everyone is just imagining it, and talking about it makes it more likely that someone will see a shadow moving and make it into a monster.'

'I knew you wouldn't believe me,' she snapped, and turned her attention back to the soup.

After a few minutes the servants took the soup bowls away and replaced them with plates piled high with slices of venison. Steaming dishes of vegetables were brought to the table, and the guests filled their plates.

'I'm sorry,' Sherlock said eventually, after several mouthfuls of the tender venison. 'I only believe what I can see with my own eyes.'

'You can't see the wind,' she pointed out, 'or the heat of the sun.'

He sighed. 'No, but I can see their effects.'

70

'And you can see the effect of the Dark Beast. It scared me. It scares the local townspeople and the fishermen as well.'

'I'm not going to win this argument, am I?'

'No,' she said with finality. 'You're not.'

Sherlock knew that pursuing the conversation would be pointless, but he couldn't help himself. He was just about to say something else when a ringing noise from the head of the table cut through the sound of conversation. Quintillan was rapping his wine glass with his knife.

'Gentlemen,' he said in his rich, dark voice. 'Thank you so much for being here this evening. Given the shape of the table there are only two places that I can directly interact with –' he nodded at Mycroft Holmes and Count Shuvalov – 'but please believe that this does not indicate any preferential treatment. The seating arrangements will be changed at each meal. I will have had the pleasure of talking directly to all of you by the time we have concluded our business.' He paused, and looked around at all the people seated at the table. 'I can also only apologize for the absence of our American friend. I am assured he will be here tomorrow. Nevertheless, I have no intention of delaying matters waiting for him to arrive. We are on schedule, and we will remain on schedule. If he misses tonight's events then it is unfortunate, but he, not you, will be the one disadvantaged.'

71

Herr Holtzbrinck and von Webenau nodded their appreciation.

'I am sure you will have noticed,' Quintillan went on, 'that Mr Albano is not present at dinner tonight. When he knows that he has to communicate with the astral plane, he does not partake of any refreshment. He finds that it interferes with his ability to communicate with the spirits of the dead. Mr Albano is currently in his rooms, preparing for tonight's séance – relaxing, meditating and summoning his mental powers. The intention of this séance tonight is to give you some indication of the scope and scale of Mr Albano's abilities. I would urge you to pay careful attention to what happens, but not to try to interfere. The spirits are sometimes agitated and excess noise or confusion can make them angry. Please, for your own sakes, stay calm and quiet whilst the séance is taking place.

'I will not be asking any of you to make any financial commitments tonight,' Quintillan went on. 'I merely want you to observe, and to reflect on what you have seen. Tomorrow we will start the negotiations.'

'He really believes all this?' Sherlock asked Niamh as the guests returned to eating.

She nodded. 'Yes, he does.'

'Dessert will be served shortly,' Quintillan continued a while later. 'When you have finished it I suggest we repair to the reception room for the séance. After that, I recommend cigars and brandy.'

Sherlock couldn't wait to see what would happen at the séance. Fortunately, everyone else at the table had the same feeling as him. Conversation died as people rushed to finish dinner.

When everyone had finished, Mrs Silman appeared, behind Sir Shadrach Quintillan's bath chair. She grasped the handles, pulled him backwards and manoeuvred him away from the table.

'Please,' he said, 'everyone – follow me.'

Mycroft Holmes, Count Shuvalov, von Webenau and Herr Holtzbrinck all got up and followed. Shuvalov made a gesture to his manservant, dismissing him.

Sherlock glanced at Niamh. 'Are you coming?' he asked.

'I wasn't specifically invited,' she admitted, 'but I'd love to see what happens.'

Sherlock escorted Niamh in the wake of the other dinner guests. They walked across the castle hall and through an archway into a room that was dark, lit only by candlelight. Thick velvet drapes blocked out any illumination from the windows. A table had been set up in the centre of the room, smaller than the dinner table, and circular. It was not covered by a cloth, and around the edge were inscribed the letters of the alphabet, along with the numbers 1 to 10 and the words 'Yes' and 'No'. Six seats were arranged around the edge of the table, with a gap for Quintillan's bath chair.

Ambrose Albano was standing by one of the windows. He was wearing evening dress and white gloves that clashed with his black clothing. His false left eye seemed to glow in the candlelight. He stood facing away from the doorway, and did not acknowledge the arrival of the guests.

'Please,' Quintillan said, 'take your seats.'

The four international representatives sat down, while Silman moved Quintillan's bath chair into the gap. This left two empty seats. One was obviously reserved for Ambrose Albano; the other for the mystery American.

Mycroft waved at Sherlock. 'Seat yourself!' he called.

Sherlock glanced at Quintillan, who looked around at the other representatives. 'Does anybody have any objections?' he asked. The Russian, Austrian and German shook their heads. Quintillan nodded at Sherlock. 'Please,' he said, 'feel free to join us.'

Sherlock turned to Niamh. 'Sorry,' he said. 'But duty calls.'

'I'll watch from the sidelines,' she said.

Silman moved to the doorway and pulled a set of drapes across the gap. With the light from the hall cut off, the room was much darker. Sherlock sat down at the table.

Ambrose Albano walked across to join the others at the table. As he sat down, Sherlock noticed how, in the shadows, his false eye looked like a black hole in his face.

From his pocket, Albano produced a wooden plaque about the size of his hand. It was rounded at the back, and pointed at the front.

'This,' he said solemnly, 'will allow the spirits to communicate with us. If they have messages to send, then they will move this wooden plaque to the letters and numbers around the edge of the table, spelling them out. In order that you don't think I am manipulating this plaque, we will all have our hands on it. I will not be able to move it myself without you all knowing, but the spirits will allow it to move regardless of my hand, or your hands. But first . . .'

Theatrically, he raised his gloved hands into the air. With his left hand he pushed his right sleeve up, almost to the elbow, and repeated the same gesture with his right hand and left sleeve.

'As the magicians say,' he proclaimed, 'I have nothing up my sleeves but my arms. There are no tricks here – only genuine communications from the dead.'

Sherlock glanced across the table at Mycroft. His brother looked at him soberly. *Watch carefully*, he seemed to be saying. *Take nothing for granted.*

Albano seemed to catch something of the

communication between the two brothers. He glanced from Mycroft to Sherlock and back. 'And in case any amongst you believe that I have secreted objects beneath the table which I will later use as props: please, go ahead and check.' He stared at Sherlock. 'Be so kind as to look beneath the table, young man.'

Sherlock glanced at his brother, who nodded in agreement. Sherlock ducked beneath the table. The underneath was bare wood, with no props or tricks attached there. Sherlock reached up and touched it, rapping it gently with his knuckles. There was no hollowness, no indication of any hidden areas.

Returning to his seat, Sherlock said, 'I can confirm that there is nothing beneath the table that shouldn't be there.'

'Thank you.' Albano raised a hand and clicked his fingers. Silman, the butler, approached him, holding an object the size of a large, thin book. Albano took it from her and handed it to Sherlock. 'Please, tell us what this object is, young man.'

Sherlock looked at it. 'It's a slate – like the kind they use in schools. You can write messages on it in chalk.'

'And is there any chalk?'

Sherlock turned the slate over and gazed at the back. 'I can't see any chalk.'

'Good. Is there anything else you can tell us about the slate?'

'It's framed in wood, and it has a wooden back.' Sherlock tried to prise the wooden back off, and failed. 'It seems to be very robust – I can't pull it apart.'

'Please – pass it around the table. Let everyone check it.' He smiled thinly. 'After all, as far as the other representatives are aware, you may be my secret assistant.'

Sherlock passed the slate to Mycroft, who glanced at it and handed it straight on to von Webenau. From him it went to Count Shuvalov, to Quintillan and then to Herr Holtzbrinck. The German representative handed it back to Ambrose Albano, who held it in both hands. 'Then let us start,' he proclaimed. 'Later I will demonstrate the power that makes me different from other psychics – the ability to specifically call on particular named spirits to communicate with – but for now I will merely see which spirits are closest and wish to communicate.' He closed his eyes and threw his head back. 'I call upon the great spirits of the astral plane! I call across the Great Divide that separates the living from the departed. Is there anybody there? Is there a spirit willing to converse with us? Is there a spirit willing to act as interlocutor for the Other Side?'

Sherlock glanced around at the faces of the others. They held a range of expressions, from rapt attention to mild disbelief. The latter expression was, of course, on his brother's face.

Sherlock looked over at the doorway, where Silman

stood. Behind her, he could just make out Niamh's face in the darkness of the hall. She smiled at him.

'I can feel someone approaching,' Albano said.

Von Webenau looked around anxiously.

'On the astral plane,' Quintillan whispered. Von Webenau settled back in his chair, relieved.

Ambrose convulsively half rose out of his chair, as if he had been electrocuted, then slumped back into a seated position. His eyes were still closed. His gloved hands, which were still holding the slate, fell to his lap. 'Identify yourself!' he called in a strained voice.

There was silence for a few moments, during which Sherlock waited for some kind of response – a voice perhaps, or some movement of the wooden plaque towards the edge of the table, but the eventual form of the reply took Sherlock by surprise. Albano brought his hands out from below the table, still holding the slate, but it wasn't blank any more. There was a message scrawled on it in chalk.

Albano held the slate up and turned it around so that everyone else could see it. 'Please,' he said in a strained voice, 'someone, read the message out.'

'*My name is Invictus,*' Herr Holtzbrinck quoted. '*I have been selected to be your guide for this night.*'

'Amazing!' von Webenau murmured.

Sherlock glanced at Mycroft, whose gaze shifted from

Sherlock to the table and back. Intuiting his intent, Sherlock ducked his head beneath the level of the tabletop, looking for some evidence that he had missed. Maybe Ambrose had a piece of chalk under there, held between his knees, or some chalk had been attached to the underneath of the table so that Albano could have written the message himself? But there was nothing. Albano's trousers were black, and there would have been some evidence of chalk dust. Sherlock straightened up and shook his head briefly. Mycroft nodded, a scowl on his face. It was obvious to Sherlock that he didn't know how the trick had been accomplished either. If it was a trick.

'Are you willing to act as our guide, seeking out those spirits of the dead who have messages for friends or relatives who are still living?' Albano called. Eyes tightly shut, he moved his head around as if looking for something. His hands, Sherlock noticed, were in his lap again, still holding the slate.

The silence in the room was heavy with expectation. After a moment or two Albano's head twitched. He brought the slate out again and held it up. It was covered with scrawled chalk marks, but they were different from last time.

'*I stand ready to assist,*' Herr Holtzbrinck read out, '*but the others do not have the power to write, as I do. They will use the plaque.*' The final words were written in smaller letters, and squeezed together, as if the spirit named Invictus had suddenly realized that it was running out of space. Somehow Sherlock found the idea of a spirit making a misjudgement like that rather comical.

Albano held the slate up in his right hand. Silman moved forward to take it from him. He reached out to place his fingertips on the wooden plaque which had been sitting on the table all that time. 'Please,' he said, 'all of you, place your fingertips alongside mine.'

The six others around the table all leaned forward and did as Albano had asked. It felt to Sherlock as if the plaque were trembling slightly. He looked around to see if anyone's hand was obviously shaking, but he couldn't see any unusual movements.

'Is there anybody there?' Albano asked.

Nothing happened for a long moment, long enough that Sherlock thought that nothing *was* going to happen, and then the plaque suddenly shot across the table towards the word 'Yes', dragging their hands with it. Count Shuvalov sucked his breath in, while von Webenau's eyebrows rose in surprise.

'Do you have a message for someone here?'

The plaque slowly drifted back to the centre of the table, and then jerked back towards the 'Yes'.

'Who is the message for?'

Again, the plaque drifted back towards the centre of

the table, and then jerked back towards the rim again, but this time, instead of heading for the 'Yes', it went off at an angle, towards the alphabet of letters that ran around the edge of the table. Laboriously, the plaque pointed to the 'H', the 'E', the 'R' . . .

'Herr Holtzbrinck,' Sherlock murmured, but if the spirit heard, then it ignored him, and kept on spelling out the name until it got to the final 'K'.

Holtzbrinck glanced around the table. 'My apologies,' he murmured. 'I had no idea . . .'

'Who are you?' Ambrose asked. 'Identify yourself.'

The plaque shuddered, and then set off again around the table. Within thirty seconds it had spelled out F-R-I-T-Z.

'Does this name mean anything to you?' Ambrose asked, looking at Holtzbrinck.

'Fritz was my brother,' the German representative said. His voice sounded tremulous, as if he were in the grip of some strong emotion.

'And has he passed across the Great Divide?'

Holtzbrinck nodded, once. 'It was a boating accident, five years ago. He drowned.'

Albano turned his attention back to the air above the table. 'What is your message, Fritz Holtzbrinck?'

The plaque moved again, from letter to letter. Sherlock found himself jerked across the table as the plaque tried to reach letters that were opposite him, and he could see the others pulled in similar directions when the plaque moved his way. He tried to spot if anyone was deliberately pushing the plaque – Albano, or any of the others – but it was impossible to tell. It did feel to him, however, as if the plaque were moving of its own accord.

I am happy here, the message read. *Do not mourn for me. Helga must stop grieving and make a new life for herself.*

'Helga was Fritz's wife,' Holtzbrinck said quietly. He seemed to be suppressing some heavy emotion. 'They had only been married for two months when he died. She was, and still is . . . how do you say it? . . . distraught.' He turned his face towards the empty air in the centre of the table. 'Are you in heaven, Fritz?' he asked. 'Or are you in hell?' There was a pleading expression on his face.

Sherlock glanced at Mycroft. He could tell what his brother was thinking – *The German is getting sucked in to the theatricality of the occasion!*

The plaque spelled out a new message. *There is no heaven and there is no hell. There is only the life beyond the veil.*

'Very cryptic,' Mycroft mouthed to Sherlock. Turning to face Albano, he said more loudly, 'The message is in English, I notice. Is that usual for German spirits?'

'The language of the spirit plane is universal,' Albano said smoothly. 'When we hold the séance in English, the messages appear in English.' He turned back to

Holtzbrinck before Mycroft could ask another question. 'Do you have any final message for your brother?' he asked.

The plaque moved again. Sherlock tried to guess what the message was from the initial letters, but it took him a while to work out that the spirit – if it was a spirit – was spelling out: *Believe in the life beyond life. Believe that we all move on to a better place. Do not mourn for us, but celebrate our lives.*

Herr Holtzbrinck was breathing heavily by the time the message was complete. His eyes glistened with unshed tears. 'Do not go,' he murmured. 'Please!'

'It is too late,' Ambrose announced. 'The spirit of your brother has returned to the formless void, whence all things come and to where all things go.' He paused. 'Another spirit approaches. Invictus tells me so.'

Sherlock glanced at the plaque, waiting for it to move, but it stayed where it was. Instead, Ambrose threw his head back and, staring at the ceiling, pronounced: 'I can feel a spirit moving within me! This is a powerful spirit. It wishes to manifest itself in this room – to become visible to us!'

Sherlock and the others seated around the table looked around, expecting to see some ghostly form moving through the room, but instead Ambrose convulsed in his chair again. He brought his arms around his body, clutching himself, and coughed once, twice. His hands came up to his head, open and grasping at the air, then they moved to cup his mouth, and he coughed into them as if trying to expel something from his lungs.

To Sherlock's astonishment, something white and misty began to emerge from Ambrose's mouth. It was as if he were breathing out some vaporous substance into the centre of the room, but instead of dissipating, the substance retained its form, expanding above the table until it began to look like a shroud concealing a face. Albano's hands waved in the air, as if trying to contain the substance, to stop it from spreading. If he concentrated, Sherlock could almost see features inside the dark centre – the features of a beautiful young woman, looking like a portrait done in oils.

He felt his heart beating fast. A strange terror edged his thoughts. This was not what he had been expecting. Table-tapping, yes. Messages, perhaps. But a spirit materializing in the centre of the room? No – absolutely not!

He tried to focus on the shape of the spirit, but it was difficult to make out details. It kept shifting, moving around, vibrating. It was white, and it looked like smoke, but it glistened as if it was wet and it moved as if it had a mind of its own.

'Ectoplasm!' von Webenau breathed.

'Poppycock!' Mycroft murmured.

Sherlock stared at the Austrian. 'What exactly *is* ectoplasm?' he asked quietly.

'It is the substance that spirits use to give form to themselves.' His face was rapt. 'It is a form of matter unlike anything we have ever seen on earth. Mediums can generate it from their own bodies. It exudes from their pores.'

'You sound like you believe in all this.'

Von Webenau glanced sideways at Sherlock. 'How can you not,' he asked, 'when you see and hear what we have seen and heard?'

Sherlock looked across to Count Shuvalov, who had remained quiet all through the séance. 'What about you?' Sherlock asked.

Shuvalov looked over at Sherlock and shrugged. 'I am Russian,' he said simply. 'I believe what I can see, and touch, and talk with.' He nodded towards the ectoplasmic mass of white vapour, which still hung above the table. 'This,' he said, 'is outside my experience. I can see it, but can I touch and talk with it? I think not.'

Sherlock looked over at Ambrose Albano, who was half standing. His gloved hands grasped the arms of his chair. His mouth was open and he was staring wide-eyed at the ectoplasmic mass, as if surprised that it had ever emerged from his body.

The lights, subdued as they were, suddenly went out.

The room was plunged into darkness. Sherlock heard gasps from around the table, and the sound of Ambrose Albano falling back into his chair.

The light suddenly appeared again: gas lamps flaring around the room, flooding it with brightness. The people around the table blinked in confusion.

The ectoplasm had vanished.

CHAPTER FIVE

After the events of the night before, breakfast was a subdued affair. All of the representatives, bar the missing American, sat quietly, wrapped in their own thoughts. Sir Shadrach Quintillan was at the head of the table, of course, and Mr Albano was absent again. Count Shuvalov was served by his own manservant, while the rest of them were served by the castle staff.

As for himself, Sherlock was intent on working out how the effects of the séance had been achieved. He could not bring himself to believe that any spirits had crossed over from the Other Side to visit them – in fact, he was pretty much convinced that there was no Other Side to begin with. What they had sat through was a set of conjuring tricks, he was sure.

Mycroft was convinced they were being fooled as well. He and Sherlock had chatted late into the night after the séance had concluded. Mycroft had summarized by saying: 'I know that we've been tricked, but I am not entirely sure how. There are various possibilities, but to be sure we need to establish exactly what techniques were used. What we saw is, as far as I can determine, pretty standard for séances. Mr Albano did not deploy any events which I was not expecting.'

'What about the other representatives?' Sherlock had asked. 'Do they know they were fooled?

Mycroft had shrugged. 'Count Shuvalov is an intelligent man: I believe that he, like us, knows that confidence tricks are being stacked up, one upon another. Von Webenau, despite his formidable reputation as a statistician and logical thinker, appears to have fallen for the tricks hook, line and sinker. I suspect that he has an existing reason for wanting to believe – a dead wife that he mourns, perhaps, and wishes to contact again. Herr Holtzbrinck could go either way. I thought it interesting that he was the one chosen to receive a message from the Other Side – Mr Albano is obviously targeting him as the easiest one to sway over to a state of belief. He will presumably work his magic on me, and on Count Shuvalov, over the next few nights.'

'Does it matter if one or more of them believe that it's true?'

'What do you mean?' Mycroft asked.

'Well, your job here is to evaluate Mr Albano's spiritual powers on behalf of the British Government. If you decide that he can contact ghosts, then your job is to outbid any other government for his services. But if you decide that he is a fake then presumably the British Government doesn't care if any other government buys his services. They will just be wasting their money.'

'That is perfectly true,' Mycroft said, nodding his large head, 'and it shows that you are developing a good grasp of the way international diplomacy works. In fact, I would rather foreign governments wasted their money on fake psychics than on, for instance, armies or weapons. I would, however, add two codicils to what you have said: firstly, I have a personal dislike of confidence tricksters being rewarded for their efforts, even if those rewards do not come from Great Britain, and secondly it is not a healthy or stable situation for governments with large armies to be guided by fake messages from ghosts. I much prefer governments to make their decisions based on logic and fact. That makes them predictable.'

'On the other hand,' Sherlock pointed out, 'knowing that a government is paying attention to a fake psychic does give you the opportunity to feed them with things you want them to believe. Fake fake messages, if you like. Presumably, if a fake psychic will take money from one government for his tricks, he will take money from anyone.'

'The thought,' Mycroft had rumbled, 'is immoral and unethical, and had never occurred to me.'

'What about Sir Shadrach?' Sherlock asked, thinking about Niamh Quintillan. 'Is he involved?'

'Mr Albano certainly requires help in order to achieve some of the effects.' Mycroft pursed his lips. 'If that help isn't coming from Quintillan and at least one servant then it must be coming from elsewhere.' He glanced across at Sherlock. 'I presume, by the way, that you have already established in your own mind the various ways in which the chalk messages, the moving plaque and the ectoplasmic materialization could have been achieved?'

'Yes,' Sherlock had said quickly, but now, as he sat at the breakfast table, he found himself stumped. The wooden plaque could, he supposed, have been pushed around pretty easily by Ambrose Albano's fingers, but the chalk messages and the ectoplasm were puzzling him. How had they been done? He had checked under the table, and there had been nothing hidden there with which messages could have been written.

Niamh was sitting opposite him, and he glanced over at her. She smiled at him, and he smiled back. He hoped he would get the chance to talk to her later. She had, as far as he knew, seen the whole thing, but from a different perspective. The séance had, he assumed, been set up to convince the people sitting around the table. Standing in the doorway, she might have seen something that none of the rest of them had.

Or, he wondered as he looked at her, did she already know how it had all been done? If Quintillan was implicated in the tricks, was his daughter also in on it? Was she part of the conspiracy? He hoped not.

He was about to ask her if she would show him more of the castle and its grounds later when one of the foot-servants unexpectedly dropped a tureen of scrambled egg on the floor. The sudden crash startled everyone. The foot-servant ran for the door, sobbing hysterically, while the other servants quickly moved to clear up the mess.

Niamh Quintillan got out of her chair and ran after her – the only person, Sherlock noticed, concerned with how the girl was feeling.

Sherlock munched on a slice of toast while he waited for her to return. Eventually she came back into the room. Her father glanced up at her questioningly, and she nodded in reassurance.

'What was all that about?' Sherlock asked as she sat down.

'Oh, she's all right. Poor Máire, she's just worried about something she saw out of her bedroom window last night.'

Sherlock raised an eyebrow. 'Don't tell me – she saw the Dark Beast!'

'Actually,' Niamh said levelly, 'that's exactly what she did see.'

'You're joking.'

'I'm not. She said she got to bed at about three o'clock

91

in the morning, after mopping down all the stone floors. She took a quick look out of her window before getting into bed. It was misty outside – there's often a mist that comes in off the sea, and she said she was just about to close the curtains when she saw something. She thought at first it was one of the guests, but she said it was too big, and too bulky. Then the wind blew the mist away for a moment, and she saw it clearly.' Niamh's face was serious. 'She says that it was a big, black shape, bigger than a man. Then the mist got blown across it again, and it disappeared.'

'What did she do?' Sherlock asked.

'What could she do? She made sure her window was locked, and then she went to bed, but she says she couldn't sleep. She just lay there, looking up at the ceiling, shaking with fear, thinking about what she'd seen. She got up this morning, exhausted through lack of sleep, and came down to serve breakfast, but she kept remembering what she'd seen.'

'Do you believe her?'

'I believe that she believes she saw something.' Niamh glanced towards the doorway. 'She's obviously panicked. But if you're asking: did she actually see the Dark Beast, or something like a deer out in the mist, or did she just dream she'd seen something? – I don't know. I honestly don't know. I told her to go down to the kitchen, get a glass of water and sit down for a few minutes until she felt better.'

'What side of the castle does her window look out from?' Sherlock asked.

'Why?' She smiled. 'Do you want to go looking for tracks?'

'If I do, do you want to come with me?'

She laughed. 'All right. Her window looks inland. I'll show you later where it is from the outside.'

'It's a . . . deal,' Sherlock said, catching himself before he could say 'date'. 'But can we wait until nearer lunchtime? Your father has said that I can take a look at the books in his library, and I wanted to get straight down to doing that.'

After breakfast, Sherlock headed for the library while his brother took Count Shuvalov's arm and engaged him in private conversation, presumably about great secrets of state. The library was empty when he pushed open the large oak door. Inside, bookcases lined the walls, running from floor to ceiling. Tall windows were covered with green baize curtains to keep the sunlight from fading the books. Ladders on wheels and runners could be pushed along the bookcases. Every spare inch of space was covered with leather-bound volumes in faded black, red and green. In the centre of the room were a couple of over-stuffed leather armchairs and side tables, along with one much larger table where bigger volumes could be opened or maps unrolled.

Sherlock spent a few minutes familiarizing himself with the arrangement of the books – local history, world history, geography, fiction and – perhaps not surprisingly – large sections devoted to the West Indies, and also to spiritualism and psychic phenomena.

Remembering what Niamh had said about the maid's vision of the night before, Sherlock glanced out of one of the windows. The library overlooked the cliffs: there was about fifty feet of grass before an abrupt cut-off line where the cliff edge was. On a clear day Sherlock supposed that he would have seen the sea in the distance, but there was still a lot of mist around, and all that Sherlock could see was a formless grey void – much the same as he had imagined the Other Side to be during the séance the previous night. It looked pretty spooky, even by daylight, and he could see how someone staring into the coiling mist might think they saw shapes being formed. Even a tree, seen through the mist, could take on the form of a monster.

He walked across to the shelves devoted to spiritualist and psychic phenomena. There were two entire floor-to-ceiling sections, with books ranging from those recently published to those dating back hundreds of years. Sherlock scanned the titles quickly, looking not so much for a book that talked about psychic phenomena as if they were true, but one that listed all the tricks and techniques that could be used to fake the effects. He was soon disappointed. The authors of the many and various books on the shelves were all, as far as he could tell, complete and total believers.

It made sense, he supposed. If Sir Shadrach Quintillan was taking part in a confidence trick then he would hardly leave books lying around that would give everything away. If he had such books, and Sherlock suspected that he did, then they were likely to be hidden somewhere. Sherlock made a mental note to continue looking in the rest of the castle – even in Sir Shadrach's own rooms, if he had to. He was, after all, working for the British Government!

Given that he was currently in a different country, he supposed that made him some kind of spy. He found the thought strangely exciting.

Perhaps he was looking for the wrong thing. Rather than search for books specifically on how to fake psychic phenomena, perhaps he ought to be looking more widely, for books on illusions and magical tricks. He walked all around the library, using the ladders to check the upper shelves, but there were none.

He gave up on looking for books on psychic trickery or magic – in the library, at least. On a whim, he crossed to the section covering local history, and looked for any books that might have listed any local legends or stories. There were a couple on the shelves; he pulled one out and took it to the nearest chair. Sitting, he flicked through the volume to see if anything was said about the Dark Beast. He half suspected that Niamh had made the whole thing up to fool him. She seemed to have that kind of challenging sense of humour.

Surprisingly, he found an entire chapter devoted to the supernatural creature. It had, he found, been seen in and around the local area for hundreds of years. Nobody had seen it clearly – it apparently mainly came out at night, or when the weather was particularly misty.

Tired of sitting and reading, he prowled around the edges of the library. He had heard about secret passages in old castles, sometimes hidden behind bookshelves that would swing out on hidden hinges, so he pulled experimentally on a couple of shelves but only succeeded in knocking a few books on to the carpet. He felt silly, and so he stopped. Remembering things that his American tutor Amyus Crowe had taught him, he turned his attention to looking for small signs, tracks and trails, things that were out of context. If there were hidden doors in the bookshelves, and if they opened into the library rather than in the opposite direction, then they might leave some traces of wear on the carpet. He got down on to his hands and knees, looking for any evidence that a bookshelf might have swung out and rubbed against the carpet, but there was nothing. Again, he just felt silly.

'What are you doing?'

He glanced up, trying to look casual rather than surprised and embarrassed. Niamh was standing in the open doorway, gazing down at him with a puzzled smile on her face. 'I dropped a coin,' he said.

'What did you need a coin for in a library? The books are free.'

'I couldn't decide what subject to research next,' he said smoothly, 'so I was going to toss a coin.'

'Oh. All right.' She put her head on one side and stared at him silently for a long moment, obviously not convinced. 'I'm bored. Did you want to go outside and look for tracks now?'

'Actually,' he said, 'I'd rather take a look around the inside of the castle first.' Standing up, he shrugged casually. 'You live here, so you're used to it, but I've never been inside a castle before. I'm curious.'

As he suspected, appealing to Niamh's sense of curiosity worked. 'All right,' she said. 'Let's start at the top and work our way downward. I'll give you the guided tour.'

She led him out into the main hall and then, ignoring the ascending room, raced him up the stone stairway that ran around the edges of the hall, all the way to the top floor. Together they headed along one of the two corridors that led in opposite directions away from the hall.

The castle, Sherlock remembered, was in the shape of a

97

rough square, with the tower of the keep located halfway along one of the sides. The sides themselves were formed by the castle walls, which on the inside had a central corridor and rooms off to either side. The castle's 'corners' were formed by three small towers and one larger one. It took them almost fifteen minutes to walk all the way around the castle walls and back to the hall again. Most of the rooms were bedrooms, or storage rooms, or were empty. Nothing startling or intriguing.

'Can we get out on to the top of the castle walls?' Sherlock asked. 'On to the battlements?'

Niamh smiled. 'Of course,' she said, and led him to a small doorway off to one side of the hall, from where a stone stairway spiralled upward. It ended in two heavy doors set opposite each other. Niamh pushed one of them open and gestured him through.

Sherlock found himself on a long, flat, stone roof, covered with wet moss and edged with battlements that had been worn down by centuries of wind and rain into shapes like rotten teeth. At the far end of the roof was another tower, with its own heavy door. The wind whistled across the roof, snatching the heat from his body and sending cold drops of rain splattering against his face. He could see, from this high vantage point, the Irish countryside extending into the distance: green and brown, undulating gently to form low, wide hills. Undergrowth surrounded the castle, copses of trees stood out as dark green clumps, and stone walls separated fields. The clouds were low, brushing the tops of the hills.

In the distance, rising from a clump of trees, he could see a stone tower, a folly of some kind. Apart from the castle it was the only other dominating feature of the landscape, and he made a mental note to visit it, if he could find it from ground level.

The door slammed shut behind him. He turned, to find himself alone on the roof. Seconds later he heard a metal bolt slam across the inside, locking the door.

'I'll meet you at the other end,' Niamh called from the other side of the door. 'I'll keep the door open for a count of ten seconds. If you don't get through in that time, you're stuck out there!'

Before he could say anything in response, he heard her footsteps running down the stone stairs.

Right now she was preparing to run along the corridor between the keep and the next tower. He had to match her, or beat her, if he wanted to get out of the cold wind. A flash of annoyance made his face feel hot. She seemed to like challenging him, and playing games. Well, if that's what she wanted . . .

He started running along the castle roof, but almost instantly his foot slipped on a patch of moss and he fell sideways, slamming his shoulder into one of the worn battlements. Sick pain flooded his body and withdrew, leaving him weak. He climbed back to his feet and set off again, knowing that Niamh was outracing him a floor below.

This time he knew to avoid the patches of moss as he ran, but as a result his progress was marked by strange little dance-steps as he had to move rapidly right or left, or had to jump across wider areas. The bare stone wasn't that much safer, he found – the rain had left it slick and slippery, and the soles of his new shoes were too smooth to get much of a grip. A couple of times he found himself sliding towards the battlements, and had to use his arms to cushion his approach and bounce off. He thanked heaven that nobody could see him – he must have looked as though he were mad. Of course, he realized, Niamh could visualize exactly how he looked. That was why she had shut him out there and made him run. For fun. For her own amusement.

The door ahead of him opened. In the darkness inside he could just see Niamh's grin, taunting him.

He forced himself to a final burst of speed, ignoring the irregular blotches of moss, trusting to his speed and his weight to get him past them. In his head he counted down the ten seconds that Niamh had promised him.

When he got to eight, and he could see her preparing to shut the door, he jumped and let his feet skid on the moss, catapulting him towards the door.

He thudded against it just as she was closing it, pushing it back open and falling into the tiny room at the top of the stairs.

'What did that prove?' he gasped, leaning against the stones and trying to catch his breath.

'It proved you can run fast,' she said.

'Faster than you.'

'I got here before you, remember.'

He straightened up. 'But you weren't running on wet moss and wet stone.'

She twisted her lips in a little moue of disappointment. 'Well, if you put it that way. All right, you won – this time.' She smiled up at him. 'Do you want to explore any more of the castle?'

She was challenging him again, waiting for him to back down.

'Bring it on,' he said. 'But I've seen enough of the roof now. Let's try for some lower floors.'

She took him around the second, first and ground floors, but they were much the same as the third floor – rooms of a similar size which were either set out as bedrooms or storerooms. Only the ballroom which occupied the ground floor of the other tower was different: a large, empty space lined with curtains with a dais at one end for a small orchestra.

'I don't think we've ever used the ballroom for anything,' Niamh said quietly as they stood there. 'As you can imagine, my father isn't one for dancing.'

As they turned to leave, Sherlock had the sudden impression that a curtain twitched at the far end of the room. For a moment a dark shape, the size of a very large man, was revealed, and then it vanished again. Sherlock turned back to stare at the curtain, wondering if someone else was in there with them – a servant, maybe – but it didn't move again.

'Seen something?' she asked.

'I'm not sure.'

'Was it the Dark Beast?'

He laughed. 'I doubt it. If it was, maybe it'll stay for luncheon. He turned away and followed Niamh.

'What about dungeons?' he asked as they stood back in the main hall where they had started.

'We've got them,' she answered. 'We keep them downstairs.'

'Very funny.'

'Mainly they're used by the servants, and for the cooking. Would you like to see?'

'I'd be worried about you locking me in a cell. I think I'll pass.'

She smiled. 'Probably a good idea. Shall we go outside now?'

'Yes please.' He checked the watch which hung from a chain on his waistcoat. 'What time is luncheon?'

'At one o'clock.'

'We've got about an hour, then. Less if we get dirty or wet and need to change when we get back.'

She raised an eyebrow. 'Afraid of getting a little bit dirty or wet?'

'Not at all. I'm just afraid of missing lunch.' He caught himself, and smiled. 'I'm beginning to sound like my brother. God forbid.'

'Do you get on well with him?'

'That's simple to ask but not so simple to answer,' he replied, uncomfortable with the question but wanting to answer it honestly. 'We've been apart for a while – well, I've been away. Abroad. We've obviously both changed since I left, and I think we're both trying to work out what our relationship is now. I don't need to rely on him the way that I did, but he needs to realize that we're closer to equals now.' He paused, wanting to change the conversation but unsure how. 'What about you? Do you have any brothers or sisters?'

'Apparently I had an older brother,' she said, 'but he died when he was a baby, before I was born.' Her expression turned serious. 'Lots of children die as babies where I come from.'

'A fair number die as babies where I come from,'

Sherlock said, thinking about cholera, and the various other diseases that ran rife through the poorer areas of the big cities. 'Not that I'm trying to draw any equivalence between your background and mine. I know I was privileged.'

'Hey, I grew up in a place of beautiful beaches and beautiful sunsets where you could just pick your meals off the trees, and I'm now living in a castle. Believe me, I feel like I'm privileged.'

'Touché.'

She punched his arm. 'Come on, let's take a tour around the outside of the castle. We won't go too far – we can save that for later.'

He followed her across to the door that led out of the great hall. The doors were half open, and she slipped between them. Sherlock followed into the central square that lay between the castle's walls. In daylight, and facing outward rather than facing towards the doors, as he had been the day before, he could see that it was mainly paved, with scattered patches of grass. In the centre was a statue of an armoured man on horseback. His arm was upraised, and holding a sword.

Niamh led the way outside through the entrance arch and crossed the moat quickly, but Sherlock paused to look down, into the moat's murky water. He couldn't see more than a foot or so into it, because of the mud and vegetation in the depths, but there were things swimming in there – sinuous shapes that could be fish or could be eels, he wasn't sure.

The bulk of the castle shielded them from the wind that had chilled Sherlock up on the roof. He stared out at the Irish landscape. The low clouds had disappeared inland, and he could see the same low hills that he had spotted from the battlements. He looked around, trying to place where the tower he'd spotted was located, but he worked out that it must be around the side of the castle.

Niamh set off in the opposite direction. 'Let's look at the sea,' she said. 'I never get tired of it. Back on my island the sea is blue and green, but here it's always grey. It's also always angry, always crashing itself on the shore rather than coming in as gentle waves.'

Sherlock thought about the different ways he had seen the ocean as he'd sailed to China and back. 'It's like people,' he ventured. 'Despite the fact that we all look basically the same – two arms and two legs and a head – there's an infinite range of personalities. The sea should be just as simple – chemically, it's not complicated – but the same stretch of sea can look completely different depending on the weather and the time of day.'

Niamh vanished around the edge of one of the towers, and Sherlock followed. He found her heading across the stretch of grass that he had seen from the library – the one that separated the castle from the cliffs. She strode right up to the edge of the cliff and stood there, hair blown back from her face by the wind. He joined her, and together they stared silently out into the majesty of the Atlantic Ocean. The waves seemed to form momentary mountain ranges, grey and bleak and topped with white. It was only the size of the gulls that rode the waves that gave away their true size.

Niamh turned her head and stared at him boldly. He returned her stare, not sure what message he was sending but aware that messages were being exchanged.

Niamh opened her mouth to speak, but Sherlock's attention had been snagged by something that he saw sticking out from a bush just the other side of her.

It was a foot. A bare foot.

'Stop a minute,' he said.

'What is it?'

Sherlock gestured at the foot. 'I think,' he said grimly, 'we need to get someone from the castle.'

Niamh took one look at the foot sticking out from the shrubbery, nodded, and ran back towards the castle as fast as she could. Sherlock moved closer to the shrubbery and carefully pushed back the leaves.

A body was lying beneath the bush. It was one of the castle servants. She was on her back, staring upward at the sky, and her face was twisted into an expression of pure terror. Sherlock checked her wrist and her neck for a pulse, but there was nothing. Her skin was cold, and her eyes had a thin coating of dust and pollen on them. She was undoubtedly dead.

This wasn't the first time that Sherlock had seen a dead body, but the sight still made him uneasy. He was amazed at how thin the line was between life and death, and how easy it was to cross. He thought he recognized the girl as well: she was the servant who had dropped the plates and run out of the dining room during breakfast. So quick then, and so still now.

Without touching the body, Sherlock made a visual examination. There was no sign of blood, no obvious trauma. She looked as if she had suddenly fallen down and died on the spot.

Something was nagging at the back of his mind, and he quietened his thoughts to let it come forward. It had something to do with what he had first seen. He stepped back, and let his eyes move over the body, from the top of the head to the soles of the feet, trying to work out exactly what it was that was bothering him.

The feet! That was it! She wasn't wearing shoes!

He heard Niamh returning from the castle, accompanied by others. He turned as they arrived. Silman was there, as were several of the house servants. They saw the girl on the ground and gasped, blessing themselves.

Silman bent to check the girl's pulse, as Sherlock had done. She straightened up, shaking her head. 'The poor girl. She must have had some kind of seizure, God rest her soul. I could tell that there was something wrong this morning, at breakfast. Perhaps her heart was weak.'

'Perhaps it was the sight of the Dark Beast that drove her mad and killed her,' someone whispered. Silman turned to glare at them. 'Fetch sheets. We'll wrap her body up and take her back to the castle. Someone go for the priest. The doctor is already on his way on other business. He'll need to examine her, and sign a certificate of death. If he finds traces of disease then he might well quarantine the castle, which would be awkward for the master.' She turned to Sherlock and Niamh. 'Mistress, young master – I'm sorry you had to see this. Thank you for alerting us. I will tell Sir Shadrach, and we will make all the necessary arrangements. There is nothing else you can do here – I suggest you go on with whatever it was you were doing when you found her.'

Niamh nodded. 'Thank you, Silman,' she said soberly. 'Please let me know if there is anything that we can do.' She paused. 'Did she have family?'

'Not in this area. I believe she had a mother and a brother down near Cork. I will write to them.' She sighed. 'Such a tragedy, when young people die for no reason.'

Niamh was obviously still shocked. 'I was only talking

to her this morning,' she said. 'How can the Lord just . . . take people away like that? Do you understand it?'

'What I don't understand,' Sherlock said thoughtfully, 'is why she was outside in bare feet. She was wearing shoes this morning. Where did they go?'

Silman suddenly made a wordless exclamation, and slapped her hands to her cheeks. 'Forgive me, young master,' she said, 'but the shock of seeing poor Máire here made me almost forget that I was already in the process of looking for you when the mistress ran in to find me.'

'What did you want me for?'

'It's your brother, sir.'

Sherlock felt his heart shift suddenly. He felt sick. 'What's happened to Mycroft?' he asked, stepping forward.

Silman hesitated, apparently trying to frame her next sentence properly. 'He's been injured. It's his head . . .'

CHAPTER SIX

Ignoring Silman and Niamh, Sherlock raced back towards the castle. The idea that his brother had been injured filled him with horror. He had only just got back to the British Isles, only just met up with his brother again. For anything to happen to Mycroft now would be unimaginable. He had always been a fixed, solid presence in Sherlock's life. He had to stay that way!

He raced across the moat and through the high arch into the open central area of the castle, heart pounding and breath rasping in his throat. The entrance to the keep was off to his left, and he pelted towards it and up the ramp without slowing.

In the hall, servants were gathered around the entrance to a room that Sherlock hadn't been in before. Guessing that was where Mycroft was, he pushed past them.

The room was a reception room, with comfortable chairs, *chaises longues* and sofas scattered around. Mycroft was sitting in one of the chairs, his large frame spilling over the arms of the chair and threatening to snap the thin legs. He was as white as the ectoplasm that Ambrose Albano had manifested the night before. It looked for a moment as though he had an enormous wound on his forehead, until Sherlock realized that the blood was a stain that had soaked through a bandage wrapped around Mycroft's head. His skin was so white that the bandage was almost invisible.

Sir Shadrach was beside Mycroft, still in his bath chair. In Silman's absence, one of the foot-servants was stationed behind the chair, ready to push it if needed. Count Shuvalov was standing in a similar manner behind Mycroft's chair with his hand on Mycroft's shoulder.

Mycroft himself had his eyes closed and a hand raised to his forehead. Sensing Sherlock's approach, he opened his eyes and waved his sausage-like fingers. 'Ah, Sherlock,' he said, voice weak. 'I apologize for disturbing your pre-prandial constitutional.'

'What happened?' Sherlock asked urgently.

'I was alone in the library. Sir Shadrach had very kindly given me his permission to conduct some research – I gather that you had the same idea earlier, and I am sorry that I missed you. As it turned out, someone did not miss me. I was struck down from behind. I am informed that the object in question was a candelabra, although I confess that I did not notice at the time. Fortunately, one of the servants entered to see whether I required a cup of tea, and found me on the floor.'

'Did you shut the door when you went into the library?' Sherlock asked.

'I did, yes.'

'And when the servant entered the library, was the door also shut?'

Sir Shadrach glanced away from Mycroft and towards one of the female servants. She curtsied briefly and said, 'Yes, sir, it was.'

'The library door leads directly out into the hall,' Sherlock pointed out. 'Anyone going in or coming out would be liable to be seen by someone – unless there's another way in or out.' He was thinking, as he had earlier, about secret passages.

'I am not aware,' Quintillan said stiffly, 'of any other ways in or out of the library, save the windows, which were and still are firmly closed.' He grimaced. 'On the other hand, there were people going through the hall all the time, and none of them saw anyone going into or out of the library between the time your brother entered and the time he was discovered unconscious.'

'How do you feel?' Sherlock asked, kneeling by his brother's side.

'I have the kind of headache I normally get the day after drinking a bottle of particularly old and crusty port, and my stomach is informing me urgently that luncheon is completely out of the question.' He smiled weakly. 'On the other hand I am alive, and that is always advantageous.'

'We have called for a doctor,' Sir Shadrach said. 'We need to check for concussion, obviously, as well as signs of skull fracture.'

'The important questions,' Count Shuvalov said in his thick Russian accent from behind Mycroft's chair, 'are why the attack was carried out, and by whom.'

'The "why" is obvious,' Quintillan pointed out. 'Someone wanted to stop the British Government from taking part in the auction for Mr Albano's services. This kind of action is despicable and deplorable, and I will not put up with it in Cloon Ard Castle.'

'You seem to imply,' Count Shuvalov said calmly, 'that either I, von Webenau or Herr Holtzbrinck are responsible. For the sake of form, I deny any involvement, although I am sure that the other two gentlemen will do the same.'

'Calm yourselves, gentlemen,' Mycroft said faintly, waving a hand again. 'There is another possibility. The attack may have been arranged as a means of making Mr Albano's services seem worth killing for, and therefore driving the price up.'

'That,' Quintillan said ominously, 'would suggest that either I or Mr Albano might be responsible. I completely—'

'I merely intended to show,' Mycroft interrupted, 'that there are a number of alternative explanations which could point towards anyone in this castle. Even young Sherlock there has had occasional reason in the past to want to hurt me, although he has kindly refrained so far. No accusations are being made, and I would suggest that no offence is taken – if only because I am not sure that my headache would stand an argument breaking out right now. Besides, that might constitute an international incident, and I have been given strict instructions to avoid those at all costs.'

Quintillan nodded. 'Of course. Wise words. You should rest, Mr Holmes. Would you like to be taken to your room to lie down until the doctor arrives?'

'In a moment.' Mycroft caught Sherlock's eye. 'I would like to remain here for a while, just until I get my strength back, then my brother can help me to my room. Perhaps a pot of tea could be arranged?'

'Of course.' Quintillan gestured to the foot-servant, who began to manoeuvre his bath chair towards the door. 'If there is anything else you need, please don't hesitate to call.'

'A plate of biscuits?' Mycroft said hopefully as Quintillan left.

Count Shuvalov patted him on the shoulder. 'Old friend,' he said, 'you have my word that—'

'Say no more,' Mycroft said, halting the Russian. 'Knowing you as I do, I am sure that if you had wanted me dead, I *would* now be dead, and in a considerably more inventive way than being struck down with a candelabra. We will talk more later, when I am feeling better.'

Shuvalov nodded to Sherlock, and left. Sherlock crossed to the door and closed it. There were still servants clustered in the hall outside. He glimpsed Niamh, just entering the hall, but he didn't have the time to explain to her what had happened.

'How are you really feeling?' he asked as he turned back towards his brother.

'Slightly better than the impression I am giving, but not much.' He reached to his forehead gingerly. 'All these years in government service, and I have managed to escape direct attack until now. I cannot recommend it. Still, on the bright side, I suppose it gives me a better insight into the perils that my agents face.' He frowned. 'I suppose.'

'Do you remember anything else apart from what you said just now?'

'Nothing. There is a period of blankness from just before I was struck down to the point where I was discovered.'

'And do you have any idea *why* you were struck down?'

'No more than was said earlier. It was either to reduce the field of bidders or to force the price up. The problem is, that doesn't allow us to exclude any suspects.'

'All right.' Sherlock crouched in front of his brother. 'What do we do now?'

'Several things. Firstly, I will be relying on you to keep involved in the séances. We must be *sure* that there is trickery involved. If you cannot prove trickery, then you must bid on behalf of the British Government. In the unlikely event that this talk of psychic phenomena is true then we cannot allow the Russians, the Germans or the Austro-Hungarians to control it.'

'Or the Americans, if they ever turn up.'

'The Americans always turn up late,' Mycroft said. 'It is a national trait.'

'Can I ask a question?'

'Have I ever been able to stop you?'

'Ambrose Albano isn't the only psychic in the world. Even if the British Government were to lose the auction for his services, surely they could just engage the services of another psychic?'

'A good point,' Mycroft conceded, 'and one that had occurred to me already. The issue is that Mr Albano claims to be able to target particular spirits, to somehow pick them out of the psychic mass and bring them to the earthly plane to communicate. All other psychics, to my belief, say that they have no control over which spirits appear – sometimes it might be a loved one, and sometimes it might be Wolfgang Amadeus Mozart.'

'All right – I stay involved with the séances, and I keep investigating behind the scenes, as I have done already. What else?'

'I need you to send a telegram for me.'

'From where?'

'There will be a telegraph office in the town. I will give you an address to which you should send the message. I am afraid that the message itself will be in code. I realize that you will feel an almost irresistible urge to break the code, but believe me when I tell you that it depends on a code book kept by the man to whom I am sending the message. You will be wasting several precious hours of your life if you try.'

'I understand.'

'Now, please pass me a sheet of paper and a pen. I will compose the message.'

Sherlock hunted around until he found paper and envelopes, along with an inkwell and a pen, in a drawer. He took them to Mycroft, along with a book to rest on as he wrote. Mycroft quickly set to work writing a string of letters in groups of four on the paper. Sherlock watched him as he wrote, but could see no rhyme or reason to the clusters of letters. They appeared to be random.

Eventually Mycroft – who was looking visibly exhausted – wrote an address at the bottom of the paper. It was somewhere in London, but not somewhere that

Sherlock was familiar with. Mycroft folded the sheet, slipped it into the envelope, sealed the envelope and handed it to Sherlock. 'Please take this to the telegraph office in town, and get them to send it. The cost will be minor.' He patted his pockets. 'I believe I have some change . . .'

'I can cover it, Mycroft. Don't worry.'

'I appreciate that, Sherlock. Thank you for being here. I could not have hoped for a more trustworthy or competent assistant in this time of need.'

Sherlock held the envelope up. 'In that case, why are you requesting help from outside?'

Mycroft's eyebrows shot up towards his hairline. 'Sherlock, you *cannot* have decoded the message. It is *impossible.*'

'You are right,' Sherlock said, partly in triumph and partly in sadness. 'I did *not* decode the message, but your reaction has confirmed a meaning that I only guessed at.'

'Very clever.' Mycroft relaxed back into his chair. 'Your mind is so sharp, Sherlock, that you will end up cutting yourself one day.' He took a breath. 'Now – I am tiring rapidly. If you will assist me, I will attempt to make my way to bed. Have the doctor sent up when he arrives – and my tea and biscuits.'

Mention of the doctor reminded Sherlock of something important that he had forgotten. 'One of the servants was found dead outside in the castle grounds,' he said suddenly.

Mycroft gazed at him with interest. 'Who found the body?'

'I did.'

'Yes, of course you did.' Mycroft paused, wincing at a sudden pain in his head. 'Were there any suspicious circumstances?'

'I couldn't see any cause of death. It looked like she just –' he shrugged – 'fell down and died. Maybe a heart attack.'

'Stranger things have happened,' Mycroft mused, 'but the timing is certainly odd.'

'Oh, and she wasn't wearing any shoes.'

'Interesting.' Mycroft winced again. 'But I cannot think about this properly now. I need to lie down. Could you help me to my room, please?'

After he had done so, Sherlock walked down the square spirals of the stone staircase. He half expected Niamh Quintillan to be waiting for him when he got to the bottom, but the hall was empty. He weighed the envelope in his hand. Mycroft had wanted it to be sent immediately. He supposed he should head down to the town to send it. He could ask a servant from the castle to take it for him, but he knew that Mycroft was expecting him to take it himself, to make sure that it got sent. It was quite a distance down to the town: he could ask Sir Shadrach Quintillan for a carriage, but he felt awkward doing that. The walk would do him good.

Strolling out of the castle he was pleased to discover that the low cloud was blowing inland, leaving blue sky behind, and the splattering of rain had ceased. The weather here certainly was changeable.

He set out on the reverse of the route that the carriage had taken the previous afternoon, taking him and Mycroft from Galway to the castle. The path was mainly downhill, of course – the castle was on top of the cliffs, and the town was at sea level. The walk was pleasant, with the sun shining down from an increasingly blue sky and the smell of wet grass accompanying him, but he was painfully aware that the walk back would be uphill all the way. Perhaps he could hitch a ride.

It took him nearly two hours to get from Salthill to the centre of Galway. Part of him wished that Niamh had been with him, to while away the time with questions and guessing games, but another part realized how annoying that would become. There was something bewitching about Niamh, but only in short doses.

He passed the hotel where he and Mycroft had stayed and taken lunch. He knew that the telegraph office would have to be somewhere central and obvious, and he eventually found it at the end of the cobbled main street, near the harbour. Entering, he found the proprietor bent over a complicated mechanical contrivance consisting of various wires and magnets terminating in a simple lever which he was tapping in a regular manner. He was in shirtsleeves, with metal bands holding his cuffs away from his wrists, and he had a green celluloid eyeshade held above his eyes by an elastic band.

'Can I help you, young master?'

'I have a telegram to send to London.'

The man raised an eyebrow. 'And have you the means of payment?'

'I have.' Sherlock handed the envelope to the man, along with a handful of change. 'The message needs to be sent with some urgency.'

'It's odd,' the man said, 'how few people come in here and say "Don't worry, it's a trivial message and it can wait for a while".'

Sherlock nodded. 'Point taken. Nevertheless . . .'

'It will be sent quickly. You have my word. What if there is a reply?'

'Then I am up at the castle at Salthill.'

'Cloon Ard Castle – as a guest of Sir Shadrach Quintillan?' The man's voice had taken on a deferential tone, but one tinged with caution. 'You're staying up there?'

'I am. With my brother.'

121

The man nodded. 'I will get a message up to you if there is a reply.' He paused, obviously wanting to say something else. 'Young master – may I ask . . . have you . . . *seen* anything up at the castle?'

Sherlock hesitated. He had seen lots of things. 'Such as what?'

'Well . . .' The man hesitated again. 'There are rumours that . . . that *the Dark Beast* has been seen again. Is it true?'

'I haven't seen it,' Sherlock said. The words seemed true when they left his lips, but he suddenly remembered the black shape he had seen in the Cloon Ard Castle ballroom, hiding behind the curtains. Surely a monster looking like a lobster wouldn't hide behind curtains? That would be . . . rather trivial.

'But is it true that the Beast has taken a life?' the man whispered, glancing around and surreptitiously crossing himself for protection.

Sherlock was amazed at how fast the news had found its way to the town. 'Someone did die, but we think it was an accident,' he said firmly. 'There is no connection to the Dark Beast.'

'But the dead girl, God rest her – she saw it, didn't she? That's why she's dead!'

'It was a heart attack,' Sherlock said. 'Or perhaps a seizure. There was nothing supernatural about the death.'

'Very well,' the man said, obviously disappointed. 'But people talk.'

'Indeed they do.' Sherlock nodded his head. 'Thank you.'

Before returning to the castle, he managed to find some lunch at a local shop. The walk had made him hungry, and he bought two pies and some fruit, and ate them as he strolled back.

He spent time looking at the landscape – the low hills, the fields, the hedges. Strangely different from the England countryside that he remembered from before he left.

As he got nearer the castle, he spotted something tall and thin rising above the trees. It was the tower he had seen from the roof earlier. The sight reminded him that he had intended to visit it, and he made a mental note to do so later.

It took him well over an hour to reach the twin pillars of stone that marked the entrance to the castle grounds. As he got there he thought he heard the clatter of distant wheels on stone, and the whinnying of horses.

Entering, he noticed a group of people standing just the other side of the castle moat. Sir Shadrach Quintillan was there, instantly recognizable in his bath chair, being pushed by Silman. Von Webenau was there as well, as was Herr Holtzbrinck, and Ambrose Albano, who was wearing a long coat and a hat, as if he were going out for a walk.

123

The psychic was arguing with Quintillan – his arms were waving, and even at that distance Sherlock could hear him shouting in his thin, reedy voice, although he couldn't make out the exact words. The Austro-Hungarian and German representatives seemed to be appealing to him to calm down – there were lots of flapping hand gestures from them, and quieter words that Sherlock couldn't hear. After a few minutes, Albano made an abrupt dismissive gesture with his hand, turned around and strode away from the group, across the moat and towards Sherlock.

Sherlock kept walking along the gravel path that led to the moat and the castle. He and Albano would pass each other at the halfway point. Albano, however, was walking fast with his head down, staring at the gravel. He hadn't seen Sherlock.

A commotion behind him, at the entrance to the castle grounds, made Sherlock turn. A black four-wheeled carriage pulled by two black horses had burst through the gap between the pillars. The driver – who had a scarf wrapped around his face – had skidded dangerously to make the turn. The carriage headed straight at Sherlock, who had to leap out of the way to avoid being hit. He rolled, trying to keep the vehicle in sight. He had a brief glimpse through a side window and inside the carriage, where three men were sitting: two facing forward and one facing back.

Albano had seen the carriage by now, or perhaps he had been alerted to shouts from the group by the moat. He stopped and stared at the black vehicle that was bearing down on him.

Just moments before Albano would have been mown down by the hoofs of the galloping horses and the wheels of the carriage, the driver snapped the reins to the left and flicked his whip at the horses' heads. The carriage slewed around so that it was side-on to both Albano and Sherlock. The force carried it off the gravel path for a few feet before the driver regained control.

As he climbed to his feet Sherlock's mind was racing, trying to explain the driver's bizarre behaviour, but before he could come to any conclusions the doors on either side of the carriage were flung open and two men – also with their faces wrapped in scarves – jumped out. Sherlock just had time to see a third man, motionless inside the carriage, before the man on Sherlock's side of the carriage ran around the back to join his companion, and together they jumped on Ambrose Albano and bore him to the ground. One of the men pulled a sack from his belt, and pulled it over Albano's head. The other man struck Albano, rendering him either unconscious or stunned. Or possibly dead. All Sherlock knew was that the man wasn't moving.

Sherlock's stunned amazement at the sudden turn of

125

events snapped, and he began to race towards the incident. 'Hey!' he called. 'You! Stop! Let that man go!'

Von Webenau and Herr Holtzbrinck ran from the castle towards the carriage, but they weren't as fast as Sherlock, and they were further away. It would take them longer to get there. Sherlock knew that he would have to manage the initial fight himself.

The two thugs with hidden faces pulled the insensible Albano towards the carriage. Picking him up, they threw him in, climbed in after him and pulled the doors closed. The driver, who had been waiting for that moment, whipped the edgy horses into life. They lunged against the straps, pulling the carriage away. The driver hauled on the reins and the horses responded, coming around and heading across the grass and towards the gravel path.

Straight for Sherlock again.

He just had time to leap out of the way once more before the carriage sped past in a blur of black. Sherlock gained a momentary impression of wild rolling eyes from the nearest horse, and then it and the carriage were past him and moving towards the gateway.

Sherlock got to his feet again, brushing himself off, and watched as the carriage rushed away from him. It was too late to catch it: the speed it was going, it would outdistance him easily.

Herr Holtzbrinck and von Webenau ran up to him, both breathing heavily.

'Are you all right?' the Austrian asked, gasping for air.

'I'm fine,' he replied. 'What's happening?'

'What you can see,' Herr Holtzbrinck said. 'Herr Albano has been abducted. Kidnapped. Taken.'

'But why?'

Von Webenau shrugged. 'We have no idea.'

As the three of them stared after the departing carriage, something unexpected happened. It seemed to swerve sideways, leaning up on to two wheels and wobbling alarmingly. Somehow the driver managed to release the horses, or perhaps the sudden twisting of the carriage snapped the straps that connected them to it. Whatever the reason, the horses bolted away, trailing the leather straps and the reins behind them, and vanished out of the castle grounds and on to the road outside. The driver, now without a job and in imminent danger of his life, jumped off the carriage, falling to one side. He seemed unhurt, judging by the way he staggered to his feet and ran off.

The carriage wasn't so lucky. Rolling at an angle, it smashed into the right-hand pillar with the sound of wood splintering. The front right-hand wheel collapsed, sending the carriage tilting forward. The two left-hand wheels came off their axles and spun away, flying over the top of the wall and vanishing beyond.

127

Sherlock, Herr Holtzbrinck and von Webenau shared a shocked look, then bolted towards the site of the crash as fast as they could.

Before they could get there, three men climbed out of the wreckage, brushing shards of wood from their clothes. All three of them had black scarves wrapped around their faces – the two men who had abducted Ambrose Albano and the third man whom Sherlock had seen in the carriage. They saw von Webenau, Holtzbrinck and Sherlock bearing down on them, panicked, and ran away, through the gap between the pillars. Within moments they were out of sight.

Sherlock had a horrible feeling about what they were going to find when they got to the smashed remnants of the carriage. There was no sign of Ambrose Albano getting up unhurt. He must have been injured in the crash, if he wasn't already dead.

The three of them got to the pile of black-painted wood that was all that remained of the carriage and started pulling at the wood, throwing the fragments over their shoulders in their attempts to uncover the psychic.

But he wasn't there.

By the time they got down to the flattened grass and scattered gravel underneath where the carriage had been they had to admit that there was no sign of Ambrose Albano. The three of them straightened up and stared around them, looking for some piece of the wreckage large enough to hide his body, but there was nothing. They had moved every fragment of debris without finding him.

'How many men did you see running away from the carriage after the crash?' Sherlock asked. He deliberately didn't name a number himself, as he wanted to hear what the other two men remembered without influencing them with his own memories.

'The driver ran away first,' Herr Holtzbrinck said, 'followed by three men from inside the carriage. They were all wearing scarves across their faces.'

Von Webenau nodded. 'Three men from inside the carriage, plus the driver.'

'Apart from the driver, how many men were inside the carriage before Ambrose Albano was kidnapped?' Sherlock went on. This was the key question. He had seen three – the two men who had taken Albano and the third man inside, but maybe he had been mistaken. Maybe there had only been two men.

'Three,' von Webenau said firmly. 'Two men jumped out of the carriage to take Herr Albano, but I saw a third man inside. I saw him clearly. He never got out.'

Herr Holtzbrinck nodded an emphatic agreement. 'Three men – one inside and two who got out.'

'So where is Ambrose Albano? What has happened to him?'

'Perhaps he was taken across to the Other Side,' von Webenau said sombrely. 'Perhaps he was rescued by his spirit friends.'

'What was he doing outside in the first place?'

'He said he was worried about the attack on your brother. He wanted to leave, straight away. Sir Shadrach was attempting to calm him down and get him to stay when—'

'May Ah ask,' a voice interrupted them, 'what exactly is goin' on here? Ah was nearly decapitated by a spinnin' wheel, then two horses nearly ran me down, then four masked men ran past me. This ain't exactly the kind of welcome Ah was expectin'.'

The voice – deep and accented – sent a shiver down Sherlock's spine. He turned towards the road outside the gates. A cart had stopped there. Stepping down from the cart was an impressively large man in a white suit with a wide-brimmed white hat on his head. His face was tanned and creased like leather, and his eyes were a faded blue.

'Mr Crowe,' Sherlock said in a voice that he hardly recognized as his own, it was so full of amazement and joy. 'I wasn't expecting you here.'

'Apparently not, otherwise Ah would have expected a calmer introduction.' He walked towards Sherlock and stuck his hand out. Sherlock did the same, and they shook hands solemnly. 'When Ah found out that Mycroft

Holmes was goin' to be here, I guessed there was a chance you might be turnin' up. Glad to see Ah was right.'

'What are you doing here?'

'You're a clever man. You work it out.'

The bright light of sheer logic flooded Sherlock's mind, revealing the obvious answer. 'You are the American representative at the bidding for Mr Albano's services,' he said.

'Exactly. Mah apologies for the late arrival, by the way.' He indicated the cart behind him with his thumb. 'We missed the ferry because mah daughter just had to go shoppin'.'

Sherlock stared over Amyus Crowe's shoulder, at the cart that had brought him up from the town. For a moment all he could see was the driver, the horses, the cart and the luggage piled inside it and strapped down.

And then, from behind the driver, Virginia Crowe leaned forward and looked over at him, and his heart broke all over again.

CHAPTER SEVEN

'Well,' Amyus Crowe said as he settled himself into a comfortable armchair, 'this ain't exactly the set of circumstances Ah imagined our next meetin' to take place under.' The springs creaked beneath his weight.

'Me neither,' Sherlock replied.

They were sitting in the castle's reception room – the same one in which Sherlock had earlier talked to his injured brother. The past twenty minutes had been a bustle of activity as Crowe had presented his credentials to Sir Shadrach Quintillan, introduced his daughter, met the other representatives and overseen the transfer of their luggage to their rooms. Virginia had avoided Sherlock all the while, although he had been painfully aware of her presence. When refreshments were offered Crowe accepted, while Virginia pleaded tiredness after the long journey. Sherlock remembered how sea travel had affected her on the way to and from New York, and wasn't surprised when she went to her room to lie down.

Or maybe, a rebellious part of his mind said, she just doesn't want to talk to you.

'Where's Holmes Senior?' Crowe asked.

'Ah. He's resting in his room after being attacked this morning in the library.'

'*Attacked?*' Crowe's face creased in concern, the leathery wrinkles almost hiding his eyes. 'An' is this somethin' to do with this psychic fellow – Albano – or is it just a random attack?'

Sherlock shrugged. 'Probably the former, but the motive is unclear. Either someone wants to improve their chances at the auction by taking out the likely competition, or someone else wants to force up the price by making it look like Albano is worth fighting for. That means the pool of suspects is pretty much everyone in the house.'

Crowe nodded. 'That's a succinct analysis of the situation. Future events will prob'ly tell us which one it is.'

'How so?'

'Well, if the attack was designed to get rid of competition then there're likely to be more attacks on other representatives. If you want to reduce the pool of contenders then you don't just take out the one.' He smiled. 'Of course, you don't take out *all* the contenders, because that kind of gives the game away as to who is responsible. Last man standin', an' all that.'

'What if the attack was designed to make Albano a more valuable commodity because he's worth fighting for?'

'Then Albano will reappear,' Crowe pointed out. 'There ain't no point in biddin' for something that's vanished. He'll come back with some kind of cockamamie story to make himself look important and powerful.' He paused for a moment. 'How *is* your brother? Will he . . . recover?'

'He was lucid and talking when he regained consciousness. The injury doesn't look too serious. Apparently a doctor has been called in to examine him. I don't know whether he's attended yet or not – I had to walk down to the town to send a telegram on Mycroft's behalf.'

'Knowin' your brother, the telegram was prob'ly somethin' along the lines of "Send fine wines and cream cakes: the catcrin' here is not ideal".'

Sherlock smiled. 'Actually the catering is very good. Certainly last night's meal met with Mycroft's approval.'

'So you've met Ambrose Albano, an' presumably had the chance to see his act?'

Sherlock was about to answer when he suddenly realized that he wasn't talking to a friend any more, he was speaking with a potential competitor. He wondered with a flash of concern what Mycroft would have wanted him to do – tell the truth, say nothing or try to make out that Albano was probably a fake in order to reduce the likelihood that Crowe would make a serious offer on behalf of the American Government. He shook his head.

This was complicated. What was the best thing to do?

The best thing, he decided, was to tell the truth and damn the consequences. He knew and trusted Amyus Crowe; and, more to the point, so did his brother. Besides, Crowe might well wonder himself whether Sherlock was telling the truth or telling a lie, in which case Sherlock might as well tell the truth anyway, on the basis that whatever he said might not be believed.

'Wise move,' Crowe said softly. 'Always tell the truth, if you can. It'll confuse the hell out of your enemies – an' you know Ah'm not an enemy.'

'How did you know what I was thinking?' demanded Sherlock.

'It's pretty simple, although it makes for a good parlour trick. You hesitated after Ah asked the question, indicatin' that you were havin' doubts about tellin' me. Your gaze flickered upward, to where Ah presume Mycroft's rooms are. You were wonderin' what he would want you to say. You looked back at me, but your eyes weren't focusin' on my face – they had that look that people get when they're rememberin' somethin'. Ah guessed that you were rememberin' everythin' you an' Ah have been through together. You then glanced down an' to the right, which is a sign that you were puttin' your thoughts in order logically before tellin' them to me. People who are lookin' to lie often glance down an' to the left. It's a strange thing, but worth knowin'. Somethin' to do with which side of the brain you're usin', Ah believe – the analytical side, or the side that we use to construct stories.'

'Very clever. You'll have to teach me how to do that.'

'If we get a chance to have any more lessons,' Crowe said, and there was a sad tone in his voice that Sherlock didn't like. 'Now,' he continued briskly, 'your thoughts on Mr Albano.'

'He's a fake,' Sherlock said immediately. 'I haven't worked out how he manages his tricks yet, but I'm certain that they *are* tricks.'

'What kind of things has he been doin'?'

'Chalk messages appearing on slates, wooden plaques moving to point to letters in order to spell out other messages, the production of some kind of substance that is apparently called "ectoplasm" that can take the shape of a supposed spirit . . .'

'The standard repertoire, then. Nothin' cleverer than that.'

'Exactly.'

'An' your brother concurs?'

'He does.'

Crowe nodded slowly. 'Ah suspect that Mycroft an' Ah are in the same position, bein' less convinced ourselves than our respective governments are. From what you've said Ah can't imagine Ah'll be any more convinced when

Ah've seen him in action mahself.'

'So how did you get to be the American representative?' Sherlock asked.

'You tell me, son.'

Sherlock thought for a moment. 'The invitation went out late enough that the American Government didn't have time to send someone over from America; or perhaps they didn't think the likely reward was worth the expense and effort of such a trip. They looked for people they trusted who were closer geographically. There would be the Embassy staff in London, of course, but for some reason they chose you instead.' Sherlock closed his eyes briefly, to help himself concentrate. 'I presume they needed someone whom they trusted and who also had a reputation for not being taken in by trickery, and that led them straight to you.'

'Precisely.'

Sherlock thought about what they had been talking about for a moment. 'That kidnapping,' he said. 'How was it arranged, do you think?'

'Ah don't know, son – Ah wasn't here. What did you see?'

Sherlock closed his eyes again, recalling the events and putting them into logical order, aware that Crowe had just pointed out that closing the eyes was a sign of remembering. 'I'd only just arrived back from town myself, so I was looking at events from out near the road. Everybody else was nearer the castle, so between us we had a view from both sides. Albano was outside the castle, apparently leaving. He was having some kind of argument with Sir Shadrach – with the benefit of hindsight I suspect it had something to do with the attack on Mycroft. Perhaps he was scared. Anyway, he had just set off, walking towards where I was, when a carriage raced in from the road. The carriage stopped by Mr Albano. Two men jumped out, but I saw a third man inside. They all had scarves over their faces. And, of course, the driver makes four men in total. The two men knocked Albano over, put a sack on his head and threw him into the carriage. They got back in, and the driver drove off, but the carriage seemed to veer off the path when it got outside the walls, and it crashed. Four men raced away, and they all still had scarves over their faces. I had the carriage in sight the whole time, from before the kidnapping until it crashed, and Mr Albano never got out, but when I and the other two representatives ran over to it he wasn't there. The carriage was empty.'

Crowe nodded slowly. 'A fine and succinct account, young man. Your brain hasn't got slack while you've been away. Now, a couple of things occur to me. Coincidences, things that stand out as being different. Firstly, it was lucky for the abductors that Mr Albano was outside the castle just at the moment they drove in. If he'd been inside, what would they have done? Gone lookin' for him?'

'Good point,' Sherlock said. 'They had to know he was going to be outside at that exact moment, and the only person who knew that was, I suppose, Albano himself.'

'Precisely. The second point is: it was lucky for us that everyone just happened to be outside *watching* Mr Albano walkin' away. Everyone got to see the abduction and, more importantly, the vanishin' trick. Every trick needs an audience.'

'Again,' Sherlock said, 'that was down to Mr Albano. He was the one who had the argument. If it started inside then people would have taken notice and moved to watch, then followed him and Sir Shadrach outside. They were the perfect audience.' He took a deep breath. 'So, it *was* a trick, and it *was* arranged by Mr Albano himself, or at least with his knowledge and assistance. Which means that we can expect him to reappear in a little while, as you said.'

'There's another point,' Crowe said.

'What is it?'

'You tell me.'

Sherlock thought for a moment. 'If we're right, and Albano arranged the kidnapping and the disappearance himself, or at least knew that they were going to happen, then it was important that the crash happened *inside* the grounds of the castle, because that was the only way those of us who were there would know that he had disappeared. If the crash had happened half a mile down the road then we wouldn't have been there, and we might, when we finally did get there, have assumed that Mr Albano had just wandered off. The mysterious disappearance only works because it happened in front of our eyes. That means the crash was deliberately arranged to occur exactly where it did. But how?'

'Oh, many ways.'

'But what about the disappearance from the carriage? How did he manage that?'

Crowe frowned in disapproval. 'Ah'm surprised at you, Sherlock. That's the simplest thing of all. There's only one answer. Go figure it out yourself.'

'Oh!' Sherlock said suddenly, changing the subject. 'I forgot to tell you. One of the servants died. I don't know if there's any connection to anything else, or whether it was just a tragic coincidence, but I found her outside. There wasn't a mark on her, but she had a horrified expression on her face, and her shoes were missing.'

'Hmm. Difficult to see how that ties in with anythin' else. That kind of horrified expression can be a sign of a weak heart givin' way – Ah've seen it before. Let's park that one for now.' His gaze softened. 'But Ah guess there's a question you've been avoiding, all the time we've been talkin'. You want to ask it now, or you want to pretend there's nothin' wrong?'

Sherlock felt a sudden obstruction in his throat that stopped him from saying anything for a moment. He wanted to ask about Virginia, but he wasn't sure he wanted to know the answer. Would it be best just to pretend that nothing was wrong, and continue onward with a smile on his face?

No, he decided. It was always better to know the truth, no matter how much it hurt, because that hurt was the kind you got when a wound was beginning to heal.

'How is Virginia?' he asked quietly.

'The short answer is: she's growin' up. She ain't the girl you knew a year or two back. Hell, she ain't the girl Ah knew a year or two back, an' Ah'm her papa.' He shook his head sadly. 'Ah know that you had feelin's for Virginia, even though Ah wasn't sure you knew it, an' Ah know she reciprocated, at least in her way. The trouble is that you were gone for over a year, an' it happened just as she was growin' up. She got to thinkin' about boys, an' marriage, an' the future, an' you just weren't there. There's an old saying, Sherlock – "A bird in the hand is worth two in the bush". It means that something you've got is better than something better that you actually haven't got. Ah think she thought about waitin' for you. Ah think she thought real hard about that, but in the end she just didn't know if you were ever comin' back. She had to make a choice –

141

wait on a promise, or take what was there in front of her.'

'So she met someone else, just like that?'

Crowe frowned. 'It wasn't "just like that", son. It took a considerable period of time. Travis an' Virginia met naturally, just like you and she met, at the cottage. He rides like he was born in the saddle, so he an' Ginnie just got talking straight away. He's a fine, upstandin', good lookin' boy, and she couldn't help bein' impressed. She kept him at arm's length for nearly six months, but eventually she came to me one night an' asked me if Ah thought you were ever comin' back.' He paused, and grimaced. 'Ah had to be honest, Sherlock. Ah had to tell her that there was a strong chance you might get caught up in some adventure, or decide to stay in one of the countries that you saw, or maybe even go to India to look for your father. You might even have met another girl and fallen for her. An' even if you did come back, Ah told her that it might be a year or more, and that you'd have changed. She thought about that, an' Ah guess she made her decision. A bird in the hand is worth two in the bush. So she an' Travis got more serious, an' he proposed to her.' He sighed deeply. 'Ah can't say Ah don't wish things were different, but hopin' for what ain't goin' to happen is just plain foolishness. We have to accept the world the way it is.'

Sherlock found that he didn't want to accept the world

the way it was. He wanted it back the way it used to be. He wanted to *change* the world.

But that wasn't fair on Virginia. She had made her choice. Trying to win her back would be like pretending her opinions had no validity, that they weren't important to him, that only *his* desires had any importance, and that wasn't a message he wanted to send. He had to let her make her own choice.

'Is there any chance,' he asked quietly, feeling the dead weight of unwanted emotion in his heart, 'that she might change her mind, now I'm back?'

Crowe shrugged. 'You know how stubborn Ginnie gets. The only thing that can change her mind is her. Best thing you can do is just be around, be a friend, talk to her and let her decide what she wants to do.' He frowned. 'But there isn't too much time. Ginnie an' me, we're leaving for the States after these psychic shenanigans are over. Ah've been called back, partly because the US Government wants me to report in person about this Mr Albano, but partly because the Pinkertons have got work for me to do. With Bryce Scobell dead, there's no threat to us any more.'

'Going back?' Sherlock whispered. His heart, which had felt heavy before, now felt like it was filled with lead and sinking through his chest.

'Things change, Sherlock,' Amyus Crowe said simply.

'When I grow up, I don't *want* things to change. I

want to live somewhere that never changes, and I don't want my friends to change either.' He knew he sounded petulant, but he couldn't help himself.

'Your brother Mycroft feels much the same. That's why he spends most of his time at the Diogenes Club. That place hasn't changed since he started it, an' it never will.' He paused. 'Speakin' of your brother, Ah ought to go and check in with him, see how he is, but before Ah do – tell me about China. What was the place like? Ah hear rumours that you did some great service for the American Navy while you were out there, an' Ah would truly like to know more about that.'

Sherlock spent the next hour or so telling Amyus Crowe in great detail about his adventures both on board the *Gloria Scott* and in Shanghai. Crowe was particularly interested in the grotesque Mr Arrhenius, and his feral daughter. Sherlock explained about the USS *Monocacy* and the plot to blow it up and start a trade war, and the way he detected the location of the bomb and the bomber. At the end of the story, Crowe applauded.

'You sure don't have a simple life, Sherlock. Ah'm jealous of the adventures that happened to you, Ah'm proud of the way you used your mind to solve problems an' get out of danger, an' Ah'm grateful on behalf of the US Government for what you did. War in the Far East may be to the benefit of certain businessmen, but it's not somethin' the President would wish to happen, an' Ah have that on the highest authority. But Ah'm concerned about the possible involvement of the Paradol Chamber. Are you an' Mycroft sure that there's a connection?'

Sherlock shrugged. 'There's no real evidence, but the indications are that the Paradol Chamber want a war in the Far East just as little as your President does. Or, rather, if there is going to be a war, then they want it to be at a time of their choosing. I'll probably never know if I was really working for them or not, but I think it's likely.'

Crowe nodded. 'They do seem to be a complicated bunch. Ah hope we've seen the last of them, but Ah suspect we haven't.' He started to lever himself out of the armchair, which was so small compared to his bulk that it threatened to come up with him, snugly fitting around his hips. He pushed it down. 'Ah'm goin' to pay mah respects to your brother now. What about you, son?'

Sherlock looked around, checking that nobody was in the doorway. 'I'm going to investigate Mr Albano's room while he's still safely disappeared. I want to see if I can work out how some of his tricks were accomplished. I need to give some thought to how he vanished, too.'

'Good idea. Let me know what the results are.'

They left the drawing room together and headed for the ascending room. Sherlock showed Crowe how to operate it, and they rose together to the second floor. Sherlock left Crowe outside his brother's room, returned to the ascending room and headed for the third floor. He walked along the corridor towards the second tower, where Sir Shadrach Quintillan, Niamh Quintillan and Ambrose Albano had their rooms.

Niamh had already shown him who was in which room, and he stopped outside Ambrose Albano's door. Nobody was around, and he twisted the doorknob and entered quickly. It was only when he was standing in the centre of the room that it occurred to him that Mr Albano might well have crept back there after his faked kidnapping – if it really had been faked – to hide out. Fortunately the place was empty.

He looked around, mentally cataloguing everything so that he could make sure he left the room looking like it hadn't been searched. Albano was fastidious and meticulous: everything was in place and carefully lined up. Sherlock started on the wardrobe, where Albano's clothes were hung. He went through all the pockets, and checked that nothing had been hidden between the garments or behind them, but he failed to find anything. He then went through the drawers in the bureau, but the folded shirts, undershirts, socks and handkerchiefs hid no secrets. Sherlock even knelt and looked beneath the bed, but apart from several pairs of highly polished shoes there was nothing of interest there either.

The next step was to check behind the paintings and framed prints that were hung up on the wall, and then to look on top of the wardrobe. Again: nothing. He pulled the bureau out from the wall and checked behind it, but apart from finding a line of dust on the floor his efforts were wasted.

Remembering the time he had searched the room of Mrs Eglantine – his aunt and uncle's former housekeeper, back at Holmes Manor – and found what he was looking for hidden on a rope hanging outside, he opened the window and looked out to see if anything had been hung down from the window ledge, but the stone brickwork of the castle was unadorned by any additions. He pulled up the rugs, but there were no papers beneath them and no areas of the stone flooring that looked like they might be capable of being levered up to reveal a hole beneath.

Coming back to the centre of the room, he looked around again in frustration. He was beginning to run out of ideas.

Glancing again at the bed, he noticed that there was a frilly valance running around the edge of the mattress. It hung in folds halfway towards the floor. Previously he had only looked at the floor under the bed, but he suddenly saw that near the foot of the bed the valance was caught up, as if someone had lifted it and tucked it beneath the mattress and then forgotten to pull it out again.

147

He got back down to his knees and pulled the valance completely clear, then looked beneath the bed again, this time paying particular attention to the underside of the mattress.

A box was hanging beneath the bed. Hooks at each corner suspended it from the metal springs. Sherlock studied it carefully, to make sure he knew exactly how to put it back again, and then he reached underneath and gently unhooked it. It was about the size of a shoebox. Placing it on the carpet, he undid the catch securing the lid and lifted it up.

Inside was a mass of white material, very fine and very light. The weight of the lid had been holding it down, but with the lid released it puffed up, lifting up with it the other object inside the box, almost as if it were bringing it to Sherlock's attention.

It took a few moments to work out what the other object was. It was white and small, and it had one rounded end and one that was flat. Something sharp was protruding from the rounded end, while the flat rear appeared to be attached to a length of cotton that finished in a small hook. Sherlock picked it up gingerly, and realized that the bit he thought was flat was actually hollowed out. That, along with its size, immediately told him what it was, and what it was for. It was a thimble, something meant to fit over the end of a finger, and the sharp bit projecting out of the end was a splinter of chalk. The length of what he had taken to be cotton was actually elastic.

He smiled to himself, and nodded. During the séance, Ambrose Albano had been wearing white gloves. If the white thimble had been hidden up his sleeve, or inside his jacket, he could have pulled it out and slipped it over a finger without it being noticed. That way he could have written messages on the slate while he was holding it underneath the table. Once he had finished, he could just have pulled the thimble off his finger and the elastic would have snapped it back out of sight. Ingenious. Simple, but ingenious.

He put the thimble to one side and examined the material. He already had an inkling of what it was, but he wanted to make sure. He pulled it from the box and spread it out. It weighed almost nothing – so light that it seemed to float in his hands. He examined it closely, and found several small tears in it.

This was almost certainly the 'ectoplasm' that had manifested from Albano's mouth during the séance. It was so fine that it would crumple up into a small ball, barely larger than the thimble. He must have had it hidden somewhere about his person.

Gingerly, he smelt the material. It had been washed recently – he could still detect the sharpness of carbolic. That was probably a good thing, if his suspicions about where Albano had been hiding it were correct. Sherlock

149

suspected that it had actually been in Albano's mouth, pressed between his cheek and his teeth. Crushed up that small, it wouldn't have soaked up much saliva, and it may have been chemically treated to repel moisture. Under the guise of choking, Albano must have pulled it free. He guessed that the material had been soaked in some kind of chemical that glowed in the dark, making it look spookier in the shadows of the séance.

This wasn't just ingenious: this was brilliant. So simple, and yet so effective.

But how had the material expanded outward and floated in the air, and what about the face that had seemed to materialize inside the shroud? There were still questions to answer, but Sherlock could see the broad strokes of the trick.

Genius.

Sherlock carefully packed the material back inside the box and placed the white thimble on top of it. He refastened the lid, replaced the box beneath the bed, and pulled the valance back into position.

He stood up and looked slowly around the room. There was, as far as he could see, no trace that he had ever been there.

Quickly he left. There was no knowing whether one of the servants would enter to turn down the bed or make up the fire or something, and it was obvious now that the servants had to be involved.

Leaving the room and closing the door carefully behind him, he returned to the castle keep and down to the ground floor. He saw nobody on the way. He stood in the hall indecisively for a few moments, then headed out into the open air. He couldn't stand being cooped up for too long.

The sky was even clearer than it had been earlier. Sherlock walked out of the castle, through the main gate and across the drawbridge. He wasn't sure where he was heading, but the sight of the wreckage of the carriage used by the kidnappers caught his attention and he wandered across to it. He was aware of the stone bulk of the castle behind him, and also painfully aware that Virginia was behind one of those windows. The thought made him feel self-conscious, and he found himself walking stiffly, unnaturally.

No, he told himself, this is stupid. Just be yourself.

When he got to the wreckage he stopped thinking about Virginia and forced himself to consider the pile of wood instead. He knelt down and started sorting through it, uncertain at first what exactly it was that he was looking for. The wood had been flung in random directions during the fruitless search for Albano, and after a few minutes Sherlock found that he was unconsciously sorting it into more ordered piles, trying as best he could to replicate the overall shape of the carriage. Left-hand door over *here*, right-hand rear wheel over *there*, driver's platform in front, and luggage rack at the back. Those bits of wood that he couldn't identify he placed to one side until he could figure out where they went.

He pulled out a long rod that was almost certainly an axle. There was no way of knowing whether it was the front or the rear axle, of course. The second axle was buried further under the wreckage, but when he finally managed to excavate it he discovered that it was in several pieces. It must have been broken in the crash. He juggled the lengths for a few seconds, trying to work out how they would fit together. The bits where the wheels would have gone were obvious – they were worn and rubbed smooth by the constant rotation – and that gave him a head start on arranging the other pieces, but as he did so he realized something strange.

The broken ends weren't broken at all – they looked as though they had been cut.

He stared at the axle for a few moments, thoughts whirling around his head. The carriage had been deliberately sabotaged. The axle had been sawn through so that it would snap if put under pressure. Albano had probably given the driver a particular manoeuvre to carry out that would do the trick at exactly the right time.

Sherlock stood up, and sighed. Crowe might think it easy to work out, but Sherlock still didn't know *how* Albano had arranged his own disappearance from the carriage. He suspected, however, that it was also a form of magic trick.

CHAPTER EIGHT

Sherlock headed upstairs to check on his brother, but Mycroft was asleep and Sherlock didn't want to wake him. He looked pale and weak, lying there in bed with a bandage around his head. Quintillan had arranged to have a footman – female, of course, given the role-reversal in the Quintillan household – standing outside Mycroft's room at all times, making sure that nobody tried to attack him again. Given Sherlock's suspicions about the servants, he wasn't sure whether that was a good idea or not, but apart from Sherlock or Amyus Crowe standing guard themselves in shifts, night and day, he couldn't think of an alternative. Besides, if Mycroft *was* attacked again, while a servant was supposedly guarding him, then suspicion would automatically fall on the castle staff and therefore Quintillan himself. Presumably Sir Shadrach wanted to avoid that happening if at all possible, which meant that Mycroft was probably safe. At least, that's what Sherlock hoped.

'Has anybody been in to see him, apart from me?' Sherlock asked the woman standing stiffly to attention outside the bedroom door.

'The doctor, sir,' she said, staring somewhere up above Sherlock's head. 'And there was a man – a large man in a white suit. He spoke with an accent.' Given her own thick Irish accent, Sherlock found that momentarily amusing.

A big man in a white suit? Almost certainly Amyus Crowe. He had said earlier that he was going to pop in and see Mycroft.

'Nobody else?'

'No, sir.'

Sherlock turned to leave, but the woman cleared her throat as if she had something else to say. He turned back and raised an eyebrow inquiringly.

'Forgive me, sir, but is it true?' she asked.

'Is what true?'

She glanced left and right, checking whether anybody else was within earshot. 'About the gentleman inside being attacked.'

'Yes, he *was* attacked.'

'By the Dark Beast?' Her gaze momentarily flickered down to meet his. 'The same one that killed poor Máire, God rest her. That's what they're saying down in the servants' area.'

Sherlock couldn't help laughing. 'No, he wasn't attacked by the Dark Beast, and your friend died of a seizure, or a heart attack. That's all there is to it.'

'But it's true that nobody knows who attacked the gentleman?'

'Yes.'

'So it *might* have been the Dark Beast.'

'I doubt it.'

'But the Beast has been *seen*. Three of the servants have spotted it, moving around outside the castle. *Máire* saw it, and now she's dead, God love her!'

'Tricks of the light, I think,' Sherlock said. 'Maybe some kind of big animal, moving in the mist. That's all it is.'

'Yes, sir. Of course.' There was something in her tone of voice that suggested she didn't believe him. As Sherlock walked away, he remembered the shadowy figure that he had seen in the castle ballroom, moving back behind the curtain. There certainly seemed to be *something* moving around in the shadows, and if it was inside the castle now, then it was unlikely to be an animal. But it couldn't be a supernatural beast. That would be against all logic and sense.

It was late afternoon now. Lunch was a distant memory, and dinner was still a while away. Sherlock wandered back to his room to wash and to change out of clothes that were muddy and crumpled after his adventures outside. He found an envelope on his pillow. It contained a handwritten note from Sir Shadrach Quintillan stating that dinner would be at eight, and that in the absence of Ambrose Albano the séance planned for that evening would have to be postponed. Based on his discussion with Amyus Crowe, Sherlock had his suspicions that Mr Albano would make a surprise reappearance at dinner so that the séance could go ahead with added excitement and interest, but only time would tell about that.

He wandered downstairs again, feeling at a loss about what to do next. He had examined Albano's room, and the wreckage of the crashed coach, so there was nothing more to do there. He supposed he could sit down somewhere quiet and try to think through how Ambrose Albano had managed his own disappearance, or alternatively he could try to work out how Mycroft had been attacked in the library.

He decided to take the latter course. That, at least, would require some kind of action – looking for secret entrances and evidence that someone else had been in the library. He wanted to be doing something active, not just sit around thinking. That was Mycroft's forte, not his.

The problem was that he had already searched the library with a view to finding secret passages. Admittedly, he'd done that before Mycroft had been attacked, but he hadn't found anything. What was the point of searching again?

He wondered whether it was worth him pacing out the

length and width of the library inside and then pacing out the same space outside, looking for discrepancies, but that would take a lot of time and be prone to small errors. People would also wonder what he was doing. The thought of trying to trace any secret passages from outside gave rise to a realization, however – a secret passage had to have two ends. One end would be in the library, obviously, but the other end would have to be somewhere else in the castle. Maybe, if he looked in all the likely places, he could trace where the other end came out.

Enthused by the idea, he spent the next half-hour walking through the corridors and the rooms around the library, looking for something that might conceal a secret entrance – a curtain or wall hanging, perhaps, a wardrobe or a tall bureau. He didn't find anything. He ended up back in front of the library door again, hands on hips, frustrated.

Maybe it wasn't a secret passage. Maybe it was a secret stairway, or a secret ladder. That would require much less space behind the walls.

Upstairs or down? Sherlock considered for a moment, and decided to see what was underneath the library. He had already spent enough time wandering the corridors of the castle without meeting anyone, and he knew his luck couldn't last forever. Heading down into the cellars would hopefully keep him away from people. Besides, he hadn't seen the lower floors yet, and he was curious.

He stood in the hall, trying to work out where a stairway leading down to the cellars might be. As he stood there, he heard a sound behind him, like leather scuffing against stone. He turned quickly.

Count Shuvalov's manservant – the burly Russian with the close-cropped hair – was standing in the shadows. He was staring at Sherlock with no expression on his face. When he saw that he had been spotted he nodded, once, and walked away.

Sherlock watched him go, feeling uneasy. What did the man want?

He shook his head to try to banish the concern. He had other things to think about. He already knew that the main staircase didn't go below the ground floor, but he had previously noticed an insignificant door near the bottom. Pushing it open, he discovered a narrow flight of stone steps leading down.

At the bottom Sherlock found a passage that led left and right. A lamp hung from a hook on the wall, providing a meagre and flickering yellow light, but the two branches of the corridor faded into darkness after twenty feet or so. The ceiling was low, nearly touching his hair, and the walls were bare stone. He tried to work out where the library was in relation to where he was now, and decided that it had to be off to the right. He unhooked the lantern and carried it with him as he headed in that direction, passing a series of arched doorways, some with wooden doors sealing them and some without. They were obviously storerooms.

Something on the ground, in the doorway of one of the rooms, attracted his attention. He stopped to look.

It was a pair of shoes.

He bent down to examine them. They were women's shoes, black, and the leather was cracked with age. They had been well looked after, but they were obviously long past the time when they should have been replaced. Obviously their owner was poor, and couldn't afford new shoes, but appearances were important to her, which is why she had taken care of them.

He remembered the dead servant. She had been barefoot. Were these her shoes? If so, did that mean she had died here, down in the cellars, and that her body had been moved up and left in the castle grounds? Her shoes might have fallen off as she was dragged away, he supposed, but why would anyone want to hide the place where she had suffered a heart attack but not hide the body? It didn't make sense.

Leaving the shoes where they were, he straightened up and moved off. This castle was just full of mysteries.

A wall suddenly appeared out of the shadows in front, where the corridor made an abrupt right-hand turn. He kept going, aware that he was moving further and further away from the location of the library but interested to see where the corridor actually led. It turned left, and then right again as he walked, with no obvious reason why.

Within a few minutes, the stone of the walls had been replaced with brickwork, old and crumbling. The flat ceiling over his head had given way to arches. Patches of green moss had taken hold in places, and were hanging on for grim life.

A dark ring around the walls appeared within the bubble of lamplight. As Sherlock got closer he saw that moss had spread all the way around the walls and across the ground. He hesitated before stepping on to it. It was only when he counted his footsteps and realized that he was now beneath the castle moat, and that the moss was almost certainly growing on the moisture that had seeped through the bricks, that he felt safe enough to continue.

He kept walking, knowing by now that he was actually outside the boundaries of the castle. The corridor – more properly a tunnel now, he supposed – was leading him out into the grounds and into . . . where? Into the Irish countryside, he assumed. It was difficult to keep track, what with the way the corridor had twisted several times, but he thought he was heading parallel to the cliffs.

Other tunnels began to sprout off from the one Sherlock was in. They led into darkness, and Sherlock didn't feel that he particularly wanted to explore them – not at the moment, anyway. Following a single tunnel in a straight line, he was unlikely to get lost. If he started turning off on a whim, then he was likely to completely lose his bearings. From some of the tunnels – usually the ones that led off to the left, towards where he estimated the cliffs to be – he could feel a faint hint of cold air on his skin. He also thought he could detect a slight downward slope to those tunnels, but it was difficult to be sure. Did they lead to caves down on the beach? Quite probably.

Next time he came down, he promised himself, he would take some paper and a pen, and make a map as he went along.

It was increasingly apparent to him that this castle had some kind of historic connection to smuggling contraband goods. The smugglers had probably landed their goods by boat on the beach and then stored them in the caves. Other people – locals – had then used the tunnels to get to the goods and transfer them inland, possibly keeping them in the dungeons of the castle if there was any sign that the police were going to search for them. Would the castle's owners have been involved, or was it more likely that the castle servants had, over many generations, dug the tunnels and were running their illegal business from beneath the castle without the owners actually knowing? There was no way of telling.

Sherlock kept walking, heading away from the castle.

The tunnel ended without warning. Suddenly, in the lamplight, Sherlock saw a wall ahead. Why would someone put a wall there? It didn't make sense, he thought, unless it had been done in a hurry to disguise the tunnel from outside, to stop anyone getting in.

The wall was odd. For a start, it was built out of a different kind of material from the tunnel walls and ceiling. They had been brick, and this was stone, but not the kind of light, granite-like stone that the castle was made from. No, this wall was made from blocks of a darker, greyer stone, and it was rougher. Running his fingers across one of the blocks he could feel a rasping sensation. Looking closer, he also thought he could see small holes in the stone – natural holes, not created ones. He had never seen anything quite like it.

Sherlock realized with some surprise that the wall had a gradual curve to it. It had to be a planned thing – but why? What was the purpose?

The bricks of the tunnel were held together with mortar, Sherlock noticed, but there was a gap between the bricks and the dark grey stone. Through that gap he thought he could detect a faint breeze, and the smell of the sea. He bent down and checked the junction between the flagstones of the floor and the wall, and found something odd. The flagstones had actually been *cut* to fit around the curve of the wall, and there was a gap there too.

He looked up at the junction of the wall and the roof. The same thing was true there: the bricks had been cut to follow the curve of the wall, as if the wall went up further than the tunnel. And down further as well.

There was no moss on the wall. That struck Sherlock as being particularly odd. The walls and the arched ceiling were both marred by occasional blotches of the green stuff, but the dark stone wall was completely clear. Maybe it was something to do with the stone itself, he mused. Perhaps that type of moss didn't like growing on that type of stone.

He stood there for a few moments, hands on hips, frustrated at the fact that he couldn't go any further. Eventually and reluctantly he turned to leave, but as he did so he put out a hand and rested it on the wall.

It was vibrating.

The sensation was very faint, but clear enough that he stopped and placed both hands against the stone. There was definitely a vibration there, but he had no idea of where it was coming from.

More frustrated than ever, he turned to walk back to the castle.

It took thirty minutes for him to get back to where the stairs led up, towards the castle, passing all the tempting side tunnels on the way but always aware of which direction he was going in. He glanced into the doorway where he had found the shoes earlier. They were still there, which somehow surprised him. Given the strange things that were happening in this castle, he had almost been convinced that they would have vanished.

When he got to the stairs he glanced up into the darkness, towards the closed door at the top, but shook his head. There was still another branch of the underground corridor to explore, and he knew that it would keep gnawing at his mind if he didn't complete his investigations now. He walked on, the centre of his glowing bubble of candlelight.

For the first few minutes the corridor to the left of the stairs was the mirror image of the corridor off to the right. He wondered if he was going to waste the next hour replicating the last one, including finding himself way outside the castle walls and being confronted by a curved wall of dark stone. Instead, just when he wasn't expecting it, the corridor abruptly turned right, and ended in another archway sealed by a wooden door. This door was bigger than the previous ones. Sherlock tried it, and to his surprise it opened.

The room he found himself staring into was large, with an arched stone ceiling. The only illumination was the lantern that he carried. It was another storage room, but there was no mistaking what was being stored in it. The room was filled, floor to ceiling, with racks containing bottles of wine. Sherlock could tell that most of the bottles had been there for a long time – dusty cobwebs covered everything, looking strangely like the ectoplasm that Ambrose Albano had produced during the séance of the night before.

The thing that struck Sherlock the most, however, wasn't the bottles, or the racks, or the cobwebs. It was the black fungus.

This wasn't the green moss that he had seen in the tunnel earlier. This was something much darker and much more alive. This stuff wasn't just clinging to the edge of existence: this stuff was actively *exploding* with life. It filled the corners of the wine cellar in the same way that seaweed covered rocks on the beach, or that snow would pile up in the winter. It crept up the wine racks and covered the lower bottles like a dark and evil tide. It hung from the ceiling in black curtains and drapes. Everywhere that Sherlock looked, he could see it. It seemed to glisten slightly in the light from the candle, as if it were wet. He imagined that, if he touched it, the fungus would squish beneath his fingers, leaking some strange and potentially toxic black fluid, but he had no intention of testing that out.

Eventually, realizing that it was almost time for dinner, he left the wine cellar and headed for the stairs that led up to the hall.

He was about to move towards Mycroft's room to see how he was when he heard voices outside the open front door. He glanced over, and noticed Count Shuvalov and his military manservant standing there. They were arguing – or, rather, Shuvalov was speaking quickly and angrily and his manservant was attempting to interrupt. Eventually Shuvalov jerked his head dismissively, and stalked off. The manservant watched him go with an expression of dismay on his usually impassive face.

Sherlock headed upstairs, towards Mycroft's room. There was a different servant standing guard outside the door. She looked at him, recognized him, and nodded.

'Sir.'

He nodded back, and entered the room.

Mycroft was awake, and reading. He glanced at Sherlock. 'Ah, good evening. I see you have been outside and also underground. I must have been asleep for longer than I thought.'

Sherlock smiled. There was no keeping of secrets from his brother, but there was also no point in asking how his brother knew the things that he knew. Unlike Amyus Crowe, he rarely gave lessons. 'Ambrose Albano is a fake,' he said, 'the coach crash was arranged in advance, and there are tunnels leading away from the castle in various directions, probably built by smugglers.'

'Very concise. Be so kind as to explain the evidence

for your first and second statements.'

Sherlock explained about searching Albano's room, and about finding the sawn-through axle. He wondered whether he should tell Mycroft about the stories of the Dark Beast, and the dark shape that he had seen moving around, but decided not to. There were all kinds of explanations for that, and none of them affected the job that Mycroft and he were there to do, as far as he knew.

'Albano will reappear tonight,' Mycroft concluded. 'It will set the scene perfectly for the second séance.'

'That was my conclusion as well.' Sherlock hesitated. 'Do you feel well enough to join us for dinner and for the séance?'

Mycroft shook his head. 'The doctor has advised me to stay in bed for the next twenty-four hours, at least. There is, fortunately, no sign of concussion, but my system has been weakened and needs to recover. Sir Shadrach has very kindly agreed to provide my dinner on a tray.' He paused momentarily. 'Actually, a series of trays. Probably a trolley carrying numerous trays. He did indicate that he wished me to participate in the séance, and suggested that I use one of his spare bath chairs, but I worry that the strain of getting out of bed would be too much at the moment. I keep falling asleep at the most inopportune moments. No, Sherlock, I fear that you will have to take my place both at dinner and at the séance.'

167

'You *fear*?' Sherlock repeated.

'An unfortunate choice of words. I have complete confidence in you.' He gazed at Sherlock for a long moment. 'I have spoken with Mr Crowe, and I understand that his daughter is here as well. Have you spoken to her?'

Sherlock shook his head. 'Not yet.'

'Then be gentle. She will be as confused and uncertain as you are.'

'That,' Sherlock said, 'I seriously doubt. Did you know, by the way, that he was going to be the American representative?'

'I suspected so, but I had no actual evidence, so I said nothing to you. It does, however, make sense from the point of view of the US Government.' He turned his attention back to the book in his lap. 'Report back to me after the evening's events. I am agog to discover what will happen.'

Sherlock nodded, and left.

A gong sounded for dinner just as he was descending the stairs. He headed for the dining room.

Most of the other guests were already assembled, with the exception of Amyus and Virginia Crowe, and of course the missing Ambrose Albano. Sherlock took his place at the table, nodding at Count Shuvalov, Herr Holtzbrinck, von Webenau, Sir Shadrach Quintillan and Niamh Quintillan. Candelabras set along the table served to illuminate the room. The curtains were open, and through the windows Sherlock could see a dark and stormy sky. Rain splattered intermittently against the glass, sounding like thrown gravel.

The servants were just preparing to serve the soup when Amyus Crowe and his daughter entered the room. He was wearing his usual white suit, while Virginia was almost unrecognizable to Sherlock in a pale violet gown that perfectly matched her eyes. Her hair was up, and she looked so much older and more assured than Sherlock remembered. She looked like a lady now, not a girl. He wondered bitterly if he looked like a man to her, rather than a boy – now that it was too late.

She glanced at him and smiled nervously.

'Many apologies for my slight delay,' Crowe boomed, holding the chair out so that Virginia could sit down. 'Sir Shadrach, you have a daughter too, an' a beautiful one. You must know, therefore, just how long it takes them to get ready for a simple evening meal.'

'Daughters are jewels beyond price,' Quintillan said, 'and so we must give them every opportunity to display themselves in the right setting.'

He smiled at his daughter. Niamh smiled at her father, then her gaze sought out Sherlock, and she shared the smile with him. Virginia glanced at Niamh too, and Sherlock thought he caught a flicker of emotion on her face, although he was unsure exactly which emotion it was. Perhaps several.

Lightning flashed outside the window, and a sudden gust of wind rattled the glass. Moments later a peal of thunder echoed through the castle's halls and corridors.

'A fine night for communicating with the dead,' Herr Holtzbrinck said. 'A shame the séance has been postponed. I presume that there is no news of Herr Albano's whereabouts?'

Quintillan opened his mouth to speak, but before he could say anything another flash of lightning, bigger this time, illuminated the room in stark black and white. The following gust of wind was so strong that it sent the dining-room windows crashing open, letting rain spill into the room and blowing the candles in the candelabras out. Darkness engulfed everything.

'Do not panic,' Quintillan's voice rang out. 'The servants will relight the candles in a—'

The candles suddenly came back to life by themselves. Their flames seemed twice as tall, twice as bright as before.

And in their light everyone could see the thin figure of Ambrose Albano standing at the end of the table, arms spread wide.

'I have returned!' he exclaimed.

CHAPTER NINE

Silence fell around the table. Everyone was thunder-struck – everyone apart from Sherlock, who had been expecting this, and probably Amyus Crowe as well.

'Good Lord!' Quintillan exclaimed. 'Ambrose, my dear fellow! What happened? Where have you been?'

Very convincing, Sherlock thought, *considering the fact that you are almost certainly part of the conspiracy.*

Albano collapsed theatrically into an empty chair. He gestured to a servant. 'Wine!' he said in his thin, reedy voice. 'I need wine! I have neither eaten nor drunk since I was taken.'

'*Who* took you?' Herr Holtzbrinck asked, but Albano just waved an arm. 'I meant when I was taken *from* my kidnappers to the Other Side.'

The servant poured a large glass of wine and placed it in front of Albano. He downed it in one go.

'Tell us everything,' Quintillan urged. 'Leave nothing out.'

'You remember that I had said I was leaving, following the attack on the British representative,' Albano said. 'I was, perhaps, being overly melodramatic, but I fully intended at the time to walk all the way down to Galway and find my way back to a large town where I could vanish for a while. You all saw the carriage that drove into the grounds of the castle, and the two masked men who leaped out and grabbed me.' He glanced sideways at Amyus Crowe. 'Except you,' he said. 'I do not believe that you were there.'

'Amyus Crowe, representing the US Government.' Crowe thrust his large hand out towards Albano. 'Pleased to make your acquaintance, sir.'

Albano gazed at the hand with palpable unease, as if Crowe were holding a fish out towards him. Eventually Crowe withdrew the hand.

'They threw me bodily into the carriage,' Albano continued, 'which then clattered away so fast that I thought my teeth would fall out! There was another man in the carriage, one who hadn't got out with the other two. Along with the driver, that made four men.'

Crowe glanced over at Sherlock meaningfully. Sherlock knew what he was thinking. Why was Albano making such a thing about the number of men who kidnapped him, unless it was somehow important?

'This other man in the carriage put his foot on my chest, and said: "You, psychic. You will provide *us* with your services now, and you will provide them for free. We will not bid for them like common folk. You will put us in contact with the dead, or you yourself will die!"'

'Did he have an accent?' Count Shuvalov asked, leaning forward earnestly.

'He did,' Albano said, 'but I cannot place it.'

Shuvalov leaned back again, disappointed.

'I was terrified, of course,' Albano continued. He glanced around the table, making eye contact with everyone sitting there. 'I knew that I had fallen into the clutches of a group of bloodthirsty bandits who would exploit my abilities without cease.' He made a fist of his right hand and banged it on the table. 'And that was when I decided to contact my spirit guides and ask for help!'

'Of course,' von Webenau murmured.

'I sent out waves of mental energy on the astral plane, through my psychic crystal.' He reached up and tapped the false eye. It made a clicking sound. 'And they responded. Feeling my distress and my terror, they came for me and took me up out of this world and into theirs. My body vanished from the carriage. I can only imagine the looks on the faces of the three men inside. After that . . .' He paused dramatically. 'I cannot speak of what happened here on earth.'

'The carriage crashed,' Quintillan said. 'Perhaps the sudden shift in weight as your corporeal body vanished somehow unbalanced it. We all saw it crash, and we saw four masked men run away. That would be the driver, the

173

two men who snatched you and the third that was inside the carriage.'

Again, Crowe glanced over at Sherlock. The message was plain: Albano and Quintillan between them were making a bit of a play over the number of men that were seen. But why?

'Did you manage to capture the men?' Albano asked. 'Who were they?'

Quintillan shook his head. 'They ran off. All attempts to trace them have failed.'

'No doubt the employees of some unscrupulous foreign power that was not invited to this auction,' Herr Holtzbrinck said grimly.

'But where did you go?' von Webenau pressed. 'What was it like?'

Albano smiled, and shook his head. 'There are no words to explain. The astral plane is . . . unlike anything you have ever experienced. Time flows differently there. The spectrum has five more colours than we are used to on earth, and there is no need of conversation as thoughts can be heard directly. Food and drink do not exist – instead, the spirits of the deceased feed off the very light itself, which provides all the nourishment they need. It is a beautiful, remarkable place. I wish I could have stayed, but my rescuers explained that I was needed back on earth. I am, they said, destined to be the bridge that connects the worlds of the living and of the dead. So, when they determined that it was safe for me to return, they placed me back here, with you –' he threw his arms wide – 'my friends.'

It was, Sherlock had to admit, a very convincing dramatic performance. If he hadn't seen the paraphernalia of Albano's tricks hidden in the man's room and discovered that the carriage had been sabotaged then he might even have been taken in.

'But surely you can tell us *something* of the astral plane?' von Webenau pressed. 'Did . . . did anybody there give you any messages for anybody here?'

'There were spirits eager to talk to me,' Albano admitted. 'I told them to wait – that there would be a chance this evening to hold another séance during which they could talk with those here.' He looked over at Quintillan. 'That will be all right, will it not? The séance will still take place?'

'I fear you may be too fatigued,' Quintillan said. 'Perhaps we should let you rest.'

Sherlock was fairly sure that Quintillan was protesting for effect rather than seriously. The sudden protests from Holtzbrinck and von Webenau made Sir Shadrach raise his hands up in surrender. 'Very well – we will go ahead. *If* you are sure you are strong enough.'

'I will have to be,' Albano said, raising a hand to his head. 'The spirits on the astral plane are depending on me.'

Dinner, when it arrived, was just as varied and as interesting as it had been the night before. The soup was seafood again, but instead of being cream of turtle it was a lobster bisque. The main course was braised rabbit in a cream and mustard sauce, with asparagus and sea kale as accompaniments. The dessert was a trifle.

All the way through the meal the talk was of what had happened to Ambrose Albano. The Austro-Hungarian, German and Russian representatives pestered him with questions about what it had been like on the astral plane, how he had felt when he was there and whether or not he had met any famous dead spirits. Albano answered the questions with long and convoluted replies, accompanied by much arm-waving and elegant, flowery descriptions, but Sherlock noticed that his answers contained a lot of words and not very many hard facts.

Sir Shadrach Quintillan acted as a kind of orchestrator, Sherlock noticed. He asked some questions, but they were very generic and easy to answer, and his main role seemed to be to interrupt politely if the questioning became too intense or pointed and move the conversation on to something simpler which Albano could illustrate with more ambiguous examples. Sherlock wasn't sure whether the other guests had spotted Quintillan's role as distracter-in-chief, but the American representative certainly had. Amyus Crowe's face was fixed in an interested smile, but his right eyebrow was raised in a manner that Sherlock knew expressed scepticism and irritation. He didn't ask any questions, which was probably for the best. Sherlock suspected that if he did, then he would try to trick or trap Albano, and with Crowe's sharp mind it would be a massacre.

Every now and then, during the meal, Sherlock became aware that either Virginia or Niamh was looking at him. He glanced back, but they looked away quickly. He felt awkward; as if there were something going on that he wasn't quite aware of, a subtext to the glances that was lost on him.

He did notice, in passing, that Count Shuvalov's manservant was missing. The burly Russian with the severe haircut wasn't at his usual place, standing behind his master. Instead, one of the castle servants was filling in.

Sherlock did ask Ambrose a few questions of his own. During a lull in the conversation, he said with apparent naivety: 'Were you scared when you were threatened in the carriage?'

Albano smiled in a kindly way. He had already answered that question during his speech when he had first reappeared, and he obviously thought that Sherlock had forgotten, in his nervousness at replacing his brother at the table. That wasn't the case: Sherlock remembered the answer very well, but he wanted Albano to repeat it so that he could use the answer as the basis for his real question. It was like bowling an easy ball to a cricket batsman, knowing that he would take the easy course and hit it to where you wanted it to go – where a fielder was waiting to catch it.

'I *was* scared,' Albano said, as if talking to a child. 'The kidnappers, whoever they were, threatened to kill me if I did not cooperate with them.'

'But if the astral realm is so warm and peaceful, and so full of interesting spirits,' Sherlock said innocently, 'then why be scared to die? Why should *anyone* be scared of death any more?'

Albano struggled with an answer. Sherlock didn't take his gaze off Albano's face, but out of the corner of his eye he could see Amyus Crowe grinning.

'Death, it is true, is merely a portal between this place and a better one,' Albano said slowly and eventually, 'but sometimes the transition can be . . . painful. There are many ways to die, and I suspect that my kidnappers would have chosen a particularly unpleasant one for me. I confess, with some embarrassment, that although I am not scared of death, I am not keen on being hurt, especially for any length of time.' He smiled. 'Does that answer your question, young man?'

'Do you wish you were still there?' Sherlock asked innocently in response.

'I beg your pardon?'

'If the astral plane is so welcoming and comfortable, do you wish you had stayed there?'

Albano frowned. 'Well, to an extent, yes, I suppose I do. Existence there is so much more peaceful than it is here.' His voice took on a more dramatic tone, as he started slipping into what Sherlock recognized as a standard answer which he had used several times, with variation. 'There is no pain, no unhappiness. There is only . . . peace and great joy.'

'Then why did you come back?' Sherlock asked simply.

'I . . . I still had work to do here.' Albano looked as if he wished he were somewhere else. 'And, of course, I could feel the mental call from the gentlemen here, who wished me to return so that I could bring them the glad tidings from the Other Side. Does that . . . does that answer your question?'

'It does, thank you,' Sherlock said. Before Albano could say anything more, he added: 'Do bad people go to the astral plane?'

'What?' Albano's face was creased in confusion.

'Well, you said that the astral plane was a warm and peaceful place filled with friendly spirits, but there have been a lot of evil people in history. Are they on the astral plane too, because you haven't mentioned them? If they *are* there, are they still evil? If your kidnappers had been

179

killed in the carriage crash, instead of escaping, would they have ended up on the astral plane with you? What would you have talked about?'

Albano's silence this time was longer than before. Quintillan tried to interrupt, but Amyus Crowe raised a hand to stop him.

'It's a good question,' Crowe said, 'and I'd like to hear the answer.'

'There are many . . . ah, degrees, or . . . or levels . . . of existence in the astral plane,' Albano said slowly. 'Which level you end up in depends on your deeds during life.'

'So it's like heaven and hell,' Virginia interrupted from further down the table. 'Just like we get taught in church.'

'It's not like heaven and hell at all,' Albano snapped. 'Those are absolute and opposite things. The astral plane is more *nuanced* than that, more subtle. The concepts taught by the Christian church need to be updated to reflect the reality.'

It would have been easier, Sherlock thought, if he'd just said that he didn't know. He's got himself into a hole now.

'So there's no concept of punishment for sin in the astral plane?' Herr Holtzbrinck asked, confused. 'That seems unreasonable and unfair.'

'No,' Albano said, and then quickly added, 'Well, yes,

but it is not punishment as we on earth would understand it . . .'

Sherlock risked a glance at Amyus Crowe. He nodded at Sherlock, and made a small clapping motion with his hands.

'You mentioned colours that the astral realm has which we do not,' Quintillan interrupted. 'Is there any way you can describe these new colours to us?'

'Ah,' Albano said, obviously relieved to have been rescued from a difficult conversation. 'Yes, there is, for instance, a new colour located between green and blue which we have no word for and no conception of, but which the spirits of the astral plane call *elichori*. Staring at that colour can bring feelings of intense focus and concentration . . .'

The conversation went on like that for a while, and Sherlock didn't feel any great desire to interrupt again. He had already shown, to his own satisfaction, that Albano was making it all up as he went along, and had no real coherent vision of the astral plane.

After plates of cheese and biscuits had been served, followed by small cups of coffee, Quintillan said to Albano, 'My friend, I have no wish to put you under any undue stress, given the terrible events that have befallen you, but do you feel strong enough to take part in a small séance? These gentlemen have travelled a great distance to

181

see you at work, and it would be a shame to deny them.'

Von Webenau and Holtzbrinck were nodding like eager puppies at this. Count Shuvalov was more restrained, sitting back in his chair casually, but he was nodding slightly in agreement. Amyus Crowe glanced at Sherlock and shrugged as if to say: *Why not? Let's let him demonstrate his tricks.*

Albano took a deep breath. 'This excellent dinner has helped to relax me,' he said. 'And the fact that I was only recently in the astral plane means that I still feel a strong connection to it. I believe I might be able to manifest a few spirit appearances, but I cannot promise anything. My passage there and back has stirred up the psychic currents, and the spirits may not have the strength to make the journey across.'

Which was, Sherlock thought, a great excuse if the séance was a failure: it sounded mysterious and convincing, but it meant absolutely nothing.

As he stood up, Sherlock surreptitiously removed a knife from the table and slipped it into his sleeve. The knife was made of silver, and was heavy. He could feel it pulling at the material. If knocked against the table in the room where the séance was going to be held it would make a loud noise, and Sherlock had a suspicion that he might need to do that, if only to throw Albano off his game.

The seven men sitting around the table – including Sherlock – made their way to the drawing room where the séance had taken place the night before. Niamh Quintillan attempted to appeal to her father to let her watch, but he said no. 'You and Miss Crowe go to the sitting room. I'm sure you have a great deal to talk about.'

Looking at the scowl on Virginia's face, Sherlock wasn't so sure, but he said nothing.

The arrangements were exactly the same as the previous night. They all sat around the table which was still marked with letters, numbers and the words 'Yes' and 'No', and the blank slate was set on the table in front of Albano. The psychic made a big thing of asking someone – Amyus Crowe this time, given that he had not been present the night before – to examine the slate and the table to ensure that there were no tricks, no hidden messages, no extra slates, but Sherlock was sure that he would already have hidden the white thimble with the chalk tip inside his jacket, held by the elastic cord so that it could be quickly pulled back when he had finished with it.

Outside the window, lightning flashed again, outlining the curtains with white light. Moments later, Sherlock heard thunder once more. It was, he thought, a perfect backdrop to a séance. Albano and Quintillan couldn't have arranged for anything better if they had tried.

183

Quintillan glanced around the table. 'Gentlemen, are we all ready?'

Everyone nodded.

Albano placed his hands on the table, palms down, and threw his head back. 'Is there anybody there?' he called. 'Spirits of the astral plane, I ask again: is there anybody there? Does anybody have a message for someone around this table? If you can, knock once for "Yes" and twice for "No".'

Nothing happened. The tension in the room was so tangible that it was, Sherlock thought, almost like a form of ectoplasm in its own right.

He wondered briefly if the spirit of the dead servant – Máire – might appear and answer questions about where she had died and why her body had been moved, but that was perhaps too much to hope for. Nothing was *that* convenient.

'I ask again: is there anybody there? Does any spirit have the strength and the will to cross the astral currents to be with us here tonight?'

Again, for a long moment, there was nothing, and then a loud *bang* echoed around the room. Von Webenau jumped in his seat.

'Do you have a message?'

Another *bang*.

'Do you wish to spell the message out using the letters,

numbers and words around this table?'

Bang! Bang!

Now that he was aware that the séance was entirely trickery, Sherlock wondered how the knocking was being done. It had to be something simple, like Albano, or possibly Quintillan, hitting their shoe against one of the legs of the table. Whoever it was might even have a wooden reinforcement on their sole to make the sound louder.

'Is this the spirit known as Invictus?'

Bang!

'Can you write the message for us on this slate?' Albano asked, touching the slate in front of him.

Bang!

Albano picked the slate up in both hands and held it up so that it was clear there was no message on it. He turned it over so that everyone could see both sides, and then clutched it to his chest with both hands. He rocked forward and backwards a few times, still holding the slate, but Sherlock noticed that as he rocked he moved the slate further and further down, until it was beneath the level of the table, relying on the movement of his body to keep everyone's attention. Sherlock watched his upper arms carefully, and spotted the moment when Albano let go of the slate with his right hand, slipped the thimble on his index finger beneath the table and blindly scribbled a quick message.

The psychic threw his head backwards as if in some kind of trance state or fit, but Sherlock noticed that he used the movement to distract attention from the fact that he had brought the slate up from beneath the table again. It wasn't that he was trying to convince the watchers that the slate had always been above the level of the table – he had already gone to some efforts to show them that there were no tricks or props beneath the table – but it was more, Sherlock assumed, that he didn't want them thinking too much about where the slate was or what was happening to it. Albano held the slate up, facing the watchers. 'Is there a message?' he asked.

That was a nice touch, Sherlock decided. Of course there was a message – he had written it himself – but asking the question made it sound to the watchers as if he were being taken by surprise.

'Yes,' von Webenau exclaimed.

'Please, read it out.'

'*Someone around this table*,' von Webenau read slowly, '*does not believe!*'

The chalk message on the slate was perfectly legible – at least, to Sherlock – but having it read out was a touch more dramatic.

Albano glanced around the table. 'Is it true?' he asked, shocked. 'Is there someone here who does not believe? It is not an easy thing for the spirits of the dead to pierce the veil between the worlds. If they thought their time was being wasted, they might decide to stop.'

Von Webenau and Holtzbrinck protested their belief loudly; Shuvalov, Crowe and Sherlock protested in slightly less voluble terms. Albano nodded. 'Very well.' He raised his voice. 'O spirit, we beseech you, please continue to communicate with us. Is there any other message – perhaps for someone specific?'

Bang! The table vibrated, knocking the wooden plaque sideways from where it rested in the centre.

Albano went through the same routine as before, rocking back and forth and holding the slate beneath the table. This time Sherlock knew that he was wiping the first chalk message away with the side of his white gloves before writing a new one.

When he brought the slate up from beneath the table, the chalk writing said: *I have a message from the wife of one present.*

Sherlock's eyes were drawn to Amyus Crowe. He knew that Crowe's wife had died on the ship that had brought the family from America to England. Crowe rarely talked about his wife, and Sherlock wondered whether the man would react now.

Crowe's jaw was clenched tight. Sherlock could see the muscles tense beneath his cheeks. He said nothing.

'Is there someone here who has lost their beloved wife?'

187

Albano asked. 'If so, rest assured that she is happy and well.'

Sherlock looked around the table. Shuvalov, he knew, was unmarried. Mycroft had mentioned it at some time in the past. Von Webenau and Holtzbrinck he wasn't sure about, but judging by the expectant looks on their faces they were both waiting for someone else to come forward. Quintillan had lost his wife, of course, but he was part of the plot, not a victim of it: none of the foreign representatives would be impressed by a message from a psychic to the man who was organizing the séance. No, this had to be aimed at Amyus Crowe, and Sherlock felt a spark of anger fan into flame within his chest. This was a step beyond trickery and into abuse. Quintillan and Albano must have researched each of the international representatives before they arrived, looking in particular for any relatives or friends who had died. They had played on Holtzbrinck's dead brother the night before, and now they were using Crowe's dead wife. There would, if Crowe came forward and accepted the communication, be some meaningless message about her being happy, and urging him not to grieve for her. For some this might be a comfort, but Crowe would know that he was being tricked, and the anger he would feel might cause him to do something that, as a representative of his government, he might later regret.

'Sir Shadrach,' Sherlock whispered, looking across the table at the man in the bath chair. 'Is it possible that the message is for you?' He knew that it wasn't, but he wanted to give Crowe the chance to calm himself down.

Quintillan's gaze flickered to Albano and then back to Sherlock. He obviously didn't want to accept the message himself – he wanted Crowe to accept it – but theoretically it *could* have been for him.

'Is the message for Sir Shadrach?' Albano asked the air above the table, coming to Quintillan's rescue.

Bang! Bang!

'Then there must be someone else here who has lost their beloved companion,' Albano persisted. He glanced around the table, not letting his gaze fix on Crowe, as that would have given away the fact that he knew very well who was being targeted, but making sure that he at least glanced at Crowe on the way. It was a battle of wills between the two men; one that Sherlock knew he had to interrupt, otherwise there might be violence. Crowe was not going to come forward and admit that his wife was dead. He would not let her memory be defiled by trickery and deceit.

'Is the message for von Webenau?' Albano continued.

Bang! Bang!

Sherlock knew what was going to happen. Albano was going to go around the table. Given that he was making

189

the knocking sound himself, he would be able to choose the man he wanted – Amyus Crowe – and Crowe would either have to accept that he was going to be the victim of their trickery or he was going to have to protest.

Sherlock slipped the knife – the one he had taken from the dinner table – from his sleeve. The weight rested in the palm of his hand beneath the table. He turned it over so he was holding the blade, and the handle – the heaviest part – was pointing up.

'Is the message for Mr Crowe?' Albano asked, deliberately not looking at Crowe.

Before Albano's foot could hit the table leg, or whatever he was doing to make the noise, Sherlock hit the handle of the knife hard against the underside of the table, twice.

Bang! Bang!

The noise wasn't quite the same as the one Albano had been making, but it was near enough. Most of the men around the table took it in their stride, but Ambrose Albano and Sir Shadrach Quintillan twitched. They knew that it wasn't Albano making that noise. More than that, they knew their plan to get Crowe to accept a fake message from his dead wife was now finished. The problem was that they couldn't say that this knocking was a fake without admitting that they had been doing the knocking up to now.

Albano's mouth twisted in anger – a momentary

expression that only Sherlock, and probably Crowe, noticed. His gaze flickered around the table, trying to spot who it was that had made the unexpected noise. One by one he asked a succession of spirits if they had a message for the rest of the men – Herr Holtzbrinck, Shuvalov, von Webenau, Sherlock himself and even the absent Mycroft – but his heart obviously wasn't in it and the repeated double-knocking was perfunctory. When he had exhausted all the possible candidates, he announced: 'I fear that the spirits must have become confused by the turbulence of the psychic currents. The message they hold must be for another person, somewhere else. Never mind. We shall press on.'

Sherlock glanced briefly across at Amyus Crowe. His friend and mentor's face was white and strained, his lips tight with anger, but he nodded his gratitude towards Sherlock.

'I sense that no more messages will be forthcoming tonight,' Albano continued testily, 'but if we are fortunate then one of the spirits may feel able to manifest itself directly in front of us. Please, everyone, concentrate on making the spirits feel welcome here. Ask them, in your minds and your hearts, to appear for us. Suppress any disbelief in your hearts.'

He bent forward and raised his hands to his face. This time, knowing what was to come, Sherlock realized that he was using the theatrical gesture to mask moving something from his hand to his mouth – almost certainly a tightly wadded pill of thin material from his hidden box, the one that he would then produce as ectoplasm – but he couldn't spot the actual moment of transfer.

Albano now waved his hands in the air. Sherlock looked closely at him, and saw that his right cheek was slightly swollen. Something was in his mouth that hadn't been there before.

'I can feel them!' he cried, his voice slightly muffled by the object in his mouth. 'They come!'

His hands were making clutching motions at the air, and Sherlock realized that he was feeling for very fine hooked threads that must be hanging from the ceiling and which would be used to pull the material into the shape of a shroud, or a spirit. In the darkness of the room, they would be invisible. The night before, his gestures had looked reasonable, if exaggerated, but now that Sherlock knew what the man was doing he couldn't see how he could have been fooled.

Albano's grasping hands must have found the hooks at the ends of the threads, because he pulled his hands back towards his mouth and coughed convulsively – once, twice – to expel the material and surreptitiously attach the threads to it. Jerking his head back, he slowly brought his hands away from his mouth again. Between them, a ghostly white shape began to expand.

Gasps filled the darkness as the Austro-Hungarian, Russian and German representatives reacted to the appearance of the spiritual form.

The hooks and threads pulled the material into a rough approximation of a shrouded human form. Inside the shroud, a face swam into existence. Last night it had been a young girl's; tonight it was an old woman's, lined and creased. Sherlock glanced around, trying to place where the light projector had to be, but he couldn't see it. The lens must be shrouded somehow, so that only the person directly in front of it – Albano – would be able to see it, but the expanding material provided a perfect screen for the illusion.

Sherlock could still feel the anger in his chest that had been there since Albano had tried to force Amyus Crowe to accept a fake message from his dead wife. He couldn't sit there and let this farce go on any more. His brother would almost certainly have let it continue, but Sherlock felt cheapened by it.

'Stop!' he cried, and stood up.

CHAPTER TEN

Before anyone could stop him, and before Albano could dispose of the fake ectoplasm, Sherlock leaned forward and snatched it from the air above the table. The light material was almost weightless in his hands, but he could feel it against his skin. The invisible threads snapped, one by one, and the material floated down and came to rest on the table.

'Turn the gas lamps up,' he said, but as the words were leaving his mouth the light in the room suddenly flared into brightness. Glancing over, Sherlock saw that Amyus Crowe was moving from gas lamp to gas lamp, turning them up to full strength.

'What is the meaning of this?' Quintillan shouted. His face was livid. 'You are a guest in my home. This is an intolerable abuse of my hospitality!'

'The intolerable thing here,' Sherlock said loudly, 'is the way you and this man –' he indicated Ambrose Albano – 'are using trickery to try to convince us that you can communicate with the dead, and you are doing it just so you can make money from governments who should know better!' He gathered up the white material on the table and held it out. 'This is not ectoplasm. It has not been produced by spirits, and it did not appear out of nowhere. It's just a magical trick.'

Holtzbrinck and von Webenau were staring at him, open-mouthed. Count Shuvalov was less emotional, but he was still paying rapt attention to Sherlock's words. 'But – the face?' he asked.

'A projection.' Sherlock pointed to the far side of the room, where he knew the light projector had to be, based on the way the light had shone on the cloth. 'You'll find it up there, hidden behind the wall. There will be a hole for the light to shine through.'

'But . . . where did the ectoplasm . . . the *material* . . . come from?' von Webenau stammered.

Sherlock said nothing, but instead wadded the material up, tighter and tighter, until it was a small knot the size of a walnut. 'Easily hidden,' he said. He ran his hand across the table until he found the black threads. Letting the material expand out again into a fluffy cloud, he laid the threads across it. They were stark: black against white. 'Manipulated from outside the room to take a particular shape.'

'The shape of a woman,' Holtzbrinck said.

'A shape which you *believed* was a woman.' Sherlock shrugged. 'Have you ever looked at a cloud in the sky and thought it looked like a dragon? The mind can play tricks.'

'You accuse me of trickery?' Albano protested in his high-pitched voice. 'Ectoplasm, when touched by human hands, becomes manifest as an ordinary substance. Every psychic knows that! You have proved nothing!' He stared defiantly around the table, his white false eye seeming to stare at everyone at once. 'I will not listen to these accusations any more!'

He turned to go, but found Amyus Crowe standing directly behind him.

'Oh, you will stay,' Crowe said genially. 'The moment you used mah dear wife's memory as a prop in your obscene game you lost any claim to bein' treated with respect. Sit *down*.'

Albano sat abruptly, white-faced.

'An' you,' Crowe added, pointing at Quintillan, who was quietly ordering a foot-servant to wheel him away, 'you stay where you are. We have things to say that we want you to hear.' He turned back to Sherlock. 'Go on, son. You're doin' fine.'

'The whole thing is a series of tricks, one after the other,' Sherlock said, 'designed to convince you that Ambrose Albano can communicate with the dead, so that you would all bid whatever resources your countries had granted you.'

'Tricks?' Von Webenau seemed mesmerized. 'But what about the writing on the slate? How was that done? I am a scientist, and I cannot see how it was accomplished.'

'Elementary,' Sherlock said. He walked around the table to where Albano was sitting and reached into the right side of his jacket, to where he knew the white thimble had to be hanging from its elastic. He had a bad moment when it wasn't where he expected, but after a few seconds of moving his fingers up and down he felt a hard object. He pulled it out into the open. As the elastic tightened it jerked Albano's jacket out of shape.

'This thimble has chalk on the end. Albano used it to write on the slate. The elastic snapped it back out of sight when he had finished with it.'

'But the messages disappeared,' Holtzbrinck pointed out.

'Wiped away by his white gloves. White chalk against white gloves – invisible.'

Holtzbrinck and von Webenau exchanged glances. They seemed genuinely shocked. Sherlock had the impression that, for whatever reason, they had really wanted to believe in Albano's powers.

Count Shuvalov leaned forward. 'You are very convincing about the writing on the slate and the ectoplasmic materialization. The information about Herr Holtzbrinck's brother Fritz and –' he glanced apologetically at Amyus Crowe – 'my American colleague's wife could have been obtained by standard investigation beforehand.

197

I work in intelligence – I know how these things are done.' He paused, staring intently at Sherlock. 'But the disappearance of Mr Albano from the carriage before it crashed – surely you must admit that such a thing would be impossible to fake. That was no trick. The man really did disappear.'

'There was a disappearance,' Sherlock said quietly, 'but it wasn't by Mr Albano.' He glanced at the four foreign dignitaries. 'The carriage crash was faked to give Mr Albano an opportunity to make himself look even more powerful – to make it look as if he was so valuable to the spirits on the astral plane that they would transport him there and back if he was threatened. But there was no kidnap.'

'We all saw four kidnappers,' Holtzbrinck pointed out.

'No, we saw three kidnappers – the driver and the two men who got out and grabbed Mr Albano. The fourth figure we saw was just a shape – a silhouette inside the carriage. It was easily accomplished by hanging up a coat with a black scarf bundled up to form a head.'

'Four men ran away,' von Webenau said.

'Yes,' Sherlock agreed. 'And one of them was Mr Albano.' He stared at the men, one after the other. Shuvalov was already ahead of him, as was Crowe, but he had to persuade von Webenau and Holtzbrinck. 'When Albano was thrown inside the carriage, he quickly put on the coat that was hanging up there, and wound the scarf around his face. When the coach crashed, which it was supposed to do, he ran away with the other three men.' He turned to Quintillan. 'Were they servants, or did you hire them from the village?'

Quintillan just stared at him darkly.

'It doesn't really matter,' Sherlock continued. I was just interested to know.' He turned to Amyus Crowe. 'Have I left anything out? I think I've covered everything of importance.'

'The attack on your brother?' Crowe prompted.

'Ah yes.' He looked from von Webenau to Holtzbrinck and then to Shuvalov. 'That was nothing to do with the séance, or the attempt to get money from your governments. That was an attempt to reduce the playing field. I presume someone thought that the British Government, being the closest and perhaps the one with the most resources, was most likely to win the auction for Mr Albano's services, so they decided to take my brother out of the running.'

'An' do you know who?' Crowe asked.

'I originally suspected that the attacker had gained access to the library from a secret passage,' Sherlock said, ignoring the question. 'However, I now suspect there was a much more prosaic explanation. I believe that the attacker was hiding behind the curtains in the library.' He glanced around at the group. 'You are all intelligent men, and the attack was clumsy – badly thought out and badly managed.' He turned suddenly, and pointed at Count Shuvalov. 'Count – why did you dismiss your manservant earlier?'

Shuvalov stared at Sherlock for a long moment. 'He was incompetent. He did not meet my standards. I sent him back home, in disgrace.'

'You mean he attacked my brother without being ordered to, therefore risking an international incident? He acted independently of you, thinking he was helping you, and so he had to go.'

Shuvalov shrugged. 'You may believe what you wish,' he said, 'but believe *this* – I would never order an attack so clumsy, especially against a man for whom I have much friendship. There are other, better ways to ensure that the Russian Empire succeeds in this auction for the psychic's services –' he gazed at Quintillan – '*if* the psychic's powers are real. I think our friend here has convincingly demonstrated that they are not, and I thank him for it.'

Quintillan stared at Crowe and Sherlock, and then scanned his gaze across the other delegates.

'I realize how this looks,' he said slowly. 'I understand that you think you have been duped – that you believe Mr Albano and I are conspiring to get you to pay us money for something that does not exist. But it *does* exist. I assure you, Mr Albano's powers are *real*.'

'Then why the tricks?' Sherlock asked.

Quintillan raised a hand to his forehead. 'It is . . . embarrassing to explain.' He gestured to Ambrose Albano. 'Would you mind?'

Albano stepped forward. 'I confess,' he said, 'that there *have* been tricks, but they were intended not to fool *you*, but to protect *me*. My powers are –' he shrugged – 'fragile. They come and they go. When Sir Shadrach arranged this demonstration I was physically in good health. I was able to demonstrate my powers at will, whenever I was called upon to do so.' He sighed. 'But in the intervening time I have suffered a fever. I was confined to bed for several weeks. The doctors feared for my health. I was on the verge of death. I recovered, thanks to the care of my good friend Sir Shadrach, but while my strength has returned, my ability to summon spirits and to cross to the Other Side has not. Not perfectly, anyway. I can sometimes receive messages from the other side, but not reliably. I begged Sir Shadrach to call off the demonstration and the auction, but he said that it had taken so long to arrange that we could not cancel now. He also pointed out that if I were to fail at some or all of the demonstration, then you would go back and tell your respective governments that I had no powers, that I was a fraud and a fake, and not a very good one either. So, yes, we cheated. We concocted a series of magical illusions that gave the impression of a

201

successful séance. I am truly sorry for that.' He held his hands out, seeking forgiveness. 'We let panic persuade us into a foolish course of action.'

'So your case,' von Webenau said, 'is that you *do* have psychic powers, but that you cannot actively control them. You do not know when and if they will work.'

'That is exactly the case,' Albano said. 'What I can add is that my powers have been gradually coming back to me, and that I fully expect, within a month, to be back at my full psychic strength.'

'And we should take your word for that?' Crowe said heavily.

'Absolutely not,' Quintillan answered quickly. 'We understand that this explanation, whilst every word is true, may not be very convincing, and so I would suggest two things. Firstly, given that Mr Albano's powers are returning by degrees, we arrange a final demonstration that cannot be faked. Everything can be inspected beforehand for evidence of trickery, and that inspection will leave you convinced that the only answer is that psychic powers are involved. Secondly, you will be convinced by the fact that the auction is conducted on the basis that we are proposing Mr Albano as a partial psychic, not a complete psychic, and that the money bid by you on behalf of your governments reflects this.' He looked from person to person. 'Is this acceptable, gentlemen?'

Crowe shook his large head. 'It is not acceptable. We have a name for people like you in America. We call you "flim-flam men". You are confidence tricksters, nothing more, and this is just a rather pathetic attempt to stop us from leaving.'

'The British Government agrees with the American Government,' Sherlock said, feeling a thrill run through him as he said the words. He liked the idea that he was speaking directly on behalf of the British Government, and he was sure that his brother would have said the same thing, albeit probably with a lot more words.

'I understand,' Quintillan said sadly. 'And I thank you, gentlemen, for your honesty.' He turned to face von Webenau, Holtzbrinck and Shuvalov. 'And what about you, gentlemen? What is your answer?'

Von Webenau and Holtzbrinck looked at Count Shuvalov, as if he was the leader of their little group. He nodded once, gravely. Von Webenau turned back to Quintillan. 'We will see your final demonstration,' he said.

'But we are sceptical,' Holtzbrinck added, 'and we will be looking at you with critical eyes. You will need to provide a demonstration that is completely convincing to us. If you can do that then the auction can go ahead.'

'With a reduced number of bidders,' von Webenau said. He glanced at Sherlock and Amyus Crowe and shrugged apologetically. 'I'm sorry, but if you are out then you are

203

out. You cannot come back in if the demonstration is convincing.'

'Suits me,' Crowe rumbled.

Sherlock nodded. 'Agreed.'

'With one proviso,' Count Shuvalov said. He spoke quietly, but he spoke so rarely that everyone listened. 'This young man has a good mind, and has exposed trickery that might have fooled some of the more credulous amongst us.' He smiled. 'And I count myself amongst that number. I insist that he be allowed to watch the final demonstration, and to look for any evidence of trickery. I also insist that Mr Crowe be present as well, on the basis that the more eyes watching this demonstration, the better. They do not take part in the auction, if there is an auction, but they watch everything.'

Quintillan looked at Albano, who nodded.

'Yes,' Quintillan said, 'your conditions are acceptable.'

'And I,' Sherlock said boldly, 'insist that the demonstration is held tomorrow, in daylight, not at night. Daylight is a great exposer of hoaxes and trickery.'

'Again,' Quintillan said, 'your condition is acceptable.' It seemed to Sherlock, however, that he didn't seem particularly happy about it.

'Now I need to rest,' Albano said, 'in order to conserve my energy for the demonstration. I propose that it occurs after lunch.'

'We will reconvene tomorrow, after lunch,' Quintillan said. 'Until then, gentlemen, you must amuse yourselves.'

He gestured to Silman, who had been standing behind him all the while, so stationary that everyone had forgotten she was there, and she wheeled him out. Ambrose Albano followed.

'Very clever,' Crowe said, approaching Sherlock. 'He's managed to turn defeat into a qualified victory. Those fools –' he gestured to where von Webenau, Holtzbrinck and Shuvalov were clustered together, talking in low voices – '*want* this thing to be true, and so they're willin' to let this pair of tricksters have another bite of the cherry.'

'At least we won't be wasting British or American money,' Sherlock pointed out. 'And we get to watch, and to see exactly how the trick is done.'

'Ah suspect that this trick will be the granddaddy of all tricks,' Crowe warned. 'We'll need to watch carefully.' He seemed to notice some expression in Sherlock's face. 'What's the problem?'

'I was just thinking,' Sherlock said, 'that Sir Shadrach's daughter isn't going to be best pleased with me.'

Crowe nodded. 'That's the problem with the truth, son. It don't please a lot of people, because it upsets the neat little applecart of their world. Don't mean that you should avoid the truth, though. You should never do that. You just need to be aware that you'll have fewer friends

205

because of it, but also that the ones who stay will be better friends.' He turned towards Shuvalov, von Webenau and Holtzbrinck. 'Ah suggest we get a good night's sleep. Let's think on what has happened tonight, an' talk it over tomorrow mornin'. Are we in agreement?'

The three other men nodded.

'What about Mr Holmes?' Count Shuvalov asked. 'Will *he* be in agreement with this plan?'

'Ah'll go an' brief him now.' Crowe glanced across at Sherlock. 'Ah'm sure he'll be interested to know what his brother has accomplished this evenin'. Ah'm sure he'll also be relieved to know who it was who clocked him from behind.' He gazed levelly at Shuvalov. 'It *was* your man, wasn't it?'

Shuvalov made an ambiguous gesture. 'Let us say that it will certainly not be happening again. Mr Holmes is not in danger any more.'

Crowe looked at Sherlock. 'You comin', Sherlock, or am Ah doin' this alone?'

Sherlock thought for a moment. He knew that his brother would want to go exhaustively over everything that had happened, but he wasn't sure he had the energy for that. Not at that moment, anyway. 'You brief him,' he said. 'You were an independent witness, anyway, so he'll put more faith in what you say. I can answer any questions he has tomorrow morning.'

'Fair enough,' Crowe said, nodding. 'In that case, goodnight, gentlemen, an' sleep well.'

'I, for one, feel the need of a stiff brandy,' von Webenau said. 'Will anybody join me?'

Holtzbrinck and Shuvalov nodded their agreement. Crowe and Sherlock left the other three men there and shared the ascending room up to the floor where their rooms were located.

'Ah meant it,' Crowe said as they left the ascending room. 'You did good work there, an' you saved me from doin' somethin' Ah might've regretted later. Ah thank you for that.'

Sherlock smiled, and said nothing.

It seemed to Sherlock that he fell asleep somewhere between taking his shoes off and removing his shirt. He awoke the next morning still half dressed, and lying diagonally across his bed. The events of the night before seemed like a bizarre dream.

When he got down to breakfast the other foreign representatives were already there. Mycroft was also there, dressed and with his head still swathed in a bandage. He was looking better: there was colour in his cheeks. He glanced over as Sherlock entered the room and nodded gravely, then went back to his discussions.

Sherlock stacked up a plate with food from the sideboard, sat down, and stared at it. A foot-servant filled a cup with coffee, but he didn't feel in the mood for anything. The events of the night before had left him elated and exhausted, and now he felt like a candle that had burned too brightly and too long, and which had been blown out to leave only a trail of smoke.

A movement at the doorway attracted his attention. Niamh Quintillan entered, saw him, and stopped dead. She glared at him with venom in her eyes.

'Ah,' he said. 'You've spoken to your father.'

She just kept staring at him for a painfully long moment, and then she turned and headed out of the dining room again.

'Not hungry, I guess,' Sherlock murmured to himself.

He had just forced himself to eat some toast and marmalade when Virginia entered the room. She saw her father, and smiled, and then saw Sherlock. The smile faded, replaced with an expression he couldn't read. It wasn't the anger that had been on Niamh's face. This was more like . . . embarrassment? Fear? He wasn't sure.

Virginia, like Niamh before her, turned and left without sitting down.

'You got a way with women, son,' Amyus Crowe called from the other end of the table.

'Yes, but it looks like the wrong way,' Sherlock rejoined.

When he had finished his toast and coffee, the meeting

at the other end of the table was still going on. He wondered whether or not to join in, but Mycroft looked up, met his gaze and shook his head. Instead, Sherlock walked out into the hall. He stood there for a moment, irresolute, wondering whether he should go back to his room and just lie down for a while, waiting for the adults to decide what to do next. Eventually he wandered down into the hall of the castle, and then out into the open space outside the keep.

Virginia was standing there, in the fresh air, staring up at the sky. She was talking with Niamh Quintillan. The two of them seemed to be getting on surprisingly well. The weather was cloudy, but dry, and the clouds weren't the grey that he associated with coming rain.

Sherlock watched from the doorway, not wanting to interrupt them. Eventually Niamh smiled, nodded, and walked away. Sherlock waited for a few moments, then approached Virginia.

'Hi,' he said.

'Hi,' she said softly.

'You were talking with Niamh,' he said awkwardly. 'I wouldn't have thought you two had much in common.'

'She has horses. Well, Connemara ponies, they're called. She said she'll take me riding later, if I want.'

Sherlock couldn't think of anything to say in response. The silence between them grew to almost unbearable

209

proportions. In order to break it, Sherlock said: 'Do you want to take a walk outside?'

'Is there anything to see?'

'There's a beach.'

Virginia nodded. 'All right. Let's walk.'

Sherlock led the way out of the castle, across the moat and off towards where he remembered the cliffs as being. He remembered that Niamh had told him about a way down to the beach, and it only took a few minutes of searching to find the steep path down the side of the cliffs. The two of them made their way down, sometimes using the steps that had been crudely carved into the cliff face and sometimes just scrambling down the mud and the rock. A wooden banister ran down most of the path, giving them a handhold in case they slipped, but sometimes it just wasn't there – swept away by landslides or weathered and broken by storms, Sherlock guessed. There wasn't any chance of talking while they were descending – the exertion took all of their energy and all of their concentration.

Far below them, but getting closer, Sherlock could see grey-green waves topped with white foam crashing against the sand and pebbles of the boulder-strewn beach. Seagulls soared around them, eyeing them with beady menace and uttering raucous cries. Sherlock hoped that the two of them didn't go anywhere near any seagull nests. He suspected that those cruelly hooked bills could cause a lot of damage if the seagulls wanted to defend their eggs.

Eventually the descent levelled out, and they half ran, half fell the last few feet to the beach. They were both covered with scratches and mud. Looking back up the side of the cliff, Sherlock wondered how they would ever be able to get back. If they couldn't climb then they would have to wander along the beach until they found an easier route up. Or starved.

He scanned the cliff for signs that the tide might come all the way in and drown them if they didn't find a way off the beach in time. There was no line of seaweed on the cliff face marking the high tide point. Turning and looking at the beach, he noticed that it sloped down noticeably, and there was a line of seaweed about ten feet away from the cliff face. The pebbles on one side of the seaweed line were damp, and the ones on the other side, closer to where Sherlock and Virginia stood, were largely dry. That would be the high-tide point, he decided.

The cliff face was pockmarked with dark holes – some just a few feet across, but some large enough to drive a horse and carriage into. These must be the caves he had heard about – the ones used by smugglers in the past. He realized with a thrill that some of them must connect up with the cellars and tunnels beneath the castle, which meant that they did have another way off the beach if they needed it. The problem was that he had no idea which caves led to the tunnels and which ones just ended blindly. He would have to try and work out a way of telling which was which.

He stared at the cliff face for a while, trying to imagine it not as it appeared – a solid mass of rock – but as something honeycombed with tunnels that wound around each other and headed up towards the top of the cliff.

He turned, to find Virginia staring out at the sea.

'Are you all right?' he asked.

'In Albuquerque, the only sand we had was desert sand. I still can't get used to the idea of sand and water together.'

'Oh.' He wasn't sure what else to say.

'Come on then,' she said, turning and heading off along the beach. 'If we're going to walk, let's walk.'

'Your father said you're going back to America,' he said after a few minutes, more to break the silence than for any other reason.

'He says we have to go to Washington DC,' she said over her shoulder. 'It freezes in the winter and it boils in the summer, but that's where Pinkertons have offered him a post, liaising with the Federal Government. That's kind of what he's doing right now – the new job. They really want him back.'

'Oh.' He paused, framing the next few words carefully. 'You're old enough that you could stay here, in England, you know. I'm sure he'd let you. He might not like it, but

Mr Crowe knows that you know your own mind.'

'Travis wants to go back to America as well,' she said.

'Ah. Travis.'

Virginia stopped and stared out to sea. Sherlock stopped behind her. Without knowing what he was going to do, he reached out and touched her shoulder, pulling her around to face him.

Her cheeks were wet with tears. Her violet eyes brimmed with them. As he watched, more spilt out and ran down her face.

He stepped forward and took her in his arms. She wrapped her arms around him and buried her face in his chest.

'It's no good,' she said, her voice muffled. 'It's all wrong. Everything is wrong.'

'It can be fixed,' he said, hoping against hope that it could.

'No, it can't. You don't understand.' She balled one of her hands into a fist and hit him on the shoulder. 'I didn't know if you were ever coming back. I had to make a decision – did I wait for you forever, or did I move on with my life? So I decided.'

'I'm here now. I'm back.'

'But it's too late. I made a promise. I have to keep it.' She pushed him away, to arm's length, and stared up at him. 'Travis loves me; at least he says he does. And I love him, I suppose. Maybe not in the way I love you, but it can grow, with time. Travis will look after me. He'll provide for me. We'll have a good life. His dad is a powerful businessman – he'll be a useful contact for Father to have.'

'Is that enough?' Sherlock asked bleakly.

'What else is there?' She stared up at him, waiting for an answer, but he wasn't even sure he understood the question. 'Maybe a year ago we might have had a chance,' she said eventually, 'but not now. We've grown in different directions. We're on different paths.'

'I'm not even sure which path I'm on,' he admitted.

'And that's part of the problem, Sherlock. Travis knows who he is and what he wants to be. He has a plan for his future, and he wants me to be a part of that plan. He intends going into politics. He wants to be a senator, and maybe a governor. What do you want to be? What's your plan?'

He shrugged uneasily. 'I'm still trying to work that out.'

'I hope you do.'

'Is there anything I can say to change your mind?' he asked quietly.

Virginia just stared at him, tears still brimming in her eyes. He had a feeling that she wanted to say 'Yes', but then she would expect him to know what it was that she wanted to hear, and he didn't. He had no idea. He could work almost anything out, given the evidence, but not that.

'Let's get back,' she said eventually, looking away from him.

They headed out along the beach, away from the castle and away, as far as Sherlock could tell, from Galway itself. Sherlock kept an eye on the cliffs above them, and was relieved to see the boundary where the limestone cut across the blue and white of the sky moving closer to them. The sea had to be at the same level, so the logical solution was that the cliffs were getting lower. Maybe there would be a chance to scramble up them soon.

'How's Matty?' Sherlock asked after a long period of silence.

'I haven't seen much of him,' Virginia admitted. 'He stays in town, mostly, and I spend my time out in the countryside. I think he's scared of my dad.' She hesitated. 'He never says anything, but I know he wishes you were around.'

'I thought he might leave Farnham, once I'd . . . once I'd gone. He seems to prefer travelling to staying in one place.'

'I think he's hoping you'll come back, one day.'

'And here I am, back again,' Sherlock murmured, but if Virginia heard his response then she gave no sign.

After a while, Sherlock realized that the cliff edge was

low enough for there to be a realistic prospect of getting back up. The boulders were smaller here and speckled with orange algae. He looked for a suitable spot, but it was Virginia who saw one first. As with their original point of descent, crude stairs had been cut into the rock and the dirt to provide footholds.

'Do you want to go back to the castle?' Sherlock asked.

Virginia stared at him for a moment. 'What do you want to do?'

He shrugged. 'I'm getting hungry. Shall we head back?'

'If that's what you want.'

A path left by who knew how many generations of feet led back towards the castle through thick furze that grew to a level that was mostly over their heads, with the occasional copse of ash trees rearing from it. It was uphill, but not steeply so. The two of them walked in silence, with Sherlock taking the lead and pushing the undergrowth back so that Virginia could get through without getting hurt. Every now and then there was a gap in the bushes, through which either the sea or the distant castle was visible.

After an hour or so, Sherlock realized that he could see something above the undergrowth – something artificial. It was the tower that he had seen a couple of times before – the folly that he knew was near the castle but which he could sometimes not see from places where it should have been easily visible. Now that he was close, he knew that he had to take the opportunity to investigate it. The chances were that he might never be able to find it again if he left it now.

'I need to look at that thing,' he said, pointing. 'Is it all right if we divert our course a little so that I can take a look?'

Virginia shook her head. 'I'm tired,' she announced, 'and I'm hungry, and I need a bath and a change of clothes before I go riding with Niamh. I'm going to head back.'

'All right,' Sherlock said, glancing at the tower again, 'I'll come with you.'

'I don't need an escort,' she said angrily. 'I can find my own way safely.'

'Look,' Sherlock suddenly snapped, 'I didn't *choose* to go away. I was *kidnapped*. I was drugged, and when I woke up I found myself on a ship heading for China. *It wasn't my choice!*'

'I know.' She nodded, then said again, 'I know. But you never wrote to me. You never bothered to get in touch.'

'I was on a ship headed for China,' he repeated, more softly. 'It wasn't like there was a scheduled postal service.'

'You wrote to your brother,' she pointed out. 'But you didn't write to me.'

'I didn't know what to say.'

'That's the problem.'

She turned and walked away. Sherlock watched her go, feeling torn. On the one hand he wanted to go with her; on the other hand he wanted to take a look at the folly.

His mind flashed up a memory from over a year ago: her sleeping in a rough stone hut on the Scottish moors while he, awake, watched her. He remembered the firelight making her face and her hair glow. He knew that he would never forget that sight, and the feelings that had filled him then, but also that he would never be in that situation again.

Sighing, he turned and followed Virginia. Women, he decided, were not logical and they were not predictable, and they seemed actively to encourage that behaviour in men. He wasn't sure that he wanted to play that game.

CHAPTER ELEVEN

Lunch had just finished when – 'Gentlemen,' a voice announced.

Sherlock, along with the other representatives – Mycroft, Crowe, von Webenau, Holtzbrinck and Shuvalov – turned to look at the doorway. Sir Shadrach Quintillan was blocking the space with his bath chair, the ever-present Silman standing behind him.

'Are you ready for the final, the conclusive, the absolutely unfakable test?' he continued. There was a smile on his face, and he looked relaxed, but Sherlock could sense a tension about him. Maybe it was the way his hands were resting on his lap, with the fingers twisted together.

'We are, I think, prepared for anything you can throw at us,' Mycroft said. 'But we warn you – after the charades of last night, we are in no mood for any more trickery.'

'There will be no trickery,' Quintillan promised. 'You will all be invited to inspect every feature of the demonstration. If you spot any sign of fraud then we will stop immediately, and I will abandon any plans that I have to further persuade you.'

'Very well,' Herr Holtzbrinck said. 'Let us proceed.'

Von Webenau coughed to attract attention. 'Will the demonstration be in the same room as before?' he asked.

'No. We required a special room – an isolated one.'

'A room, I suppose, that has already been chosen and prepared by you?' Mycroft said acerbically.

Quintillan grimaced. 'Unfortunately, for reasons that will become obvious once we get there, the room needs to be on the top floor, where it cannot be observed or overseen by anyone outside, but I am happy for you to choose which room it is yourself. In fact, I anticipated your request.' He beckoned forward a foor-servant who was holding a bowl containing many slips of paper. 'I have had my servants chalk numbers on all the rooms on the top floor,' he said. 'There are equivalent numbers on the slips of paper in this bowl. Please – will someone take a number?'

The representatives looked at each other for a moment, then at some unspoken agreement von Webenau walked over and took a slip of paper from the bowl. He unfolded it, and read out, 'Twenty-four.'

'Is everyone happy for that to be the number chosen?' Quintillan asked.

'No,' Mycroft said loudly. 'I wish von Webenau to choose another number.'

'Very well.' Quintillan gestured to von Webenau, who screwed up the first piece of paper, placed it on the table beside the bowl and plucked another out. He opened it up. 'Thirty-five,' he announced.

Quintillan turned to Mycroft. 'Mr Holmes?'

'I am content,' Mycroft rumbled. 'I merely wanted to establish that the bowl wasn't filled with slips of paper all of which had "Twenty-four" written on them.'

'Then if we are happy to use room thirty-five, please – follow me.'

Silman pulled Quintillan out of the doorway, turned the bath chair around and pushed him out of sight. Everybody else followed, but Mycroft paused by the table. He reached into the bowl and removed a handful of slips of paper. He opened them up, one after the other, and glanced at them.

'What's the verdict?' Sherlock asked.

'They are all different.' Mycroft threw the papers back into the bowl. 'I felt that I had to make absolutely sure.'

Out in the hall, Silman pushed Quintillan across to the ascending room. Ambrose Albano was already standing there, looking pale but resolute. The sun, shining from high in the sky, reflected off his false eye and created a blaze of white light on his cheek.

'We will travel to the top floor,' Quintillan announced. 'It will be a tight squeeze, but I suggest that I travel first, with Mr Crowe, Herr Holtzbrinck and von Webenau. I will send the ascending room back down again, and

221

Mr Ambrose can follow with the two Mr Holmeses, plus Count Shuvalov. Does anybody disagree with this intention?'

Nobody spoke out, so Silman opened the door and pulled Quintillan backwards into the ascending room. Holtzbrinck, Crowe and von Webenau followed. The door closed, and the contraption began to rise.

The group left in the hall looked at each awkwardly. No words were exchanged.

Once they were all together again on the top floor, Silman pushed Quintillan along one of the connecting corridors and the other men followed. Each of the doors had a number chalked on it, but Sherlock noticed that they were not in consecutive order. He made a mental note of the numbers as he passed the doors: 15, 42, 11, 49, 27 . . .

Silman kept pushing the bath chair down the corridor to a room which had the number 35 on it. A key was sticking out of the lock.

'This is where the demonstration will take place,' Quintillan announced.

Silman turned the key, pulled it out of the lock and pushed the door open, and Quintillan gestured to the assembled representatives to enter.

'Why aren't the numbers in order?' Sherlock asked.

Quintillan turned to look at Sherlock. 'I am informed

that those who dwell in the spirit world have a dislike of order and organization,' he explained. 'They much prefer things to be random – more like nature than mathematics.'

'It is true,' Albano confirmed from the back of the group. 'Many times I have been informed by those who have crossed over to the Other Side that they much prefer things to be disordered.'

'Oh, I see,' Sherlock said, but he was remembering the letters on the table for the séances on the previous nights. They had been in alphabetical order, and nobody had made a comment then – not the spirits and not Ambrose Albano. There was something odd here about the random numbers.

The group all entered the room with the exception of Albano. He hung back, saying, 'For reasons that you will understand shortly, I should stay here. It will make the demonstration even more convincing.'

The room was empty – no carpets, no curtains, no paintings on the wall. There were two openings – the door that they had come through and a window. There was also a hook on one wall where a painting would have hung, and a patch of lighter wall beneath it that showed where a painting had been. The room was so bare that it looked as though it had been pre-prepared for their arrival. Sherlock was about to say something when Count Shuvalov beat him to it.

223

'Are all the rooms on this level so bare?' he asked.

'This level of the castle is not used,' Quintillan confirmed. 'There is, therefore, no point in furnishing them.'

'Could we check another room?' Mycroft asked.

Quintillan stared at him. 'There comes a point,' he said, 'when suspicion turns into active insult. You were allowed to choose a room at random, and you were allowed to then change the choice. There was no way I could have known that we would end up in this room. That should be enough for you, Mr Holmes.'

Mycroft subsided, but Sherlock caught a flash of expression on his face. Rather than annoyance, it was a look of amusement. Mycroft obviously had some suspicion that this was still a trick, albeit a more complicated one. Sherlock was of the same opinion.

'Now, gentlemen,' Quintillan announced. 'Please feel free to examine this room from top to bottom and from side to side. Check all of the stones in the wall and the flagstones in the floor for secret entrances. I want you to be assured that there is no way in and no way out.'

While Mycroft, Sherlock and Amyus Crowe stood off to one side, the other three men thoroughly investigated the walls, floor and ceiling. They all conferred for a few moments, and then turned to Quintillan.

'There is, as you indicate, no way into or out of the room with the exception of the window and the door,' Holtzbrinck stated firmly. 'We have also checked for holes through which someone might observe the room or influence what is inside. There are no holes or other gaps, and all the stones are secure.'

'Excellent,' Quintillan said. 'Now, please examine the window. I wish you to assure yourself that nobody could climb up here from outside.'

Von Webenau went across to the window and opened it. He leaned out, looking left and right, up and down. 'The wall is sheer,' he said, pulling himself back inside, 'with no handholds or footholds.'

'What about ivy?' Shuvalov asked.

'No plants of any kind,' von Webenau confirmed. 'Nothing that would allow a climber any purchase.'

'What about upward?' Mycroft called. 'Could a climber get down from the roof?'

Von Webenau leaned out again and stared up. 'There is a considerable overhang,' he shouted back into the room. 'I cannot see any way that a person could climb down from above.'

'Besides,' Quintillan said as von Webenau pulled his head in and closed the window, 'I will be demonstrating shortly that nobody could climb down without leaving traces.' He glanced at Count Shuvalov. 'Count, could you

225

please confirm that there is no way that anybody outside could see into this room.'

Shuvalov walked across to the window. Von Webenau moved out of his way. Shuvalov gazed out for a few moments. 'I can see no way that any person outside could see in,' he said eventually. 'The trees and bushes are too low to permit a sight of anything apart from the ceiling, even with a telescope.'

'Thank you,' Quintillan said. 'I think that we are ready to proceed.'

'What about a curtain?' Amyus Crowe asked. 'That would ensure nobody could see in.'

'Ah,' Quintillan said, 'but we must allow a means of entry for the spirits. A curtain could block their access.'

'Really?' Crowe look sceptical, but he didn't pursue the question.

'Indeed. Also –' Quintillan smiled – 'either you or Mr Holmes could argue that someone was concealing themselves in the curtains. If there are no curtains then there is nowhere for anyone to be concealed, yes?'

Crowe shrugged. 'If you say so, Sir Shadrach.'

A noise at the door made them all turn. Four servants entered, each carrying a large painting in a heavy, ornate frame. One was a painting of a man in military uniform, one of a horse, one a classical scene with men in togas standing and arguing in a temple, and one a landscape with trees and hills. They placed the paintings in a line against the wall with the hook in it, and left.

'We have four paintings,' Quintillan announced. 'Each painting is different from the others. In a moment we will all leave, with the exception of Mr Sherlock Holmes. While the rest of us go up to the roof and I demonstrate that no climber could get down without leaving a trace, young Mr Holmes will choose one, and one only, of the paintings and hang it on the wall. Only he will know which painting he chose. I would also ask Mr Holmes to choose which way he hangs it: normally, upside down, or rotated either to the left or to the right. Mr Albano will already have been blindfolded and will have wax earplugs placed into his ears. He will be completely unable to see or hear anything, and yet, through the aid and assistance of the spirits, he will know which painting Mr Holmes chose to hang on the wall and what orientation he has chosen.' He looked over at Sherlock. 'Is your role in this clear, young man?'

'It is.'

'And you know why I have chosen you for this important task?'

'Presumably because I was the one who exposed the tricks last night,' Sherlock said.

'That is correct. Of all of us, you are the one who cannot be in league with any trickery.' He looked around.

'Now, gentlemen, let us leave young Mr Holmes to make his choice.' He glanced back at Sherlock. 'Wait until we have all left and the door is closed,' he said. 'Place the key in the lock so that nobody can see in through the keyhole, then choose and hang a painting. Wait until you hear my voice calling from above. Do you understand?'

'I do.'

'And do not, on your life, tell anyone which painting you have hung up, or which way you have hung it.' He paused. 'Very well.' He gestured to Silman, who handed the room key to Sherlock then wheeled Quintillan out. The others followed.

Through the open door, Sherlock could see Ambrose Albano. One of the servants had tied a thick piece of material around his eyes. He stood there, blindfolded, head cocked to one side as if wondering what was going on around him.

Another foot-servant appeared from the corridor. She was holding a long wooden pole. She handed it through the door to Sherlock.

'Keep the pole,' Quintillan said. 'You will need it later.'

Mycroft was last out. He turned and raised an eyebrow at Sherlock. Sherlock nodded, and Mycroft left, closing the door behind him.

Sherlock was left alone.

He took a deep breath, and savoured the silence for a

moment. Then, remembering his instructions, he placed the pole against the wall and walked across and put the key in the lock so that nobody could see through the keyhole. He also looked the door over to make sure there were no spy holes in it, but it was a solid block of wood.

Glancing at the paintings, he wondered whether there had been any surreptitious words or phrases that Quintillan had used to persuade him to choose a particular canvas. He couldn't think of anything. He should, he decided, make the choice as random as he could. He thought for a moment. 'All right,' he said to himself. 'How many letters in the name "Virginia"? Eight.' He started counting from the left-hand painting, restarting when he got to four. That meant that when he got to eight he was pointing at the last canvas: the landscape of hills and trees. He crossed over to it and tried to pick it up. The painting was heavy – probably more because of the large frame than anything else. He turned it until the picture was upside down. He lifted it and placed it on the hook in the wall. Standing back, arms extended in case it fell, he waited for a few moments, but it was stable.

He crossed to the window and stared out at the countryside. As von Webenau had said, there was no way that anybody could see inside the room from outside: the window was too high, and there were no tall trees that Sherlock could see. The tower that he had seen a couple of times before, from various points around the castle, might have provided a suitable platform for an observer, but he couldn't spot it. It must have been on a different side of the castle – it was difficult to tell, sometimes, as the landscape tended to look the same in all directions apart from towards the cliffs.

He opened the window, leaned out and stared downward. The castle grounds were down below, along with the wall that marked the boundary between the grounds and the outside world. The wall was too low for anyone to get a view inside the room.

'Mr Holmes!' a voice called from above. 'Can you hear me?'

Sherlock turned his head and looked up, but the overhang of the roof prevented him from seeing anyone. 'Yes, I can hear you!'

'Can you fetch the wooden pole, please?'

Sherlock crossed the room, picked up the pole and returned to the window. 'I have it.'

'Now, please push the pole out of the window whilst keeping hold of one end.'

With some difficulty, Sherlock balanced the pole on the windowsill and slid it out, keeping enough of it inside the room to stop it from falling. 'Done!' he called.

From somewhere above, Sherlock heard Quintillan say: 'Gentlemen, please confirm that you can see the pole below us, thus proving that we are directly above the room you saw earlier.'

There was a brief pause, followed by a quiet murmur of voices agreeing that yes, they could see the pole.

'Forgive me,' Mycroft said, 'but you might have led us to a point above a different room, and that pole might be in the hands of one of your servants. We need to establish that it is Sherlock who is holding the pole.'

'What do you propose?' Quintillan asked.

'Sherlock!' Mycroft called. 'Can you hear me?'

'I can hear you!'

'I am going to call out some letters, chosen at random. When I reach the letter that is the first letter of the first name of a friend of yours who is not here, and who lives on a canal, then pull the pole back in. Do you understand?'

'I understand.'

'Very well. "A", "T", "L", "V", "F", "G", "M"—'

When he heard Mycroft say 'M', Sherlock pulled the pole back in.

'Are you satisfied?' he heard Quintillan's voice ask his brother.

'Reasonably,' Mycroft responded.

'Mr Holmes!' Quintillan called down. 'Please stay where you are until you see us on the grass down below the window, then leave the room, lock the door and stand

231

guard outside. I will send a servant for you in due course. Do you understand?'

'Perfectly!' he shouted.

He stayed at the window for what must have been half an hour. The room behind him was quiet, and the landscape that he was looking at was stunning in its beauty. The sun was low in the sky, and the shadow of the castle boundary wall lengthened on the grass.

Eventually a door opened in the castle wall below, and he could see a group of figures emerging. One of them was in a bath chair, and another was being led by a servant.

'Mr Holmes!' Quintillan called up. Distance made his voice very quiet. 'Can you hear me?'

'Barely,' Sherlock called back.

'Can you confirm that the room has remained undisturbed since we left?'

'I can. Nobody apart from me has been in this room, and nobody has tried to see in.'

'Very good. Please now go outside, lock the door and wait for a servant to come and fetch you. We will maintain watch from here.'

With one last glance to check that there was no way of seeing into the room from outside from any vantage point in the landscape, Sherlock left, taking the key from the lock and locking the door behind him from the outside.

The corridor was empty. He stood there, back against

232

the door, key in his pocket, looking first left, and then right, and then left again, making sure that nobody approached him. He also listened, in case he could hear anyone moving around inside the room, but it was perfectly quiet.

Twenty minutes passed. Nothing happened, and Sherlock found his mind racing, trying to work out how Quintillan and Albano were going to manage their trick – because it had to be a trick. The problem was that he couldn't think of any way it could be accomplished. Quintillan seemed to have covered all of the possibilities, and eliminated them.

Eventually, a servant entered the corridor from Sherlock's left. 'The master says would you follow me downstairs.' She handed him a small cloth bag. Sherlock glanced inside. It was filled with blue chalk dust. 'The master says to please scatter this powder around outside the door, so that any entry to the room will be spotted.'

Sherlock did as he was instructed, scattering the dust not only in front of the door but also down the corridor in both directions. Even if someone tried to sweep it up, get in the room and then replace the chalk with more chalk, there would be traces left – of that he was sure. The corridor would have to be washed down to remove chalk traces from all the cracks between the flagstones.

Sherlock followed the foot-servant down the stairs to

233

the hall, and then through various corridors which he had not seen before to a door that led outside, into the open air. The foot-servant gestured to Sherlock to go through. 'Please, sir – the master is waiting for you outside.'

The five international representatives, along with Quintillan and the blindfolded Albano, were standing outside. The sun was so low that it was nearly behind the boundary wall.

Sherlock crossed to where Mycroft was standing. 'What's been going on?' he asked.

Mycroft shrugged. 'Lots of theatrics,' he said. 'We went out on to the castle roof, above the room you were in. The roof is, as you know, a very unpleasant and possibly dangerous place. We looked over the edge, to where you were in the room. The business with the wooden pole persuaded me that we were in the correct place. After that had been done, Sir Shadrach had von Webenau sprinkle blue chalk powder all over the roof. I do not think it can be removed easily without leaving traces, and so I am reasonably content that nobody can get on the roof and lower themselves to that room without us knowing. Not that I think it will be attempted: we came straight down here, and you were still in the room. Since you left the room, we have been watching the window and the roof, and nobody has attempted any descent. What happened up in the room?'

234

Sherlock told him.

'Gentlemen,' Quintillan called. 'May I have your attention, please? Are you of the opinion that the only way into or out of that room is by the door or the window?'

There was a general nodding and murmuring of 'Yes.'

'And are you of the opinion that there is no way anybody could get into that room via the door, or via the window, without leaving traces in the chalk dust?'

Again, there was general assent.

'And are you of the opinion that the window is so high, and the surrounding landscape so low, that nobody could look into the room from outside and see the painting that young Mr Holmes placed on the wall?'

Everyone agreed that was the case. 'They could only see the ceiling,' Herr Holtzbrinck added. 'The wall would be too low for them to see.'

'Then I believe we can place ourselves in the hands of Mr Albano.'

One of the servants tapped Albano on the shoulder. He stepped forward, still blindfolded. He reached up and plucked two small balls of wax from his ears and threw them away, then he spread his hands out in a gesture of openness. 'Gentlemen,' he said. 'Friends, if I may call you that. To my eternal shame there has been a degree of deceit in our dealings with you thus far. I deeply regret that deceit, but Sir Shadrach was not sure that my physical and mental state was strong enough for me to successfully carry off two convincing séances. Perhaps we should have tried regardless. Perhaps we should have postponed the demonstration and the auction until I was stronger. However, as a very wise man once said, "We are where we are", and we cannot go back and change time. I hope that by exerting my powers to their utmost now, in an environment where you have exhaustively searched for signs of trickery without finding them, we can persuade you that what has occurred has been an unfortunate but minor event in an otherwise successful demonstration. Now, you have agreed, have you not, that no human agency could know which of the four paintings young Mr Holmes hung on the wall?'

Holtzbrinck, von Webenau and Shuvalov agreed, yet again. Crowe and Mycroft just glanced non-committally.

'The mark of the confidence trickster,' Crowe muttered, low enough that only Mycroft and Sherlock could hear him, 'is to get his audience to agree with him as much as possible. That puts them into a frame of mind where, when he says something untrue or unprovable, they will be more likely to agree with him again.'

'You agree too that I, having been blindfolded since before young Mr Holmes made his choice, cannot have seen anything, or have been passed any message. I have been in your sight all the time.' He pulled the blindfold off with a theatrical flourish. 'In which case I do not need this any more. The choice has been made, the die has been cast, and it remains for me to determine which choice was made. I will now commune with the psychic plane,' Albano continued, 'and persuade one of the spirits resident there to materialize in the room above. Please – be as quiet as you possibly can. This is a very delicate and easily disrupted operation.'

He looked at each man present for a few seconds. When his gaze turned to Sherlock, the boy felt transfixed by the way Albano's false eye seemed to glow white in the light of the approaching sunset.

The silence was almost unbearable. Eventually it was broken when Albano clapped his hands together, then turned around and walked away from the group, towards the boundary wall. He stood there, staring out into the gathering shadows. He extended his arms, threw his head back, and started to chant softly.

'It occurs to me,' Mycroft said quietly, 'that even if he guesses, he has a one-in-sixteen chance of getting it right. There are four paintings, and four ways to hang each painting.'

'Those are pretty steep odds,' Crowe pointed out. 'It's not like he can repeat these shenanigans another fifteen times with different international representatives until he manages to guess right. He has one go at this, and he has

237

to get it right first time if anyone is to believe him.' He paused. 'Not that Ah'm inclined to believe him even if he gets it right. Ah know there's still a trick involved – Ah just don't know what the trick is.'

'I agree,' Mycroft said. 'There has been a large degree of theatricality about the proceedings – the chalk, the waving of the wooden pole, the blindfold and the ear plugs. I suspect that is meant to distract us from the more unusual parts of the proceedings.'

'Which are?' Sherlock asked.

'Why don't you tell us?' Crowe said.

Sherlock collected his thoughts. 'Well, the whole thing about hanging paintings on a wall is strange. He could have chosen a whole range of different things. Why use something so large and heavy?'

Mycroft nodded. 'Good so far. Continue.'

'The random numbering of the rooms is strange as well. I don't believe that stuff about spirits not liking ordered things. The letters on the séance table were ordered alphabetically.'

'Again, a good point, and I suspect that the trick depends on that random numbering. We were always meant to end up in that room, I believe.'

'The third point is the room itself. You mentioned the lack of curtains, Mr Crowe. Sir Shadrach's explanation didn't really make much sense. The trick must have something to do with the fact that the window is not blocked, but even so I can't see how.' He indicated the room, several storeys above, with a nod of his head. 'There really is no way to see in from ground level, or from anywhere outside the walls. It's impossible.'

'And yet,' Crowe murmured, 'it is going to happen.'

They talked quietly for a while longer, as the sun settled towards the horizon and the sky turned from blue to purple, from purple to red and from red to black. The warmth was sucked out of the air, and Sherlock found himself shivering. A servant emerged from the castle with a blanket, which Silman put over Quintillan's legs. All the time Albano stood out in the open, alone with his hands outstretched, muttering to himself, apparently communing with the spirits.

Eventually Albano turned around and walked back towards the group. Everybody clustered around him – three eagerly and three with some scepticism.

'I have managed to persuade a spirit to accede to my request,' he said. 'It is my old friend and spirit guide, the one who now calls himself Invictus. He has returned from the room above, and he tells me that the answer is . . .' He paused dramatically. 'The painting of the landscape has been hung in the room, and it has been hung upside down.'

Everyone turned to Sherlock.

'Is that true?' Herr Holtzbrinck asked breathlessly.

For a moment Sherlock had the almost overpowering desire to lie, but he couldn't do that. He knew there was a trick here, but he had to be completely honest.

'Yes,' he said. 'I hung the landscape on the wall, and I hung it upside down.'

Albano threw his head back and laughed, while von Webenau, Holtzbrinck and Count Shuvalov applauded wildly.

CHAPTER TWELVE

Dinner was a bizarre, excitable affair.

From Sherlock's point of view it was as if his revelation of trickery during the second séance, the night before, had never happened. Count Shuvalov, von Webenau and Herr Holtzbrinck were clustered together at one end of the table. They were all talking together animatedly about psychic phenomena and the 'spiritual plane', suggesting ways in which communication with the dead might benefit the living, and debating what it might mean for organized religion. Sir Shadrach Quintillan and Ambrose Albano were absent, presumably to give their 'guests' time to talk among themselves. Niamh Quintillan and Virginia Crowe were further down the table, talking to each other – probably, Sherlock thought, about horses. They formed a barrier like an ocean between the continent of belief at the top end of the table and the island of disbelief at the other – Sherlock, Mycroft and Amyus Crowe.

'I just can't believe it,' Sherlock said as he took a forkful of lamb. 'Did that second séance actually happen, or did I just dream it?'

'It's human nature,' Crowe pointed out. 'If people are

predisposed to believe a thing then they will accept any and all evidence that it is true and they will do their best to reject any evidence that it is false. Our international colleagues at the other end of the table really do want to believe that spiritualism and psychic phenomena exist. The three of us down here are much more likely to be guided by logic than by wishful thinkin'.'

'But *why?*'

It was Mycroft who answered, in a low voice. 'In the case of von Webenau and Herr Holtzbrinck, I suspect that they have both lost someone dear to them, and they do not wish to believe that the person has gone forever. They cannot let go, and so they will cling to any shred of evidence that might mean that their loved ones are happy and that they can still communicate with those of their family who are still alive.'

'You may have noticed that neither of them was happy when you demonstrated the trickery in the séance,' Crowe pointed out. 'Ah thought at the time it was because they were angry that they had been duped, but now Ah realize it was because they'd had something precious taken away from them. Albano and Quintillan have waved that precious thing under their noses again, and they're goin' for it.'

'In the case of Count Shuvalov,' Mycroft continued, as if Crowe hadn't interrupted, 'I believe that the answer is more to do with his nationality than with his personal history. In my experience the Russians are a highly religious and fatalistic people. They are already inclined to believe in all kinds of things that would seem bizarre to those who are not Russian.' He smiled. 'I remember that a military acquaintance of mine once said that if you put a British general, a Russian general, an American general and a German general in a room together and give them a problem to solve, the British, American and German generals would come up with one solution and the Russian general would come up with a completely different one. The Russians do not think like us, and the world will get itself into a lot of trouble if it ever forgets that.'

'They've all fallen for Ambrose's explanation that he was ill, and therefore his powers were unpredictable.' Crowe shook his head, and his voice took on an oratorical quality. '"Hear now this, O foolish people, and without understanding; which have eyes, and see not; which have ears, and hear not," as the Good Book says.'

'Can we persuade them that this is still trickery?' Sherlock asked. 'Or is it too late?'

Crowe sighed heavily and looked at Mycroft.

'That,' Mycroft said judiciously, 'depends entirely upon whether we can work out how the trick with the painting was done. If we can't explain that logically then the explanation might just as well involve psychic phenomena.'

'The first step – choosing the right room – is pretty clear,' Crowe pointed out.

Mycroft nodded. 'Yes, you are correct. That part is childishly simple.'

Sherlock looked from his brother to his mentor and back again. 'Do either of you want to explain it to me?'

'Surely it is obvious?' Mycroft stared down at his plate sadly. 'One of the unfortunate side-effects of being struck on the head is that it does interfere with one's appetite. I am not sure I can eat any more.'

'No,' Sherlock said patiently, 'it's not obvious. The slip of paper with the room number on was chosen randomly, and we know that all of the slips in the bowl had different numbers. Quintillan couldn't have known in advance which number was going to be chosen.'

'That is correct,' Mycroft said, 'but what if I reminded you about the apparent random numbering of the rooms along the corridor. Would that help?'

'No.'

'Then what if I said that I believe none of the numbers in the bowl actually appeared on any doors?'

Sherlock thought for a moment, and then the answer hit him like a bolt of lightning. 'Of course!'

'Then please explain to us, just to check you have the right answer.'

'All of the rooms on the top floor were numbered

244

with chalk marks, with the exception of the room that Quintillan wanted to use. That was left blank. The bowl was filled with numbers written on scraps of paper, but none of the numbers on the scraps matched any of the numbers on the doors.'

'An easy way to do it would be to make sure that the numbers in the bowl were odd numbers and the numbers of the doors were even numbers,' Crowe said, 'although Ah believe a more sophisticated scheme was used in this case.'

'When von Webenau chose the number and called it out, a servant outside the dining room rushed upstairs with a piece of chalk and wrote that number on the blank door that Quintillan had already chosen.'

'Exactly.' Mycroft speared a mushroom with his fork. 'Well, perhaps a few more bites. Just to keep my strength up.'

'But why were the numbers on the doors random?' Crowe asked.

'Easy. Since Quintillan didn't know which number would be chosen, he couldn't have the numbers sequential, because it would have been obvious that the one von Webenau chose – the one written rapidly on the blank door – was out of sequence.'

'Bravo,' Mycroft said, chewing. 'But do any of us know how the trick with the painting was done? Sherlock – you spent more time in the room than we did. Do you not know?'

Sherlock shrugged. 'I didn't see anything that might help. Someone must have gone into the room, or observed it from outside, but I don't know how. We all inspected the chalk in the corridor and on the roof afterwards – Quintillan insisted that we did. It was obviously undisturbed. Nobody had walked along that corridor or along that roof after the chalk was scattered, and we were all outside watching the window. It was impossible. I thought maybe a balloon – but I was looking and I saw nothing.'

'I think we can eliminate the impossible explanations,' Mycroft said. 'Which means that we must start working our way through the improbable ones.'

That statement stopped the conversation for a long while, as each of them tried to come up with some improbable explanations, and failed.

Lying in bed later, Sherlock felt fragments of fact, observation and supposition flying around his skull. The attack on his brother had been explained – at least, as explained as it was going to be – and he was as certain as he could be that the performance with the painting was just an elaborate trick, but he still hadn't figured out how it was done. Then there were the sightings of the Dark Beast – were they real, or just rumours, hearsay and illusions? And did the death of the servant Máire fit into it somehow – had her body been moved, and if it had, then why? Did the moving of her body indicate that she had been murdered – and if that was so, then, again, *why*? He had too many questions and not enough answers.

He fell asleep without realizing, and drifted through dreams in which shattered mirrors reflected fragments of scenes in fractured ways, and somewhere behind it all Niamh was staring at him. Or was it Virginia?

Sir Shadrach wasn't present at breakfast the next morning. Ambrose Albano was, although he looked ill at ease. He kept picking up his cutlery then putting it down again without eating anything. Perhaps he hadn't slept very well. He kept on looking at Silman, the butler, and she kept staring back at him. Sherlock thought there was something odd about her expression – it seemed like she was trying to warn him about something, or warn him against doing something. Either way, it wasn't the normal expression he would have expected on a butler's face.

At the end of breakfast Silman nodded towards Albano, giving him a signal. He stood up and rapped the table for attention. Sherlock remembered the knocking on the table at the séances and stifled a laugh.

'Gentlemen, esteemed international colleagues, ladies,' Albano started. 'I am sorry to tell you that Sir Shadrach has been taken ill during the night, and will not be available today.'

247

Niamh Shadrach glanced up, concern in her eyes. Obviously she didn't know anything about this. 'Is father—?'

Albano raised a hand. 'He is perfectly fine,' he said, although there was something about his expression which meant Sherlock didn't quite believe him. 'He is just tired, and needs to rest.' He looked quickly at Silman, and then away again. 'The auction will proceed as planned, after lunch. It will take the servants a while to set up the room. Instead of Sir Shadrach conducting the auction, I will be conducting it myself, with the aid of Silman. I trust that will be acceptable.'

There was a general murmur of assent around the table. Niamh got up and rushed towards the door, but Albano called after her. 'Miss Quintillan – your father is asleep. Please do not disturb him.'

'Please convey our regards to Sir Shadrach,' Mycroft said, 'and wish him a speedy recovery.'

'We all wish him that,' Albano said quietly.

After breakfast, Sherlock went wandering. He headed for the library, with some vague idea of continuing to look for secret passages, but was surprised to find that Ambrose Albano had got there first. He was sitting at a long table reading a book. His jacket was slung across the back of his chair.

Albano stared at Sherlock. 'Have you come to discredit

me some more?' he asked, but he seemed amused rather than angry.

'No,' Sherlock said. 'Actually, I didn't know you were here at all, but now that I know you are, may I ask you some questions about magic? You obviously have a considerable amount of skill.'

'I did spend some time on stage as a magician,' he admitted, 'although that was under another name, and before I had my accident and discovered that I could communicate with the dead.' He tilted his head on one side and stared at Sherlock. 'How exactly did you see through my tricks at the séances?' he asked. 'Everyone else was convinced, or on the way to being convinced.'

'You might even have convinced me, if I hadn't searched your rooms and found the evidence of how you had performed the tricks beneath the bed.'

'I should be angry,' Albano murmured, 'but I haven't the energy. Besides, it would be petty of me. After all, I searched everybody else's room, looking for things that I could use in my performance. I found a letter from Herr Holtzbrinck's brother that he keeps with him. I can hardly complain if my own rooms are searched.'

'So what can you tell me about magic tricks?' Sherlock asked, trying not to think about the psychic poking around in his room.

Albano smiled to himself. He stood up. 'It's all to do

with misdirection,' he said. 'For instance –' he tugged at his right shirtsleeve with his left hand, pulling it up to display his right wrist, while he held his right hand up with the fingers held apart – 'as you can see, there is nothing hidden in my right hand or up my right sleeve, and –' he did the same with the other arm, pulling the left sleeve up to expose his left wrist and splaying out the fingers of his left hand – 'neither is there anything hidden in my left hand or up my left sleeve. Do you agree?'

'I agree,' Sherlock said, knowing that a trick was coming but unsure from which direction.

Albano shook his head. 'Then you weren't watching carefully enough.' He brought the fingers of his right hand and left hand together until they touched and then moved them apart again. He was suddenly holding a banknote between his fingertips. 'So where did this come from?'

'I don't know,' Sherlock said honestly. 'It wasn't up your sleeves, or in your hands. It must have been hidden somewhere else.'

'Of course it was.' Albano smiled. 'Watch again.'

He folded the banknote in two, rolled it up carefully into a thin tube, pulled his right and left sleeves back down to cover his wrists again, and then carefully tucked the rolled banknote into a fold of his left sleeve that was located in the crook of his elbow. He stopped it from falling out by keeping his left arm bent, but he held his left hand with his right in front of him to make the position look natural. 'Now, can we agree that there is nothing hidden in my right hand?' he said, pulling his right sleeve up again, as before.

'Agreed,' Sherlock said.

Albano used his right hand to pull his left sleeve up again, but this time Sherlock spotted that while his left hand was held up, splayed open, his right hand plucked the rolled-up banknote from the fold in the sleeve's material and palmed it. 'And there is nothing up my left sleeve, as you can plainly see.'

'Again, agreed, but the sleeves are the misdirection, aren't they?'

'Exactly.' Albano brought his fingers together again, with the right hand concealing the banknote that he had plucked from his sleeve. He took a corner with his left hand and pulled the note open. 'Now do you see?'

'It's so simple,' Sherlock said, 'that I almost feel cheated.'

'That is the shameful secret of professional magicians. What we call magic is actually a set of obvious ways of hiding things. The trick is in the way we take your attention away from the place where the things are hidden. The first lesson about magic is: if our audience only knew how obvious are the hiding places, and how much effort we go to in order to distract attention from them, then magic would suddenly lose all its attraction.'

'But you must already have had that banknote folded and rolled up somewhere, ready to hide in your sleeve. You didn't know that I was coming.'

'You're right.' Albano smiled, and this was a natural smile, not a fake, theatrical one. 'So, the second lesson about magic: always have several prepared tricks in your pockets, ready to go. Preparation takes time, and you never know when you might get the opportunity to perform a trick.' He frowned. 'Now, let me see what else I have to show you.' He took his jacket from the back of the chair and slipped it on, patting the pockets and sliding his hands inside as if looking for something.

Sherlock smiled to himself. He recognized in Albano's theatrical gestures a typical misdirection. Somehow the man had already started another trick.

'Oh, that's a shame. I seem to have lost it.' Albano took his hands out from inside his jacket, holding them flat, palms towards Sherlock. 'Nothing there, you see?' He closed his right hand into a fist and opened it again, and suddenly he was holding a playing card. 'Ah, there it is!' He handed it to Sherlock. It was the eight of clubs. With a sudden flourish he made the same movement with his left hand, and another card – the nine of diamonds – appeared from thin air. 'Oh, and another one!' He handed that to Sherlock as well.

Sherlock laughed. He couldn't help himself. There was something so engaging about Albano's simple pleasure in the tricks. 'All right,' he said. 'You were somehow hiding the cards in your hands, but how?'

'Watch carefully.' Albano took one of the cards back. He held it in his right hand, between his thumb and his fingers, then bent his second and third fingers so that the knuckles were pressed against the back of the card. He then curled his first and fourth fingers around to grip the edges of the card, and straightened his fingers out again. The card rotated around to the back of his hand, still held between his first and fourth fingers. He held his hand out to Sherlock, showing how the card was bent between the fingers. From the palm side it was invisible. 'Lesson Three: this is called a "back palm", for obvious reasons. It is one of the foundations of card magic. Once you get this right, once you can perform it invisibly, again and again, you can produce cards from the air to your heart's content.'

'Can you show me another trick?'

The man sighed. 'Always it's another trick.' He collected the other card from Sherlock, then reached inside his jacket and pulled out a full pack. 'Very well, let me tell you the story of the four burglars. Sit down.'

Sherlock pulled out a chair and he and Albano sat at opposite sides of the table. Albano shuffled the cards, riffled them open and pulled out the four Jacks. Leaving

253

the rest of the pack face down on the table, he showed them to Sherlock. 'There were once four burglars named Jack, who set out to burgle a house that had been left empty for the evening by the owners.'

'I don't need the story,' Sherlock pointed out. 'Just the trick.'

'Lesson Four: the story *is* the trick. Or, at least, it is part of the misdirection. Remember, every trick is a performance, and you must entertain the audience as well as amaze them. You must lead them on a journey that you have pre-planned for them. Now . . .' He placed the four Jacks face down on top of the pack. 'The four burglars all got on to the roof of the house and lowered themselves down on ropes. The first burglar broke into the basement.' As he spoke, he took the first card from the top of the pack and inserted it lower down, near the bottom, pushing it in until it was flush with the rest. 'The second burglar managed to get in through a kitchen window.' He took a second card from the top and inserted it halfway up the pack. 'The third burglar broke in through an upstairs window.' Suiting the words, he took a third card from the top and pushed in into the pack above the first two, just a little way down from the top. 'The fourth burglar stayed on top of the house, watching out for trouble.' He turned the top card over to show that it was the fourth Jack, and then turned it back again. Abruptly he rapped his knuckles on top of the pack. 'After a few minutes the burglar on the roof saw the owners returning to the house, so he called to his friends. They all quickly ran upstairs, got on to the roof and made their getaway down a drainpipe.' He slid the top four cards from the pack and turned them face up. They were, of course, the four Jacks again, even though Sherlock had thought that three of them had been pushed into the pack lower down and were hidden among the other cards. 'So, I challenge you: how was the trick done?'

Sherlock thought for a moment. 'If the Jacks are on top now, then the three cards you pushed into the deck couldn't have been Jacks. Therefore they were something else. So, when you picked the four Jacks from the pack and showed them to me, you must have had three cards hidden behind them. When you put the Jacks face down on top of the pack, those three cards were on top of them, and they were the ones you removed and inserted lower down.' He finished, and took a deep breath. 'It's obvious.'

'Exactly. The trick is in how smoothly you can pick up seven cards rather than four, and how well you can disguise the three spare ones behind the four Jacks. That depends on never showing your audience the cards edge on, just front on. The trick is actually over before the story starts, and that is the misdirection.'

'Can you teach me?' Sherlock asked quietly.

'You exposed my . . . unfortunate and ill-conceived

tricks,' Albano pointed out in a calm voice, 'and you made it harder for me to convince those here to bid for my services that I really do have psychic powers. I don't owe you anything.'

'No.' Sherlock nodded. 'You are right, you don't owe me anything, but I think you want to show someone your tricks. You want other people to know how clever you are. Taking money is one thing, but if nobody knows it was a trick then you don't feel satisfied. So teach me. Show me the tricks. You know by now that I am probably the only person in this castle who will properly appreciate them.' He stared intently at Albano. 'You've already started. You've given me four lessons already. You want to pass on your knowledge.'

Albano nodded slowly. 'Perhaps I do. It's the dream of every sorcerer, to have an apprentice.' He sighed. 'Very well. Let's start with the basics of card tricks, as we happen to have a pack here . . .'

Sherlock stayed with Ambrose Albano for several hours. During that time Albano taught him different ways to hold a pack of cards – the dealer's grip, the mechanic's grip and the biddle grip – and the many ways to cut the cards – including the swing cut and the Charlier cut. After that they moved on to ways of secretly getting a glimpse of the bottom or the top card on a deck. Albano then showed Sherlock ways of controlling a card – moving a card from the top or the bottom of the deck to wherever you wanted it to be. 'This,' he said, 'is the essence of card magic – knowing where a particular card is, and then knowing that you can move it anywhere you want.' Finally he showed Sherlock the difficult art of getting a spectator to take what they thought was a card at random but which was actually the card that the magician had already identified and moved. By the time he had finished, Sherlock's head was spinning.

'It's all just simple trickery,' Sherlock said, amazed. 'But it depends so much on being able to handle a pack of cards perfectly, without anyone knowing what you are doing.'

'The real and only secret is practice,' Albano pointed out. 'You need to keep handling that pack of cards until you can manipulate it with your eyes shut. Never go anywhere without it. If you are travelling anywhere, take that park of cards out and just move it through your fingers. Fan them out, riffle them, deal them, do anything and everything with them. They need to become your best friends.' He handed the pack of cards across. 'Keep practising. You never know when you might need these skills.'

'Thank you.' Sherlock shook hands with Albano, and left, feeling an unusual spring in his step. He felt revived, refreshed. He felt as if he had been given a glimpse into his own future. He even felt able to talk with Virginia again, but when he asked a servant where she was he was told that she had gone riding with 'the mistress' – which, he presumed, meant Niamh Quintillan. It was strange, and rather disturbing, how well those two seemed to be getting on.

He wondered if they were talking about him.

Sherlock found that he needed a breath of fresh air before lunch after the concentration of the past few hours, so he headed outside. Remembering his walk with Virginia, and his sight of the mysterious folly that he hadn't been able to investigate then, he set out to find it again.

It took about twenty minutes before he was emerging from the undergrowth into a clearing at the base of the folly. It was narrower than he had thought: probably ten feet or so across and about fifty feet high, constructed from a dark grey stone that felt rough to his fingers when he touched it. He walked around it. The lines where the stones met were so thin as to be almost invisible. The workmanship was impressive. In the weak sunlight that filtered through the clouds above he could also see that the stones were riddled with tiny holes. There was something about the sight that provoked a memory, and it took him a few seconds to realize that the folly was actually built from the same material as the smooth, curved wall that had blocked the tunnel beneath the castle.

He looked in the direction of the castle. How far was it? He tried to estimate the distance. Was it about the same as the distance he had walked in the tunnels underground? Had he gone as far then as he had now? Was the curved wall that he had found beneath the ground the same as the curved wall of the folly that he was looking at? It seemed crazy, but he thought that it might just be true. The trouble was that it added new questions to the list. Why would the tower continue beneath the ground in the same way that it did above the ground? What was the point? Surely a folly like that would be built on a foundation on flat ground. Why excavate the ground so that the folly could be extended down as well as up?

The point of follies, he reminded himself, was that they *were* follies. They didn't necessarily follow any sensible rules. They were things built by the wealthy landowners and had little rhyme or reason to them other than to show how rich the owners were. Why was he even looking for logic?

Sherlock could see dark spaces in the wall of the folly: all in a line leading up to the top. They looked like windows. The problem was that he couldn't see a doorway at ground level. What was the point of that? What was the architect trying to do?

If he strained his eyes, he thought he could see ramparts, or battlements, around the very top of the folly. The thing looked from below, he thought, like an elongated version

259

of the piece known as the 'rook', or the 'castle', in the game of chess.

He walked around the folly again, this time in the opposite direction. There was definitely no way in from the ground level, but the presence of windows suggested that there were rooms within the tower, and what was the point of having rooms if you couldn't get into them?

He stood there for a long while, just staring at the tower, trying to work out some explanation for the oddities in its construction. Following through the thought that the tower continued below ground in the same way that it continued above, he moved towards the curved wall and knelt down to examine the point where the tower entered the ground. It was overgrown with grass and small furze bushes, but he found that he could slide his fingers down between the side of the tower and the ground. There was a gap.

A little further along he noticed a stone block sticking out of the tower wall. It was lighter in colour than the tower: made of a different stone. He hadn't seen it before because a small shrub was growing in front of it. Sherlock could only see it because he was off to one side.

He moved across to take a look. It was about the size of his body, and it nestled in a hole in the side of the tower, fitting so snugly that there was no space around it. A large iron ring, battered and crusted with age, was set into the end, for reasons that he couldn't fathom.

He moved around the tower for a third time and found another three blocks, exactly the same as the first, equally spaced around the circumference. Based on the position of the sun and the time of day, they seemed to be oriented along the points of the compass. Was that significant? He wasn't sure.

He sat back, letting the facts slide around in his mind like pieces in a child's wooden puzzle, hoping that some coherent picture would emerge, but nothing came.

The only answer, he decided, was to climb the tower and see what was in the rooms, and what was on top.

The stone wall of the tower seemed sheer, and the fact that the joins between the stones were all but invisible meant that he wouldn't be able to jam anything, like a knife blade, into any gap to act as a makeshift step. For a few moments he wondered whether it would be possible to carve notches in the stone with an axe so that he could climb up, but that seemed close to an act of vandalism. Also of course, he didn't have an axe either. The alternative was to go back to the castle and get some rope, in the hope that he could form a loop and fling it up high enough to hook on to one of the projecting battlements, but he would have to go all the way back to the castle and hope that they had some rope somewhere that he could borrow, and he really wanted to investigate the folly *now*, not later.

It occurred to Sherlock that the nearest window was

only about twelve feet off the ground. If he could find a way of getting up *that* high then he could investigate what was inside. It might at least give him some clues as to what the folly was all about.

He looked around. There were a few ash trees growing among the furze bushes, but none of them had branches close enough to the folly to use as a jumping-off point.

He wandered a little way into the undergrowth and climbed up one of the trees until he was on a level with the lowest window. Unfortunately the sun was at the wrong angle and he couldn't see inside.

The branch creaked beneath his weight, and he shuffled backwards quickly, lest it break. Looking along its length he noticed that it split into two after a few feet, and the two separate lengths also each split into two. Suddenly an entire plan sprang fully formed into his mind. If he could break the branch off then he could lean it against the tower and use it as a ladder!

Before his logical brain could give him sixteen reasons why the plan would not work, he started bouncing up and down on the branch. It creaked and bent beneath his weight, but it didn't break. He edged a little way along it, using a higher branch to hold on to, and stood up. The branch he was standing on abruptly gave way. Sherlock nearly fell, saving himself only by grabbing the higher branch with both hands.

He swung himself down the tree and pulled the broken branch over to the folly. The branch was about twelve feet long, and Sherlock found that if he set the thicker end on the ground so that it did not slip, he could raise the thinner end up to rest against the edge of the lowest window. Sherlock clambered up like a monkey until his head was level with the dark opening in the wall.

He lunged for the ledge, fingers catching on the rough grey stone, and his chest crashed against the side of the tower. He hung there for a few moments before he pulled himself up and over the ledge.

He lay inside the window, breathing heavily.

The room was circular, with only the one entrance, and it was entirely empty. Well, empty apart from some splinters of wood on the floor that looked like they came not from a branch but from a box of some kind. Maybe a crate.

The sunlight barely penetrated the room but even so, Sherlock saw that one of the flagstones was darker than the rest. He moved across to examine it, and discovered that it wasn't a flagstone at all – it was actually a hole in the floor. He reached down and waved his hand around. There seemed to be plenty of space down there. Perhaps it was a way into a lower room, one that was at ground level but had no door to the outside? He supposed he could climb down and check, but he was reluctant to do that without a lamp. He could break his ankle or his leg if he fell badly, and he wouldn't be able to get out again.

A sudden thought struck him, and he looked upward, at the ceiling of the circular room. There was a hole there as well, offset from the one in the floor. Looking at the holes in the floor and the ceiling of the room he was in, he decided that they must have been put there to allow for a short ladder to climb from one room to another: that's why they were offset. The ladder could presumably be pulled up from each room into the next, and used again. With luck, the holes would lead all the way to the top of the tower. If only he had a ladder . . .

He had the next best thing: a strong pair of arms and a strong pair of legs. Crouching, he leaped for the hole above. His fingers clutched at the edge of the hole and, arms straining, he pulled himself up.

The room above was exactly the same as the room below, with the exception that the view from the window was higher. And he had been right – there *was* another hole in the ceiling.

It took him an exhausting five leaps and straining pulls to get from room to room until he was finally at the top, on the flat platform that capped the tower.

There he found Sir Shadrach Quintillan's dead body, still in its bath chair, looking over his lands with blind, unseeing eyes, the front of his shirt and jacket stained red with drying blood.

CHAPTER THIRTEEN

'The obvious question,' Amyus Crowe said, 'is: How on earth did he get *up* there?'

'Not so,' Mycroft Holmes countered. 'The obvious question is: *Why* was he *put* up there? Most murder victims are either left where they were murdered or hidden somewhere else in the hope that they will not be found. For the murderer to go to all the trouble of getting the body up on top of the folly indicates that they had a strong motivation. What was it?'

It was hours after Sherlock had found Sir Shadrach's body. His immediate reaction had been, of course, to check that Sir Shadrach was actually dead, but the gash across the man's throat and the blood that had soaked into his shirt and pooled in his lap was proof enough, in Sherlock's eyes. His second reaction had been to gaze around, looking for some way that the body could have been placed, in its bath chair, on top of the tower, but there was nothing – no ropes, no ladders, no mechanism for moving something the size and weight of a man that far in the air. His third reaction had been to climb down the tower the same way he had got up and go back to the castle, to report Sir Shadrach's death, and that descent, and the following run, had felt like one of the longest periods of his life.

Mycroft and Crowe had believed him instantly, of course, but it had taken a while before he could persuade von Webenau, Herr Holtzbrinck and Count Shuvalov. Eventually, all six of them had trooped back to the folly, along with a handful of shocked servants and a clearly distressed Silman, the butler. Niamh Quintillan was still out, and could not be found. Two of the foot-servants had climbed up the tower, using the same route that Sherlock had taken. They called down from the top, confirming the fact that Sir Shadrach was really there, and that he was really dead.

'Could this be a way of hiding the body?' Sherlock asked, staring up at the tower. 'I mean, nobody could have anticipated that I was going to climb up there, and the body is invisible from down here, on the ground.'

'But why go to all that trouble?' Mycroft repeated. He kept looking around for somewhere to sit, and kept scowling when he realized that there wasn't anywhere suitable. 'Why not just dig a hole and bury him in the shrubbery?'

'It's a message,' Crowe said. 'Perhaps the murderer didn't care whether the body was discovered or not, but wanted to make some kind of point. Or perhaps there was goin' to be some kind of note sent or letter written tellin' us where the body was, an' young Sherlock here merely anticipated it.'

Sherlock was still gazing up the length of the tower. 'I suppose the body could have been manoeuvred through all those holes in the floors,' he said, 'but Sir Shadrach would have had to be alive for that to happen, otherwise there would be traces of blood everywhere. I guess he would have had to be unconscious, though, otherwise he would have struggled. The odd bit is the bath chair. That couldn't fit through the holes. It must have been pulled up on ropes, but that would have taken hours, and for what purpose?'

'From what you described,' Mycroft said, 'there is no doubt about cause of death. The man's throat has been cut.'

'That's what I saw,' Sherlock confirmed.

'What exactly *is* this thing?' Mycroft stared up at the tower. 'It seems to have no practical purpose.'

'It's a folly,' Sherlock pointed out.

Crowe frowned. 'What's a "folly" when it's at home?'

'A decorative and unfeasibly large garden ornament,' Mycroft explained. He shook his head. 'Why people can't be satisfied with garden gnomes I don't know.'

Silman, who had been speaking with von Webenau, Holtzbrinck and Shuvalov, came over to them.

'Gentlemen,' she started, 'I am . . . sorry that this terrible thing has happened. I am at a loss to know what to do.'

'When did you last see Sir Shadrach?' Mycroft asked.

'He was feeling ill, so he took breakfast in his room. That was the last time I saw him. I went to look for him later, but he wasn't there. I assumed that he had got one of the other servants, or perhaps his daughter, to move him.'

'Nobody saw him leave the castle?'

'Nobody,' she said.

'The police must be notified,' Mycroft said firmly. 'And nobody who is here can be allowed to leave.'

'But the foreign gentlemen are talking about leaving immediately,' Silman protested. 'They have asked for transport to be arranged.'

'Absolutely not,' Mycroft insisted. 'They were present at the castle when the murder occurred, and therefore they are suspects, whether they like it or not.'

'Don't they have immunity as diplomats?' Crowe asked quietly.

'The Congress of Vienna does grant certain rights,' Mycroft admitted, 'but only to certified diplomats, not to ordinary visitors. I don't know about the other three gentlemen, but do you, Mr Crowe, possess diplomatic papers?'

Crowe's mouth twitched. 'Not as such. Am Ah a suspect?'

'Not as such,' Mycroft countered. 'I am merely making a point. Only those people with diplomatic papers are entitled to immunity, and even then such immunity can be withdrawn by their own governments if they are involved in a serious crime separate from their diplomatic duties. But we are getting ahead of ourselves – firstly, there has to be an official crime, and that means the involvement of the police. We must all stay here until the police arrive and have concluded their examination and questioning.'

'The Irish police?' Crowe questioned. 'From Galway? This ain't a case of a disappearin' cow, you know. This is murder.'

'And I am sure that Galway Town on a Friday night sees its fair share of violence.' Mycroft glanced at Silman, who was standing patiently listening to the discussion. 'Firstly, do not arrange any travel for anyone. Secondly, send someone down to the town to fetch the police, in force if possible. Thirdly, sort out some means of getting Sir Shadrach's body down from the tower. I suppose the police will want to see it *in situ*, but we need to be prepared to move it as soon as we are permitted.'

'And fourth,' Sherlock added, 'find Niamh. She needs to be told.'

Mycroft nodded. 'A valid point, Sherlock. Now, I will go and smooth the feathers of those gentlemen. If you will excuse me . . .'

He moved across to the other group. Crowe stared after him for a moment, and then said: 'Ah need to go an' talk to Virginia. Ah'd rather she hears about what has happened from me, rather than from one of the servants, or by overhearin' some passin' conversation.'

'What about Niamh?' Sherlock asked.

'If Ah see her, Ah'll tell her as well. What about you?'

'I'll hang around here and see if anything occurs to me.'

Crowe nodded, and left. Sherlock moved back to the edge of the clearing in which the folly stood and found an old tree trunk on which he could sit. He stayed there for several hours, watching as the police arrived from Galway and briefly examined the scene, and then as firstly the body and secondly the bath chair of Sir Shadrach Quintillan were lowered on ropes from the top of the folly. He overheard, from where he sat, the police sergeant telling Silman that this was obviously a murder, and that he would need to talk to everyone at the castle. The two of them left, and a couple of servants took the now-shrouded body away, wheeling it in the bath chair in just the way they would have done had Sir Shadrach been alive.

He stayed there for a long while afterwards, just staring at the folly, letting thoughts swirl around in his brain until, every now and then, they touched each other and stuck together. He was beginning to develop a theory, and it depended on this folly being where it was, and what it was.

He heard a quiet movement behind him, and said, 'It's all right. I'm just sitting here. You can come into the open, if you want.'

Niamh Quintillan stepped out of the bushes. She had obviously been crying: her eyes were red and the skin beneath them was swollen.

'You killed him,' she said quietly, but with an intense ferocity.

'I didn't,' he replied, feeling breathless at the force of her accusation. 'I had no reason to.'

'You exposed the tricks he and Mr Albano were using during the séances. If you hadn't exposed him, he would still be alive.'

'Actually, that's not true,' Sherlock said calmly, hoping Niamh would calm down as well. 'He and Mr Albano had managed to recover a lot of the ground they had lost when I showed everyone the tricks they were using. The auction was going to go ahead this afternoon, with the Germans, the Russians and the Austro-Hungarians bidding. The situation had more or less returned to the way it was before I said anything.' He paused. 'That, I think, is why he was killed – because the auction was going ahead. I think that if the other international delegates had listened to me, and the auction had been cancelled, then he would still be alive.'

'Then maybe you should have explained away the trick

with the painting as well. If you'd done that, then the auction *would* have been cancelled.'

'I'm afraid your father was too clever for me,' Sherlock admitted, 'although I *am* on the verge of working out how it was done.'

'Too late,' Niamh said. She walked a little way off, but Sherlock didn't turn to watch her.

'Yes, too late,' he agreed quietly, feeling sick at the thought that she blamed him, 'but I still didn't kill him. I wasn't the one who held the knife against his throat and cut it open. I wasn't the one who watched him bleed to death.' His words were harsh, deliberately so, but she had hurt him with her accusation and he wanted to hurt her back.

There was silence for a while. Sherlock thought that Niamh had left, but eventually she said: 'I will always blame you.'

'I know,' he said, and then: 'Niamh, did you know about the tricks that your father was involved in? Did you know that the séances were faked?' When she didn't answer, he added, 'Did you help set up those threads to hang the material on, or was it you operating the light projector maybe?'

Still there was no reply. When he turned around, she had gone.

He walked towards the tower. He thought he knew

now how the trick with the painting had been done, but he had to make sure. Having a theory was no use unless you had the evidence to back it up.

He started with the four lighter-coloured stones that stuck out of the base of the tower, the ones with iron rings set into them. Standing beside one of them, he did what he should have done earlier, when he had first noticed them, and looked up the side of the tower. Yes! There, about twenty feet up, was a dark space that had to be a hole in the stonework. It looked about the same size as the holes at ground level that the stones were set in. About twenty more feet up, there was another hole. He walked around the circumference of the tower, noticing that there were equivalent gaps above each of the four stones. They seemed to continue up to the top of the tower, every twenty feet or so.

There was one more thing that he needed to know. Choosing one of the lighter stones at random, he walked directly away from the tower, keeping it at his back. He found that there was a faint path through the underbrush where no bushes grew, and where the grass was stunted. Turning, he looked back at the lighter stone. If, he thought, a rope was attached to the iron ring and a donkey or a horse was attached to the rope then the stone could be pulled out of the tower. If all four of the stones were pulled out . . .

273

Now he had enough evidence, but if he wanted to persuade Mycroft and Amyus Crowe then he would have to build a scale model. Words wouldn't be enough.

Before leaving for the castle, he went back to the tower and searched around the base. He quickly found what he was looking for: fragments of the darker stone that the tower itself was made from: the stone that was riddled with tiny air holes. They were surprisingly light in his hand, and he slipped them into his pocket for later.

Back at the castle, the police sergeant was interviewing servants in the reception room. He had obviously finished with the more important foreign representatives. Sherlock noticed a bell on a side table in the main hall. He rang it, and waited. After a few minutes Silman appeared. She looked, if anything, even more dour and vinegary than usual. The death of Sir Shadrach had obviously shocked her.

'Yes, sir?' she said smoothly.

'I need a large bowl of water and some sheets of card,' he said. 'Oh, and a jug of water as well. And some scissors.' He thought for a moment. 'And four knives. And some pins. Oh, and some sealing wax and a lit candle.'

She raised an eyebrow, but just said: 'Yes, sir. Of course.'

'And could you have them sent to the dining room for me?'

274

'Given the circumstances, a cold collation has been set out in the dining room so that lunch can be taken whenever people wish. The table is nearly full.'

'Ah. All right – can you have the stuff brought to the library?' It suddenly occurred to him that he hadn't eaten lunch. 'And can one of the servants put together a plate of cold meat for me and bring it in?'

'Yes, sir.'

In a fever of excitement, Sherlock went to the library to wait. While waiting he checked the shelves for books on geography and geology, and soon found what he was looking for.

When the material and the food arrived he set to work. First he set the bowl on a table, and cut a circular cover for it out of card – its diameter a few inches larger than the diameter of the bowl. In the centre of the cover he cut a hole. Next he made a long tube by rolling a sheet of the card up and fastening it with pins. He made a circular base for the tube, smaller than the cover on the bowl but wider than the tube itself, and fastened it to one end of the tube with some melted sealing wax.

Looking at it critically, he realized that he had to make some modifications to the tube. Using one of the knives he cut openings up the side to represent the windows in the folly, and then, to finish it off, he made a series of small slices in the card of the tube. He made them in groups of four, spaced equally around the circumference, and separated the groups of four along the length of the tube by a few inches.

Now he was ready. Almost. He grabbed some food from the tray and stuffed it in his mouth, working while he chewed.

He slid the cardboard tube through the hole in the bowl cover, so that the circular base on the tube was pressed against the underneath of the cover. The tube was slightly narrower than the hole, so it slid easily back and forth. Then, because he didn't want the underside of the tube's base to get waterlogged, he melted some sealing wax and spread it over the base to seal it.

Now to set the whole thing up. He put the card cover on the bowl of water so that the tube of card stuck up into the air, and he let the tube drop down so that the circular base, the one he had covered with sealing wax to waterproof it, was resting on the surface of the water. He then set the four knives out on top of the bowl's cover around the circumference of the tube.

He stepped back to examine his handiwork, and realized with a curse that he had forgotten something. He needed to be able to get water into the bowl. Grabbing one of the knives, he carefully cut a square hole in the bowl's cover.

Now he was ready.

Without wanting to waste a precious second, he rushed out into the hall. As luck would have it, Mycroft and Amyus Crowe were standing by the door seeing the police sergeant out. They all shook hands, and the policeman left. Mycroft turned and caught sight of Sherlock.

'What on earth is it?' he asked. 'You look like you used to do when you found a frog in the back garden and brought it into the house to show Mother.'

'I know how the painting trick was done,' he announced. 'Come with me and I will demonstrate.'

Mycroft and Crowe followed him into the library. Mycroft took one look at the cardboard model on the table and said: 'Of course! How could I have been so blind?'

Crowe stared from him to Sherlock and back again. 'Someone want to let me into the secret?'

Sherlock gestured to the model. 'This is the folly – the tower out in the castle grounds.'

'Right. I can see that.'

'Did it seem to you that the tower is made of a rather unusual stone?'

'Ah guess,' Crowe admitted. 'Quite porous, an' quite dark.'

'It's actually called "pumice stone". It's produced in volcanoes when the molten lava cools down.' He took the flakes he had collected from his pocket and handed them to Mycroft and to Amyus Crowe to examine.

277

'Not many volcanoes in Ireland,' Crowe noted.

'Exactly. The stone was brought here from somewhere else. The key thing about pumice is that it has a lower density than water. Pumice stone *floats* on water.'

'Ah think Ah see where you are goin' with this.'

'The tower is *made* out of pumice stone,' Sherlock went on. 'The pumice must have been shipped here from some volcanic location, carved into blocks and made into a tower. The thing is that the tower doesn't stop at the ground: it goes beneath the surface of the ground. I know that because I found its outer wall when I was investigating the tunnels beneath the castle. I thought it was just a blockage in the tunnel, but it was actually the tower itself.'

'Down to where?' Crowe asked.

'Down to where the sea comes in through a series of caves. This whole area is riddled with caves. Somewhere at the base of the tower is a big block of pumice stone resting on the surface of the sea – or at least, it does when the sea comes in. When the sea is out then the pumice stone rests on the ground.'

'And when the sea comes in,' Crowe breathed, 'the tower floats, and starts to rise.'

'Exactly.' Sherlock took the jug of water from the table and emptied it into the bowl through the hole that he had made. The increasing water level pushed the circular base

278

of the tower up, beneath the bowl's cover, and the tower slowly grew in height.

'I couldn't understand,' he said, 'why I could sometimes see the tower and sometimes couldn't. At first I thought it was due to the landscape, but the real answer is that it was sometimes taller and sometimes shorter.'

Crowe shook his head. 'But we would have spotted the fact that the tower was growin'. We were there for hours, an' it never changed.'

'That was because the anchors were in,' Mycroft said. 'Show him, Sherlock. I presume that is what the knives are for?'

Sherlock nodded. He had stopped pouring water into the bowl when four of the slits he had made in the cardboard folly had appeared above the level of the bowl cover. He put the jug down and slid the knives across the card, one at a time, until they were all stuck in the tower's wall, in the slits. He picked up the jug again and poured more water into the bowl. The knives anchored the tower in place. In the bowl, the water level crept up above the tower's base, making the card wet, but Sherlock didn't mind. He had made his point.

'There are four large chunks of stone set around the tower,' he said. 'I wondered at first what they were, until I realized that they were *wedges*. When the tower gets to a certain height they can be hammered in to fix it in place.

279

When the tower is meant to get smaller again, the wedges can be pulled out.'

Mycroft was frowning. 'I presume that such an action could only occur at the time the water level is at a certain point, otherwise the tower might suddenly drop vertically through many feet, and that could be catastrophic.'

'I'm sure there's a whole instruction book about how to raise and lower the tower,' Sherlock said. 'I'm still trying to work it all out.'

'Ah presume this is somethin' to do with smugglin'?' Crowe asked. 'Ah know that this part of the coastline was known for smugglin', some years ago. The tower would have given them a perfect place to hide their illegal goods. Put it in a room of the tower, wait till the tide goes out, an' then fix the tower in place so that the stuff is below the ground. Ingenious!'

Sherlock pointed to the model. 'And that explains the trick with the paintings. When we all looked out of the window of the room on top of the castle, the tower was at its lowest point – below the line of bushes and trees. After we'd all trooped out of the castle, the wedges were removed and the tower was allowed to rise up to its maximum height. I guess there was a servant up there with a telescope, able to see into the room. They saw which painting I had hung up, and which way I had hung it, and then got a message to Ambrose Albano while he was staring away from us and pretending to communicate with the dead.'

Crowe shook his head. 'Such a complicated plan.'

'Magic tricks are always complicated,' Sherlock said. 'I've learned that from Mr Albano. And they always use some kind of distraction. In this case, all the business with the blue chalk dust was the distraction. It got us thinking about something completely different.'

Mycroft's face took on a grim expression. 'And Sir Shadrach's death? How does that factor in to your explanation?'

'I don't know who killed him, or why,' Sherlock said, 'but I know how. The tower was allowed to sink to its lowest point, at low tide. The top of the tower is probably at ground level then. Sir Shadrach was killed, and his bath chair was just wheeled on to the tower's top. When the tide came back in, the tower rose up again, and the stone wedges were put in place.'

'There's a flaw in your argument,' Crowe pointed out. 'I doubt the sea level around here varies from low tide to high tide as much as the height of that tower. How do you explain that?'

'I think there are two things at work there. The first is that the sea is probably channelled through small tunnels and cracks, all the way into the cliff, and develops a much higher pressure that way. That hydraulic pressure is what

281

pushes the tower up and down.' He hesitated, thinking. 'When Mycroft and I arrived, Sir Shadrach told us that the ascending room was operated by hydraulic power, driven by the tides. The tower works in the same way, on a much more massive scale. The tower, when he discovered it, must have given him the idea for the ascending room.'

'And the second thing?'

'I don't think smugglers would have wanted to be pinned to the rising and falling of the tides. I'm guessing that they had some kind of system of dams so they could pen up the seawater and stop it getting to the base of the folly, or suddenly release that pent-up water and raise the folly whenever they wanted.'

Mycroft clapped his hands together. 'Fascinating though this is – and it is fascinating, of that you should have no doubt – it still brings us no closer to solving the mystery of who killed Sir Shadrach.'

'Do we *need* to solve it?' Crowe's face was serious. 'The police are involved, and the auction will not take place. Our role here is finished.'

'No,' Sherlock said simply. 'We can't leave without finding the murderer.'

'Why not?'

'Sir Shadrach is dead because we are all here. His murder has something to do with the auction. We didn't directly *cause* his death, but if none of us had turned up then he would still be alive. I think we have a moral responsibility to find his murderer and bring him or her to justice.'

There was silence in the room for a few moments.

'I recognize the expression on his face,' Mycroft said sadly. 'It means that we are not getting out of here until he is satisfied.'

'Must be a family trait,' Crowe murmured.

Mycroft checked his watch. 'Gentlemen, I think that the time has come for us to take some positive action. Come with me.'

He moved towards the door of the library. Sherlock and Crowe exchanged glances, and then followed.

Mycroft led them out into the castle hall and towards the main door. Silman was in the hall, and moved to intercept him.

'As you requested, Mr Holmes, all of the other representatives are remaining here. I presume that you will also be staying?'

'I will,' Mycroft boomed, 'but I have just realized that my brother has not been questioned by the police. He was out in the castle grounds all morning. By the time he returned, the police sergeant was leaving. I will take him into Galway now, if you would be so kind as to arrange a carriage. Mr Crowe here has kindly offered to go with us, just in case anyone was worried that we are going to head straight for the train station and leave.'

283

Silman looked uncertain. Crowe smiled reassuringly. 'We all have to stay until the investigation is complete, ma'am,' he said. 'Ah have no reason to disbelieve Mr Holmes when he says that he an' his brother will return, but there's an old saying in mah country – "Put your faith in God, but always tie your horse up". You know Ah'll be back because Ah'm leavin' mah daughter under your roof.'

Silman nodded. 'Thank you, Mr Crowe. I will organize a carriage right away.'

When she was out of earshot, Crowe said: 'Where *are* we goin'?'

Mycroft's face was unreadable. 'As I said, we are going into Galway.'

The carriage arrived barely ten minutes later – a four-wheeler with a single horse attached. They all climbed in, and the carriage set off towards the main gates of the castle. Watching the castle recede in the distance, Sherlock found that he had mixed feelings. Although it wasn't home, he had got used to it over the past few days.

Then again, he thought, where *was* home now?

The carriage rattled downhill, along rutted roads and past irregular fields, overgrown furze bushes, clumps of ash and rowan trees and the occasional thatched cottage, until it reached Galway. Mycroft banged on the roof as they approached the hotel in which he and Sherlock had stayed just after Sherlock's arrival on the *Gloria Scott*.

'Wait here for us,' he called up to the driver as the carriage slowed to a halt. 'We will be less than an hour, in my estimation. If you wish to take a break then do so, as long as you are back within the hour.'

The three of them headed into the hotel.

'Still not sure what we are doin' here,' Crowe rumbled.

'We are seeking reinforcements,' Mycroft replied enigmatically.

Sherlock glanced around to see who these potential reinforcements might be. Within a handful of seconds it was obvious, and he felt his heart suddenly get a lot lighter.

Matty Arnatt and Rufus Stone were sitting in armchairs in the hotel lobby.

CHAPTER FOURTEEN

'Sherlock!' Matty shouted across the lobby, making heads turn. He rushed across and skidded to a halt in front of his friend. He didn't seem to know whether to hug Sherlock or shake his hand. In the end he settled for punching Sherlock hard in the shoulder. 'I wasn't sure you were ever coming back!'

'There were times,' Sherlock admitted, smiling in delight, 'when I wasn't sure either.'

''Ow long you been away?'

'Don't you know?'

'Don't have a calendar, nor a watch. There's been a whole load of snow between you leaving and you coming back, so I reckon it's been nearly a year.'

'That much and some more,' Sherlock said ruefully.

'Albert's dead.' Matty's face was serious. 'Just stopped trottin' one day, fell down and died, right in front of me.'

'Virginia told me, in a letter.'

'Got a new 'orse, though, name of 'Arold.'

Mycroft placed his hands on their shoulders. 'Heart-warming though this reunion is, there are some important matters we need to discuss. Let us make ourselves comfortable and talk.'

Rufus Stone was standing up when Sherlock and the others got over to him. He nodded at Mycroft and at Amyus Crowe, but he shook Sherlock's hand warmly.

'Good to see you again, kid. I had visions of you settling down in China and learning how to play one of those abominable stringed instruments that you see in waterfront bars in Limehouse.'

'Tempting,' Sherlock replied, 'but the violin is hard enough. I have been practising, by the way. All the time.'

'There's always going to be at least one fiddle player on a working ship,' Stone said, smiling. 'The trouble is they rarely practise their scales, despite the proximity of so many fish.'

Sherlock winced at the joke. 'It's good to be back,' he said.

Mycroft gestured at them all to sit down. 'No doubt you are wondering,' he said to Sherlock and Crowe, 'why these two unsavoury characters are here.'

'You sent them a telegram.' Sherlock shrugged. 'It's obvious.'

'You did *not* decode that telegram.' Mycroft scowled.

'No, but you asked me to send an urgent telegram after you were attacked, and now Rufus and Matty are here. There's a clear connection to be made.'

'Indeed.' Mycroft didn't seem mollified. 'Knowing that I was coming here to Galway, and knowing that I would be meeting you and that we might end up with a situation that we could not handle, I took the precaution of putting Mr Stone on alert. I did not specifically ask him to bring young Matthew, but I did not rule the possibility out.'

'We relocated to Liverpool,' Stone said, 'and waited for further instructions. The minute we got Mr Holmes's telegram, we set out for Ireland.'

'But I sent the telegram to London,' Sherlock said, and then caught himself with an exclamation. 'Of course – you had someone resend the telegram to the intended recipients.'

'Never, if you can help it, give away either your intentions or your agents,' Mycroft said. He clapped his hands together. 'Now – I need to brief the two of you on recent events.'

Succinctly, Mycroft summarized everything that had happened. While he spoke, pots of tea and plates of sandwiches and cakes were brought to them.

'You're taller than you used to be,' Matty whispered to Sherlock while Mycroft was speaking. 'And you're thinner as well. And you've got a tan.'

'You're smaller than you used to be,' Sherlock countered.

'That don't make any sense. People don't get smaller as

they grow up. That's why it's called growing *up.*'

'I was joking.' Sherlock paused for a moment. 'But you are bigger around the waist. Too many pies filched from the market stalls?'

'There's this woman who runs a baker's,' Matty explained with a sniff. 'She's kind of adopted me. She feeds me stuff all the time, even when I don't want it.' A puzzled look crossed his face. 'I've never not wanted food before. It's a strange feeling.'

'It's called "feeling full",' Sherlock pointed out. 'Get used to it.'

'So,' Mycroft said, glaring at the two of them, 'we have something of a conundrum. Who killed Sir Shadrach Quintillan, and why?'

'From the sound of it, there are three different groups of villains involved,' Stone said, picking up a sandwich. 'Firstly, you have Sir Shadrach and Mr Albano, supported by the castle staff and possibly Quintillan's daughter. They were involved in faking the psychic events so they could make a tidy profit from auctioning off Albano's services, and in arranging the fake kidnapping in order to make him seem more important.'

'Agreed, and obvious,' Mycroft said.

'Secondly, you have the person who attacked you – Count Shuvalov's assistant, but acting outside his authority.'

'Again,' Mycroft said, 'you state the obvious.'

'And thirdly, you have the mysterious person or persons who want to sabotage the entire auction process, and have done so by killing Sir Shadrach Quintillan.'

Sherlock frowned. 'How can you be sure they want to sabotage the auction process? The whole thing was trickery from start to finish.'

'But from what your brother has said, the knowledge that the third demonstration of psychic powers was a trick is known only to the five of us here. For that reason, it couldn't have been any of the international representatives who killed Sir Shadrach. They obviously still believe in Ambrose Albano's powers, and want the auction to happen. They wouldn't have sabotaged it.'

'The violinist has a point,' Crowe rumbled. 'There's a third party somewhere here, an' we don't know who they are.'

'We know some things about them,' Sherlock pointed out. 'We know that they believe in Ambrose Albano's psychic abilities, we know that they don't want any of the great international nations to have access to those abilities, and we know that they want to use those abilities themselves.'

''Ow do you figure that out?' Matty asked. He was following the conversation with interest.

'Because they killed Sir Shadrach, but left Ambrose

Albano alive. If they wanted to stop any of the Empires from using the psychic then they would have killed Albano instead.'

Matty nodded. 'Fair point.' He frowned, thinking. 'So why didn't they kidnap this Albano bloke earlier? If it 'ad been me, I would've grabbed 'im first chance I got.'

'They didn't grab him earlier,' Mycroft explained, 'because your friend Sherlock had exposed him as a fake during the second séance. They were probably getting ready to pack up and go home, knowing that the international representatives were going to do the same thing, when Sir Shadrach staged that miracle come-back using the trick with the painting. That put them on the alert again. We need to arrange an opportunity for them, and not give them enough time to make anything more than a rudimentary plan.'

'We also know that they have an agent inside the house,' Sherlock added. 'They must have, in order to get information on the progress of negotiations, and also to have got Sir Shadrach out without anyone noticing. That gives us an edge.'

Mycroft nodded. 'We can provide them with false information to bring them out into the open, just by discussing it openly in the house.'

'Ah see,' Crowe said. 'Make them think that there's a deal goin' down an' that Ambrose Albano is about to be

291

whisked away by one of us. They'll have to move rapidly then to keep hold of him.'

Sherlock frowned. 'Where *is* Albano? I haven't seen him since last night.'

'He has locked himself in his room,' Mycroft said. 'He is terrified that he might be killed next. He was interviewed by the police, but through a locked door. I think we can assume he'll want to stay there.' He looked around the group. 'What I propose is this. First: Sherlock, Mr Crowe and I return to the castle. Second: I brief Ambrose Albano to keep quiet and stay in his room. Third: Mr Crowe makes a big noise about having been ordered by the US President to make a deal with Mr Albano and tells everyone that he and Albano will be leaving within the hour. Fourth: Mr Stone and young Matty hire a coach and horses and get them to turn up at the castle later this afternoon. Fifth: Mr Stone and I work out where, along the route that the coach will take back to Galway, would be the logical place for an attack to take place. Sixth: Mr Stone and young Matty wait there, along with some locals that Mr Stone will have to hire. Seventh—'

'I think we understand the plan,' Sherlock interrupted, 'but how will we make it look like Mr Crowe is taking Mr Albano away if he's locked in his room?'

'That,' Mycroft said, 'is a very good question.' He

turned to Rufus Stone. 'Did you bring the things that I asked for?'

'I did.' Stone lifted up a case that was beside his chair. 'Theatrical make-up, wigs, all kinds of stuff to make one person look like another.'

Mycroft looked at Sherlock. 'You, Sherlock, have the general build and the thinness of Mr Albano. With some pale make-up and a black wig you could, at a distance, be an acceptable substitute – and we know that this mysterious third party *will* be observing from a distance. They have to.'

Crowe shifted in his seat in concern. 'What about that singular crystal eye of his? Difficult to fake that. Could give the game away.'

'Ah.' Mycroft thought for a moment. 'An eyepatch is probably the only answer. That or Sherlock has to keep his head down.'

'Not so,' Sherlock said. 'Leave it to me – I think I can do better.'

Mycroft looked around the group again, meeting everyone's gaze. 'Does everyone know their assigned parts in this? Is everyone reasonably content that those parts can be accomplished?'

'One question,' Rufus Stone said. 'When I and these local thugs that I have yet to hire leap out from hiding and stop the kidnap attempt, what is our aim? I doubt we can make arrests, and I don't want to get anyone into a fight to the death with a desperate criminal.'

'I want to flush out whoever is responsible for giving the orders.' Mycroft's face was stony. 'If there is an obvious leader then take them, and let the rest escape. If not then take anyone you can and we can question them at our leisure to find out who they are working for and where they are based.' He looked around the table. 'Are we all clear?'

Crowe, Stone, Sherlock and Matty looked at each other, then back at Mycroft. They all nodded at once.

'Very well, let us begin. I do not need to tell you how important this is, or how dangerous.'

'Nobody told me this trip was going to be dangerous,' Matty murmured to nobody in particular. 'Is it too late to go back home?'

Outside, the carriage was waiting to take Sherlock, Mycroft and Crowe back to the castle. As they got in, Sherlock spotted Rufus Stone and Matty leaving the hotel and heading towards the quayside.

'Do you think they'll be able to find enough men to help them?' he asked.

Mycroft nodded. 'You can usually find enough men on a quayside to do almost anything, up to and including taking control of a small country. In this case, Mr Stone merely needs five or six reliable men who aren't worried that they might – actually, that they almost certainly *will* – get involved in a fight. Or perhaps double or triple that number if, when he examines the map of the local area, he finds several places that would serve equally well as the site of a hijack and kidnapping. The problem he will have is making sure they understand and follow their instructions, but he is naturally at home in their environment, and he talks the same language as the working man.' A wistful expression flashed across his face, so briefly that Sherlock almost missed it. 'I doubt that I would have that ability. I would merely get their backs up, while Mr Stone will have them eating out of his hand.' He paused, considering the words he had just uttered. 'That was a badly mixed set of metaphors, but I think you understand what I am trying to say.'

The carriage rattled along, taking them back to the castle. As they got closer, Mycroft beckoned to Amyus Crowe, who was staring out of the window, and said: 'While Sherlock takes Mr Stone's theatrical make-up kit up to his room and begins the process of disguising himself as Mr Albano, you and I need to stage a loud argument in the hall, so that the agents of this mysterious third party can hear us.'

'What do we need to say?'

'You need to tell me that you have made a separate deal with Mr Albano, on behalf of the US Government, and that you will be taking him away shortly. Oh, and that reminds me – you need to ensure that this carriage and its driver wait outside the castle to take you away later. It would be embarrassing if, after making all that noise about leaving, you were not able to do so.'

'Point noted,' Crowe said. 'What else?'

'I, of course, will remonstrate loudly with you, telling you that you have no authority to make a separate deal. You will respond that, with the death of Sir Shadrach Quintillan, the arrangement as originally struck, with the auction process and the four bidders, is dead, and that you are making your own arrangements. Throw your weight around. Make yourself unpleasant and boorish.'

'Do you think that will be believed?'

Mycroft smiled. 'The perception of Americans, especially American businessmen, is that they believe money is the solution to any problem. It isn't, of course – it is actually the *cause* of most problems. But that is immaterial – the other international representatives and, more importantly, the agents of the third party, will quite happily believe that an American would go outside the agreed process and make a side deal in a way that they wouldn't believe about any of the others.'

'The perception of an Englishman, of course,' Crowe added, 'is that he'd still take part in an auction if he was the only bidder, and happily bid against himself, just because he'd given his word that an auction would be the way things were done.'

'And quite right too.' Mycroft nodded firmly. 'If we were all to renege on our agreements, what kind of world would this be? We English have to provide a good example for others to follow.'

'It's a good thing Ah know you're jokin' with me, Mr Holmes.'

Mycroft raised an eyebrow, but said nothing.

As the carriage entered the grounds of the castle, Sherlock reached down to check that he still had the theatrical make-up box with him.

'Are you happy with being left to apply your disguise on your own?' Mycroft asked him.

Sherlock nodded. 'Yes. After the time you and I spent in Moscow, when I completely failed to recognize a dining room full of disguised Paradol Chamber agents, even though I had spent the past few days with them, I spent a while studying the techniques of theatrical make-up. There's a theatre in Farnham, and I used to go down there and watch the actors putting on their make-up. They ended up teaching me a lot about the things you can do with putty, greasepaint, hair and spirit gum. I got pretty good at it.'

'Did they ever offer you a job on stage?'

Sherlock smiled. 'I did a couple of walk-on roles in some

297

plays they were doing. I really enjoyed the experience. I'd like to do it again.'

Mycroft shuddered. 'The theatrical life is not one for a Holmes to live. Too Bohemian. I still see you in banking, Sherlock.'

'I wouldn't enjoy banking, but I could make it *look* like I did.'

'Yes, very funny.'

The carriage clattered across the drawbridge and into the central area of the castle. As it drew up to the main doors, Sherlock realized that he had been using humour to disguise his own feelings of nervousness. It had suddenly dawned on him that he was going to put himself in danger, disguised as a man who was of interest to some mysterious gang who were quite happy to commit murder to further their own aims. This was not what he had thought he was coming back home to do.

It did, however, seem to be the kind of thing that kept happening to him.

He thought about what his brother had said, about him taking up a career in banking. He honestly couldn't see that happening. He wasn't going to go into the Civil Service, like his brother, either, and he *certainly* wasn't going to join the Army like his father. But what did that leave? Going back to sea? Setting up a trading company and importing foodstuffs and silk from China?

It suddenly occurred to him that the past few days, when he had been set a series of problems to solve and had pretty much solved them all, had been some of the best fun he'd had for ages. He *liked* solving problems. It satisfied an itch inside his brain. He had particularly liked seeing the expressions on the faces of von Webenau, Herr Holtzbrinck and Count Shuvalov when he explained how the séances had been arranged, and the expression on his own brother's face when Mycroft had seen the cardboard model of the tower. It had been a thrill, and he wanted to see if he could get that thrill again. The problem was that he didn't see how he could make that into a career. The closest he could come to it would be joining the police force, but he really didn't see himself in uniform, and his experience of the police, albeit limited so far, was that they turned up at the scene of a crime, said some things that were already obvious to everyone, and arrested the nearest suspicious-looking man.

Mycroft and Amyus Crowe got out of the carriage, and Sherlock followed with the box of theatrical make-up. While Mycroft strode into the hall and Crowe talked to the carriage driver, Sherlock headed for the stairs.

He went directly to Ambrose Albano's room, making sure that he was not observed by any of the servants. Fortunately the corridor was empty when he arrived, and he knocked on the door.

Albano's voice came from inside: 'Go away! I've already told you – I don't intend coming out of this room until I have a police escort that will take me to safety! It's *dangerous* out there!'

'It's Sherlock Holmes. I wanted to ask you a question.'

A pause, then: 'You may ask any question you like, as long as the answer doesn't involve me opening that door.'

'That could be a problem. I wanted to borrow one of your suits, and your hat.'

'On the face of it, that would require me to open the door, so the answer is "No".'

Sherlock thought rapidly. 'What if you were to bundle a suit and your hat up and drop them out of the window? I could go downstairs and catch them when you dropped them.'

'That would work,' Albano replied. 'But I would need to know why you wanted them. It sounds as if you intend something suspicious, and I don't like suspicious things.'

'I can't tell you what I'm doing,' Sherlock said patiently, 'but I can assure you that it's intended to ensure your safety.' He paused, then said: 'It's misdirection, of a sort. You should appreciate that.'

Albano seemed to think for a while, then he said: 'Then the answer is "Yes". You have a quick mind, agile fingers and a natural ability with magic tricks. I can see you making a fine magician, one day. If your misdirection distracts attention from me then all the better. So, yes, I will lend you a suit and my hat, and I will await with interest the results. You will come back and tell me what you've done?'

'I will,' Sherlock promised. 'Give me five minutes to get downstairs, then open your window and look for me.'

It all went perfectly smoothly. Sherlock made his way outside the castle and waiting on the grass until a window opened far above him. He gestured to Albano to wait until he had checked left and right for watchers, and then indicated that the psychic should throw down the bundle. It fell straight into his arms, wrapped in a belt. He waved his thanks and heard the window close above him.

Part of him had wanted to tell Albano that he had figured out how the trick with the paintings had been done, but he knew that would have been a bad idea. He knew he hadn't been observed getting the clothes, but there was no knowing who might be listening, and it would have destroyed Mycroft's plan if it had become common knowledge that the last demonstration of Albano's powers had been as fake as the first two.

He headed back into the castle, and up to his room.

Once there, he locked the door and set to work making himself look like Ambrose Albano. He used a white foundation layer on his skin, and then brushed it with powder to make it even whiter, using the reverse end of the

301

brush to make a series of pockmarks in the make-up. His face was thin enough to match Albano's, but he did insert a couple of pads between his gums and his cheeks to bring his lips away from his teeth and to emphasize his incisors in the same rather horsey way as Albano, and he put some springy material inside his nostrils to make them flare in a similar fashion. There was a selection of wigs in the box as well; he picked one that more or less approximated the length, straightness and colour of Albano's hair, greased and brushed his own hair back so that it was flat against his scalp, and slipped the wig on. He examined himself critically in the mirror. It wasn't a bad likeness, he had to admit. The only problem was that his eyebrows were too dark, so he carefully covered them with fake strips of hair in the same colour as the wig, attached to his own eyebrows by spirit gum. If he was doing this for longer, or if he was going to be observed close up, then he might have cut his own hair short, and perhaps shaved his eyebrows off, so that the illusion would be better, but he only had to look like Albano from a distance.

He stripped off his own clothes and dressed in Albano's suit. It was slightly too large, but it wasn't going to make him look like a child dressing up in his father's clothes.

The last thing he did was to take a ball of theatrical putty from the box and mould it into a curve, like a fragment of a hollow sphere. Using a bright white make-up that was usually used for Oriental characters, he coloured the outer surface of the putty. Once he was happy with the result, he closed his left eye and pressed the putty against his eyelid, pushing hard around the edge so that it stuck.

Now he really did look like Ambrose Albano, fake eye and all. At least, from a distance.

As he was slipping the hat on to his head there was a knock on the door.

'Who is it?' he called.

'Amyus Crowe. Your brother an' I have caused all kinds of ruckus downstairs. He's now talkin' about breach of contract an' all kinds of stuff in the drawin' room, so we can get down the stairs an' out without any close observation. You ready?'

'Ready as I'll ever be,' Sherlock muttered. 'Yes,' he called, and headed for the door.

Crowe looked him up and down critically. 'Ah'm no judge of the dramatic arts,' he said, 'but Ah'd be convinced, if Ah saw you on a stage from a distance, that you were Albano.'

They went down in the ascending room, as it removed the chance of them meeting someone on the stairs. When they got to the bottom, Crowe hustled Sherlock towards the door. Sherlock saw that the carriage was still waiting outside. As they got to the doorway, Sherlock heard his brother shouting out, 'There they go! That Yankee rogue is taking Albano away!'

'Get in the carriage.' Crowe muttered. 'Fast, before they can see anything more than your back.'

Sherlock climbed in and settled back into the seat, pulling the hat down over his eyes. Crowe climbed in beside him. From the corner of his eye Sherlock could see a group of people clustering in the doorway of the castle. He thought he could spot Mycroft's impressive bulk at their head, but he didn't dare turn his head to look in case they glimpsed his face.

'Go!' Crowe called to the driver, who cracked the whip over the horse's head. The carriage set off with a jolt. Sherlock felt himself pushed back into the padded seats. Somewhere behind them he could hear voices shouting, but he was more concerned now with what was ahead of them. Somewhere in the next few minutes, on the way to Galway, there would be an attack on the carriage, with the intention of kidnapping him, and it was up to Rufus Stone and whatever rag-tag band he'd managed to hire in the past two hours to stop them.

The carriage approached the castle gates. Sherlock braced himself for a sudden right turn as they went through.

Instead, they turned left.

Sherlock, braced for a turn in the opposite direction,

felt himself sliding to one side. Crowe, similarly braced, fell into Sherlock. As they turned, Sherlock glanced out of the window to his right, looking down the road that they should have taken. He saw another carriage, similar to theirs, that had been hidden by the wall. It started off in the opposite direction.

'Hey!' Crowe shouted up to the driver. 'Wrong way!'

The driver ignored him. The speed of the carriage increased as it cleared the turn.

Crowe grabbed at the door handle and tried to turn it. He couldn't. It was fixed in place. Sherlock tried the handle next to him, but that didn't move either.

'Did you see that other carriage?' he asked breathlessly.

'We've been taken,' Crowe snapped. 'They switched carriages on us. Damn it, I should've checked out the driver's face!'

'It might have been the same driver,' Sherlock pointed out. 'They might have given him so much money that he went along with their plans.'

'No.' Crowe shook his head firmly. 'They might well have paid off the driver, but it's a different carriage. The one waitin' outside the gates was the one we were supposed to get into. That way, when it gets to Galway it'll look like a real mystery. The driver'll swear blind that we got in, an' Stone an' the kid'll swear blind that it cantered past them with no problems.'

305

'Just like the supposed disappearance of Ambrose Albano,' Sherlock pointed out grimly.

'Whoever's taken us has a sense of humour.' Crowe's face showed that he was anything but amused. 'They're turnin' Quintillan and Albano's tricks back against them.' He stood up and gestured to Sherlock to do the same. Sherlock tried to hang on to the ceiling of the carriage to keep himself upright, while Crowe tore at the padding that covered the seats at the back, hoping to find some panels that he could tear out so they could escape through the back. Not that jumping from something travelling at the speed they were going would be a safer option, Sherlock thought. They could well break bones if they misjudged the jump.

He looked out of the window, but couldn't see anything apart from bushes and trees rushing past.

'It's no good!' Crowe slammed his fist against the carriage door in frustration.

The carriage came to an abrupt stop, throwing Sherlock and Crowe forward. As they picked themselves up, the door opened. They waited for a long moment, but nobody appeared.

'Well, Ah ain't one to wait around on a promise,' Crowe said, and got out of the carriage. Sherlock sighed, and followed.

The carriage had stopped in a clearing in the middle

of undergrowth and trees. Sherlock could smell the salty tang of the ocean nearby, and he could hear waves. There were probably ten men standing around the carriage, but it was the two in front that caught Sherlock's attention. He felt his mouth fall open in shock.

'Gentlemen, thank you so much for joining us,' the first man said in a thin, whispery voice that made Sherlock's hair stand on end.

'Do you want to introduce me to your friend?' Crowe asked.

'Amyus Crowe,' Sherlock replied, his voice almost as thin and whispery as the man who had spoken. 'May I introduce Baron Maupertuis? He works for the Paradol Chamber.'

CHAPTER FIFTEEN

Baron Maupertuis was, if possible, even more fragile than he had appeared the last time Sherlock had seen him. That had been two years before, when Maupertuis had been trying to destroy the British Army with killer bees. Then he had been strapped into an elaborate harness of ropes, cords and wires that had enabled his servants to move him around like a puppet. That, however, had been on his own ground, in his own manor house. Now, out in the open and surrounded by bodyguards, he looked like an animated skeleton dressed in military uniform. Sherlock could clearly see the joints of his fingers and his wrists — swellings where the stick-thin bones met and articulated. The gold braid on the front of his black uniform seemed thicker than his fingers. His face was a skull papered over with parchment. Prominent veins wormed their way across his scalp, startlingly purple against the white skin. His eyes were the only things about him that looked alive, and they had enough life for several men. They glared at Sherlock with a maniacal hatred that the boy could feel as a physical force pushing him backwards.

The men standing with him moved so that they were

now surrounding Sherlock and Crowe. They were, with the exception of the giant who was standing directly behind Maupertuis, all armed. They held various medieval weapons – some had swords, some large axes, and some had pikes or halberds. It looked to Sherlock as if the thugs had scavenged the weapons from some storeroom in the cellars of the castle.

Maupertuis was clearly unable to stand unaided, but there he was, with no visible means of support. Sherlock tried to work out what it was that was keeping him up, and then realized with a shock that Maupertuis was held in some kind of complicated sling attached to the body of the man standing behind him. That man was tall, and wide, and heavily muscled, but he was wearing clothes that were a dull grey in colour, dappled in different shades, while the straps attaching Maupertuis to him were of the same colour as the Baron's uniform. A hood made out of the same material covered the man's head, peaking in two horn-like projections above his ears. Two slits had been cut for him to see through. The effect was to make him fade into the background, as if he wasn't there at all. Maupertuis stood out in sharp relief, his head located at the level of his carrier's chest.

Maupertuis's arms and legs were attached to the arms and legs of the giant behind him. When the man stepped forward, at some hidden command, the Baron's legs moved as though they were actually propelling him forward. When the man raised his arm it was as if the Baron were pointing at Sherlock.

'You,' the Baron announced, his voice barely louder than the wind but still coated with venom, 'are not Ambrose Albano.'

Now that the trick had failed, Sherlock peeled off his disguise. 'No,' he said quietly, 'but we have met before.'

'Of course.' Maupertuis's features twisted in rage. 'The boy, Sherlock Holmes. I knew you were at the castle, and I knew you had been interfering with Quintillan's plans and exposing his stupid tricks, but I did not expect you to be here, replacing the psychic. I did not think you would be so foolish!'

'Ah should have guessed that the Paradol Chamber was involved in this . . . farrago of nonsense,' Crowe announced, trying to attract the Baron's rage.

Maupertuis's thin lips formed a sneer. He didn't even glance at Crowe as he said: 'You do not have the wit to understand anything. I know about you, Amyus Thaddeus Crowe. I have studied you, ever since you briefly crossed my path in Farnham two years ago. I always make a point of understanding my enemies. I know your secrets and I know your history, from when you were born to the moment you will die – which will be in a few minutes from now. Your life has not been one of great accomplishment.

Few people will mourn your passing, and fewer still will remember it in fifty years, but the name of Baron Maupertuis will resound through the centuries! That is what happens when—'

Something about the shape that Baron Maupertuis made in conjunction with the giant standing behind him sparked a thought in Sherlock's brain. He followed the glinting connection until it suddenly sparked against a set of other facts that had been lurking in Sherlock's memory.

'The Dark Beast!' he announced, interrupting the Baron's rant. '*You* are the Dark Beast!'

It seemed so obvious, now that he was staring at Maupertuis. The bulky, misshapen outline of the two attached men . . . Sherlock didn't know what it was that people had reported seeing years ago, but he knew now as surely as he knew anything that the recent sightings of the Dark Beast had actually been sightings of Baron Maupertuis strapped to the chest of his massive carrier, glimpsed in darkness, or in mist, or in shadows, moving around the castle and its grounds.

'A stupid legend,' the Baron said, 'but one that was useful to me. It kept the local peasants from investigating, and gave me free rein to move around.'

'To what end?' Crowe asked. 'What exactly is it that you've been doin' here, at Cloon Ard Castle?'

Maupertuis moved his fierce gaze from Sherlock to

Amyus Crowe, and the big American took a small step back as he felt the force of Maupertuis's fanatical willpower. That worried Sherlock. He'd once seen Crowe stare down an enraged bear just by the force of his own will.

'You will die without knowing,' the Baron said. 'That is the smallest of the pleasures I will gain from your deaths.'

'Actually,' Sherlock said, 'it's obvious. It's been obvious all along. The Paradol Chamber is the invisible sixth bidder. You have been in discussion with Sir Shadrach Quintillan. What happened? Was he too honourable, in his own way, or did he think that he would get a better price from an open competition?'

'What Ah don't understand,' Crowe said conversationally, 'is why you wanted him in the first place. Ah mean, the man is a fraud. Young Sherlock here proved that quite conclusively.' He glanced at Sherlock. 'Do you have any theories about that, son? 'Bout why the Paradol Chamber wanted Albano so badly despite the fact he is a fraud?'

For some reason the big American seemed to want to waste time, to keep Maupertuis talking. Actually, if that was the alternative to Maupertuis killing them both, then Sherlock was happy with it.

'I think Albano and Quintillan fooled the Paradol Chamber just like they fooled Herr Holtzbrinck and von Webenau.'

'So Count Shuvalov wasn't fooled?' Crowe nodded. 'He's a smart guy. An' your brother too – he saw through it from the start.'

'Herr Holtzbrinck and von Webenau wanted to believe,' Sherlock pointed out. Fear made him want to talk faster, but he suppressed the impulse. Crowe wanted to slow things down for some reason, and he needed to go along with the plan. Whatever the plan was. 'If I've learned one thing about confidence tricks it's that people who already want to believe are the most easily fooled.'

'Albano's powers are real,' Maupertuis hissed. 'And they will be in the service of the Paradol Chamber when we finally take him! He will serve us, and the dead will tell us their secrets!'

Crowe laughed. 'Now that's just plain stupid. Young Sherlock here showed quite clearly that the séances were just flim-flam!'

'The first two séances, yes.' Maupertuis's thin frame shook with the anger he constantly felt. 'The psychic was weak, and his powers were unreliable. Stupidly, he and Quintillan faked the séances to keep interest going. But the tower and the paintings? How could that have been done, if not through communicating with the dead? How?'

Sherlock stared at Maupertuis for a moment, and what he saw wasn't a psychotic criminal, but a painfully thin

313

human being who, like any human, was capable of being fooled – if he wanted to be. In the same way a man could be fooled, then so could a country, if it took the advice of that man. Someone had once described the Paradol Chamber to him as a country without territory or borders, and it seemed they were just as capable of following bad advice as the German and Austro-Hungarian Empires.

'Who did you lose,' he asked softly, 'that you so desperately want to believe is not dead?'

'It's not another person,' Crowe pointed out softly. 'Look at him. He's hoverin' close to death every moment of his existence. He desperately wants to believe that death ain't the end; that it's possible to survive it, an' keep goin'.'

'It is possible,' Maupertuis shrieked, 'and Ambrose Albano proves it!'

'Then why did you kill Sir Shadrach?' Sherlock stepped forward, towards Maupertuis. He really wanted to know the answer to the question.

'We met with him, in his rooms.' The shift in subject had caught Maupertuis off-guard. His trembling subsided somewhat, and his eyes, which had seemed violent enough to make dry twigs catch fire, became calmer. 'We offered him money, for him and the psychic to work with us – willing volunteers are more use than forced slaves – but he argued. He wanted more money than we were prepared to pay. His death is an annoyance, but one we can live with. Albano is the one with the power.'

'You lost your temper,' Sherlock guessed. 'He went against your will, so you had him killed.' The casual brutality of it shouldn't have surprised him – he knew exactly what the Paradol Chamber was capable of – but, he reminded himself, the Baron was clearly insane. If his desires were different from those of the Paradol Chamber then he would follow those personal desires, even if it put the organization's goals in jeopardy.

'Why hide the body on top of the tower?' Crowe asked. Sherlock suspected that he had already worked the answer out himself, but he was still trying to delay events, to keep Maupertuis from acting. Waiting for something.

'That's easy.' Sherlock shrugged. 'It wasn't Baron Maupertuis who had Sir Shadrach's body displayed on top of the tower. It didn't matter to him whether the body was found or not – he wanted Albano, and was determined to kidnap him when he couldn't buy him.'

'You're not going to tell me it was the spirits of the dead?' Crowe laughed, but it was a forced laugh. There was a lot of tension in it.

'No,' Sherlock confirmed. 'It was the butler, Silman, along with Ambrose Albano. They knew the way the tower worked, so they hid the body on top with the help of the servants. Their aim was to keep the body from being found until they could run the auction themselves.

315

They were probably worried that Niamh would search the castle for her father if he wasn't in his rooms. Albano said as much this morning. He clearly knew something had happened – he was edgy and nervous. He just wanted to get the auction over and done with and get under the protection of whichever international power won. It was sheer bad luck for them that I stumbled across the body while I was exploring.'

'That explains it.' Crowe nodded. 'An' the servin' girl you told me about? The one who was discovered dead, with an expression of terror on her face?'

'She saw something in the castle cellars – probably the Baron, moving around. I presume she had a weak heart and died of fright, but her body had to be moved from the cellars because the Baron and his men were using them as a base. Of course, her shoes came off during the move, but nobody noticed.'

'You did,' Crowe observed.

The giant to whose chest and limbs Maupertuis was strapped shifted slightly, in response to some hidden command, and the Baron's head appeared to tilt to one side, as if he were thinking. 'You claim that the third demonstration was faked as well? Prove it! Tell me how it was done!'

'And you will let us live?' Sherlock asked quietly.

'No,' the Baron said, just as quietly, 'but I will kill

316

you quickly, rather than slowly. Your death has been on my mind for a long while now, and I will not be cheated of it.'

Sherlock briefly explained the way the tides had been used to raise the folly and allow one of the servants – or maybe, it occurred to him, Niamh Quintillan herself – to observe the inside of a castle room that no human being could apparently have seen into. Maupertuis was quiet for a minute or two afterwards, eyes closed. Sherlock was about to say something else when the Baron's eyes snapped open again.

'You are lying,' he said. 'You want the psychic for the British Empire. You cannot have him – he works for the Paradol Chamber now, whether he wants to or not.' His arm, attached to the larger arm behind him, rose up, and his hand made a gesture to the men surrounding them. 'Kill them both now. They have wasted enough of my time.'

'Ah, but do you know why we've wasted it?' Crowe asked.

'To delay the inevitable, of course.'

'No. To delay until this happened!'

Before Sherlock could react, a group of men burst out of the bushes and shrubs that surrounded them. They were dressed in rough jackets and trousers, and most of them were wearing cloth caps and scarves. They were carrying heavy sticks and pitchforks, and they fell on the Paradol Chamber's men like wolves on lambs. Shouts rang out, some of anger and some of pain.

Sherlock was about to ask what the hell was going on, but then he saw Rufus Stone among the ruffians, raising a club and bringing it down hard on an arm that was holding a sword. A scream pierced the air, and the arm bent in a way that arms normally don't.

'How did they know we were here?' Sherlock called to Crowe.

'Ah saw Matty on the back of the other carriage,' Crowe called back. 'Stone must've got him to hide there when the carriage was on its way up to the castle. When he spotted us goin' in the other direction, he must've hopped off to warn Stone, an' the violinist got his bunch of heavies to come up here after us. Ah was holdin' Maupertuis off until they got here.'

'Good thinking!'

A halberd – an axe blade set on a shaft almost as long as Sherlock was tall and with a spear point on top – fell near him, dropped by one of Maupertuis's thugs. He picked it up, ready to use it on anyone who came close. The fight seemed to be self-contained, though, and the Irish contingent was clearly winning.

But where was the Baron?

He had moved – or his giant carrier had moved him –

318

away from the fight. Sherlock caught a glimpse of them heading off into the furze.

He chased after them.

'Sherlock – come back!' Crowe yelled. 'He's not worth it! Whatever plan he had, it's all over now, an' we know the Paradol Chamber killed Sir Shadrach!'

'It'll never be over until he's dead or in custody!' Sherlock shouted back. 'He hates me, and he wants me dead.'

And, he thought, he's *insane*.

Just beyond the nearest bushes, which were higher than Sherlock's head, the undergrowth thinned out. Emerging at a run, Sherlock found himself at the edge of a cliff. He skidded to a halt before he could fall over. He could see the white-capped waves far below. In the distance, off to the left, the battlements of Cloon Ard Castle were visible.

There was no sign of Baron Maupertuis.

Sherlock glanced in all directions, frustrated. A narrow path led away along the edge of the cliff, but he could see for a few hundred yards in each direction before the cliff curved away and there was no sign of anyone. Had the Baron doubled back into the undergrowth? Was he creeping up on Sherlock from behind, even now?

He whirled around, but nobody was there. In the near distance he could still hear the sound of fighting.

Sherlock turned back to the cliff edge and, on instinct,

walked right up to the edge. He gazed straight down.

A narrow ledge led downward, hard against the rock.

Sherlock glanced around one more time, trying to convince himself that this was the best thing to do, and then he followed, still holding the halberd.

Pebbles skittered away from his feet as he moved down the ledge. The wind alternately blew him against the face of the cliff and then tried to pull him away from it. The path was only just wide enough for him to go down; he wondered how Baron Maupertuis's giant carrier could have managed it. *If* he had managed it. *If* he had gone this way at all.

A strong gust of wind nearly plucked him away. He flattened himself against the rock until it abated, the fingers of his free hand clutching at cracks, pebbly projections and tufts of grass. If he fell he would plummet hundreds of feet down to the sea. He would be lucky if he didn't get smashed against the cliff by the wind as he fell. He would be even luckier if he didn't hit a boulder in the sea, or smash himself to pulp on a stretch of sand. His heart raced, and he could feel the prickle of sweat breaking out down his back.

After a moment he forced himself to go on.

The ledge narrowed to a few inches just moments before he spotted the dark hole of a cave in the cliff face. That had to be where Maupertuis had gone. The Baron knew the area around here better than Sherlock – he had been there for longer.

Sherlock moved carefully along the narrowing ledge, chest flat against the rock. He could feel his heels hanging over the long drop down to the sea as he slowly slid one foot after the other: right then left, right then left.

The rock beneath his right foot began to give way.

Sherlock jumped awkwardly, flinging the halberd ahead of him and then landing in the cave mouth. His shoulder hit the floor, sending pain lancing up his arm, but he didn't care. At least he was off the ledge, and safe.

Relatively safe.

He glanced back at the ledge. A stretch of six feet or more had vanished, falling into the sea. Maybe it had been weakened by the passage of the giant carrying Baron Maupertuis. Perhaps millennia of storms and wind had just eaten it away. Whatever the reason, there was no way back for him there.

He looked around warily. In the scant sunlight that penetrated the cave he could only see a few tens of feet inside. There were scuff marks in the dirt – made recently, which indicated that the Baron had indeed come this way – but they vanished into the darkness.

He had to follow. He knew he did.

Screwing his courage up and holding it close, he went deeper into the cave.

321

The darkness swallowed him. He moved carefully, testing each step before he put his full weight down in case there was a sudden drop, or a sharp section of rock. He trailed his fingers against the rough rock of the wall, making sure that he didn't miss any openings, or turns.

A breeze gusted into his face, from deeper inside the cave. There must be a way back to the surface somewhere in there, he thought, otherwise there would be nowhere for it to blow from, but there was a smell of decay on the air. Something had died down here. Perhaps many things, over the years. Perhaps the bones of smugglers littered the floor, and he just couldn't see them in the darkness.

Something thin and brittle crunched beneath his shoe, and he cursed his over-active imagination. It was probably just a twig, he told himself, or the skeleton of a seabird.

Somewhere ahead, the cave had to join up with the others that he had explored – the ones that joined up with the base of the folly and the cellars of the castle. All the caves in the cliff were probably connected, in some great warren of tunnels, like a huge anthill.

Which only meant, he thought, that he could wander down here for days, maybe weeks, before he died of starvation and dehydration.

No, this was stupid, he told himself. Where there was a breeze, there was a way out. He just had to follow the breeze.

And hope it wasn't coming out of a crack no wider than his hand.

Up ahead, something made a sound.

Sherlock froze.

His heart hammered in his chest, and he could feel the breath rasping in his throat. Surely whoever was there could hear them too? If it was a person. His mind flashed back to the blind albino dogs that he had seen in the sewers beneath the streets of Moscow. What kinds of things might be in here? Wild boar that hadn't seen the sun for generations, and had adapted to life in total darkness? Or perhaps something stranger, something that no human had ever seen and lived to tell about?

He took a deep breath. This was getting stupid. He was panicking over nothing. It was just a sound.

But something had to have made that sound.

After a few minutes of silence, and trying to keep his breath and his heartbeat under control, Sherlock started to move again. Whatever had made the sound was either an illusion, had gone, or was standing in the darkness waiting for him. Whatever the explanation, he couldn't delay any longer. He had to move.

He inched forward as quietly as he could. Nothing leaped out at him from the darkness, and with each step he felt slightly more relieved.

His eyes had become completely accustomed to the

323

dark now, so when a faint glow shone around a bend in the tunnel ahead it hit his eyes like a lantern pointed directly into them. He had to wait for a few minutes for his eyes to get used to the idea of light again before he could move towards it.

The light intensified as he went further. It was a warm, buttery illumination that caused the projections in the rocky walls to cast long shadows towards him, like clutching fingers. He moved cautiously towards the bend and poked his head around to see what was there.

It was, of course, another tunnel, but at least this one was illuminated by a lantern set on a wooden crate.

By the light of the lantern, Sherlock could see a body lying on the tunnel floor. It was thin, and twisted, and it looked like the skeleton of some long-ago smuggler who had died down there and been left to rot.

It was the body of Baron Maupertuis.

Cautiously, Sherlock moved closer, worried that it might be some kind of trick, but by the time he was staring down at the grotesque corpse it was obvious that the Baron was dead. The straps that had held him on to his giant carrier were draped over him like ribbons. His eyes were open, but the force of his maniacal willpower was gone. All the energy that had kept him alive had ebbed away now, leaving him looking like a bundle of sticks that had been carelessly dropped in a pile.

'He died while I was carrying him,' a deep voice said, echoing along the tunnel. 'I didn't even notice for a while. He always was just one step away from death, and it was only his willpower that kept him going. Maybe his heart gave out, or maybe I jogged him too much and his neck snapped. At least he's at rest now, and at least that means I can finally take care of you, you interfering whelp!'

'Mr Kyte,' Sherlock said softly. 'I rather thought it might be you under that hood.'

CHAPTER SIXTEEN

Sherlock glanced further along the tunnel. Up ahead, blocking the light from another lantern like a boulder blocking a stream so that the water spilt around it, was the figure of a large man. A very large man. Sherlock couldn't see his face, but he recognized the voice. He had last seen the man briefly on a railway station platform as he was heading up towards Edinburgh almost two years ago, and before that driving a carriage in Moscow. His name was Kyte, and he was an agent of the Paradol Chamber.

'A little beneath your station, isn't it, carrying a man like the Baron around?' Sherlock asked, straightening up. 'It's a bit like carrying luggage, which makes you just a porter.'

'The Baron made the mistake of actually listening to you,' Kyte said. He stepped forward, and the light from the lantern beside the Baron's body illuminated his ruddy face and his massive red beard. They had been hidden beneath the hood that he had been wearing outside, but he had thrown that away now. He had also thrown away the grey clothing that he had been wearing, and was now clad in black trousers and a black shirt with the sleeves rolled up. Some kind of leather cuffs were attached to his forearms, stretching from wrists to elbows. His arms were enormous, and his hands were the size of spades.

'We don't have to do this,' Sherlock said.

'Oh, but we do. You've got in our way too many times, young Holmes. There has to be a reckoning.'

Kyte knocked his wrists together, and twin blades sprang out of the cuffs strapped to his forearms. They made a deadly *click-click* sound as they locked into place. They extended past his hands, which he clenched to keep them out of the way of the blades. In the guttering light of the lanterns, they seemed to glow like gold.

Sherlock braced himself: right leg back, left leg forward, halberd held ready in both hands.

Kyte rushed at Sherlock, whirling his blades in front of his chest as he ran.

Sherlock took a step back and jabbed the halberd at Kyte's face. Kyte ducked to his right, still moving forward, using his blades to push the axe out of the way. Sherlock flung himself in the opposite direction, pressing himself against the wall of the tunnel. As Kyte thundered past, Sherlock swung the halberd around and jabbed the long shaft between Kyte's legs. As his legs came together, they clamped on the shaft, almost wrenching it out of Sherlock's grip but sending Kyte stumbling forward, off-balance. Sherlock pulled the halberd back and turned it to

327

jab the spear-point at Kyte, but despite his bulk the man had rolled gymnastically out of the way and was springing to his feet. He turned, snarling, and barrelled straight for Sherlock again, this time with the blades held straight out in front of him like horns on a charging bull.

Holding the halberd two-handed, Sherlock desperately scythed the blade diagonally down from his right shoulder to his left knee. Kyte sprang backwards to avoid being slashed. There were two curved projections behind the blade – probably used to hook riders and pull them from their horses, Sherlock realized – and he managed to lunge forward and entangle one of them in Kyte's shirt sleeve. He pulled the halberd back, jerking Kyte off balance, but Kyte twisted, and the blade attached to his right arm slid under the shaft of the halberd, ripping straight through Sherlock's shirt and drawing a line of fiery agony along his ribs.

He felt blood trickle down from the wound as he pulled away rapidly, scraping his back against the tunnel wall.

Kyte's lips were twisted in fury, and his eyes blazed in the same fanatical way that Maupertuis's had, but he seemed to have no interest in talking. He just wanted to remove Sherlock's head from his body. Drawing back and rearing up to his full height, he lashed out at Sherlock with one blade after another, like a boxer raining punches at his opponent but with swords instead of fists. Sherlock desperately backed away, parrying the blows with his halberd, wishing that fate had given him something less clumsy than the long and heavy weapon.

His foot caught on a rock projecting from the tunnel floor, and he stumbled backwards. Kyte was on him in a flash, right arm extended like a spear. Sherlock rolled sideways and the blade sparked as it hit the rock that had, just moments before, been beneath him. He scrabbled backwards on hands and feet, still somehow holding on to the halberd, hearing it clatter against the tunnel floor. Kyte followed, lunging time after time with his blades but just missing Sherlock as the boy jerked from side to side.

Glancing quickly over his shoulder to make sure he wasn't going to bump into anything that might halt his progress, Sherlock noticed the lantern that had been silhouetting Kyte earlier. Like the previous one, it was balanced on an old crate. Without thinking it through, Sherlock reached out over his head with the halberd and caught its handle with one of the curved spikes on the back of the axe blade. He jerked it hard, pulling it over the top of his body and flinging it towards Kyte.

The big man jumped backwards, but too late. Instead of hitting him, the lantern smashed against the tunnel wall, sending oil splattering over him. The wick, still alight, caught his shirt.

And set it alight.

329

Flames flashed across Kyte's chest and beard. Sherlock heard the hairs crackling as they burned. A horrible smell filled the tunnel. Kyte flapped at the flames with his hands, trying to put them out, but the blades came perilously close to his eyes and he had to stop. Instead, he threw himself to the tunnel floor and rolled around, using the sand and the dirt that had drifted in over the years to smother the fire.

Sherlock rolled over, pushed himself to his feet and ran down the tunnel in the opposite direction to the cave mouth. The halberd in his hands seemed heavier than ever, dragging him down, but he wasn't going to abandon it now. Lanterns attached to hooks in the walls now lit his way. Presumably Maupertuis's thugs had kept them going, for their own convenience. Either that, or smugglers were still operating there, and Sherlock had a feeling that the Paradol Chamber would have cleared them all out. Or paid them off.

The tunnel twisted and turned, but he kept pounding away. He thought he could hear Kyte's heavy footsteps behind him, but that might just have been the pounding of his heart. He wasn't going to stop to find out. He wasn't even going to look over his shoulder, just in case he stumbled and fell again. If he was caught, then it was all over. He was dead.

If Kyte was still chasing him.

Dark openings started appearing in the tunnel walls: caves leading off in other directions, deeper into the cliffs, or towards the beach. He was so tired and so disoriented that he couldn't tell. The breeze was still in his face, though, so he kept following the main tunnel.

It came to an abrupt end, far ahead, in a curved wall of dark stone, just like the one he had seen a few days before. Patches of moss were spread across the tunnel walls and ground in front of it, like the marks of some terrible disease.

He kept running, but there were no tunnel openings off to either side between him and the wall. He could turn around, he supposed, and go back, but he was worried that Kyte was only a few yards behind him, blades extended towards his back.

He knew where he was. The wall was the wall of the pumice-stone folly, continuing underground. He'd seen it from the other side, when he investigated the cellars beneath the castle.

He heard a grating noise behind him. It was the sound of Kyte's blades banging against the tunnel wall as he ran, arms swinging wildly. There really was no way back, but there was no way forward either.

His frantic gaze caught sight of something – a darker patch on the wall of the folly, half disappeared beneath the floor of the tunnel – one of the window openings. It got smaller as he watched. The folly was actually sinking into the ground! Somehow, someone was operating it!

He knew what he had to do.

Still holding the halberd, he raced towards the wall, so fast that if he ran into it he would knock himself out. Breathing was like inhaling fire. In some strange optical illusion caused by tiredness and pain, the door at the far end seemed to be receding rather than getting closer. He forced himself to a final burst of speed, feet thudding into the patches of moss and squishing them before he could slip on them.

This was just like the race to the tower door against Niamh, up on the castle battlements. In his head he started to count down ten seconds again.

When he got to *eight*, and the dark shape of the window had reduced to a third of its normal size, he leaped and, when he landed, let his feet skid on the moss, shooting him towards the gap, the halberd clutched to his chest with its shaft running down to his knees and the blade dangerously close to his face. He slipped over, taking the impact on his shoulder, and started sliding on his back. His feet passed through the gap and inside the tower room, and for a terrible moment he thought his hips or his chest would stick and the descending folly would cut him in half, but he grabbed the edges of the tower window with both hands and pulled himself through, falling into the tiny circular room. His back hit the floor hard, knocking the wind out of him for the second time in three seconds. He twisted to look at the gap, which was now no bigger than a plank of wood. A dog would have problems squeezing through. As he watched, the gap narrowed to the height of a clenched fist, then a wooden ruler, then . . .

A sharp blade slid through the gap, heading straight for his right eye.

It stopped an inch away, the hand behind it – Kyte's hand – having hit the top of the window outside. The tower continued to drop, and with an echoing *chink* the blade snapped at the far end, and fell into the room with him.

He was alone, in total darkness.

He knew he couldn't afford to waste time recovering. He seemed to remember that the next set of windows were set at right angles to these, meaning that there was likely to be another set of corridors coming in from the sides, but eventually another window would line up with the tunnel that Kyte was standing in, and he would enter the tower. There were gaps in the floors between the tower rooms – he had used the gaps the day before in order to climb up to the top. He wasn't sure if Kyte would be able to squeeze through the gaps, but he wasn't going to wait around to find out. He had to get moving.

Down.

Before the thought could even complete itself he was scrabbling across the invisible floor, looking for the hole. He found it by almost falling in, then turned around, threw the halberd through and heard it clatter on the stone floor below, slipped his legs through and slid down into the next room, and then the next, and the next.

The fourth room had no hole in the floor, and it took him a moment to see that there was a faint light coming through the two windows. He crossed to the one opposite the one he had slid through, and looked out . . .

Into a circular natural cavern, illuminated by beams of diagonal light that had filtered their way through cracks in the rock from the surface.

He climbed out of the window, and on to a narrow, circular platform of pumice stone on which the tower had been built. The platform floated on a calm underground lake of sea water. The beams of faint sunlight reflected off the surface of the lake and cast rippling turquoise shadows across the rock. Cave mouths around the edge of the cavern had been plugged with thick doors of wood. The doors could be pulled up or lowered using ropes that led up and vanished inside holes that had been cut into the roof of the cavern. These must be the dams that he had theorized about earlier. By raising or lowering them, the water entering the cavern from the sea could be contained or released, raising or lowering the level of the lake and thus raising or lowering the folly.

Several of the doors had already been raised, and Sherlock could see that water was pouring out of the lake and into the caves, where presumably it would rejoin the sea. Someone, high above, had obviously decided to lower the tower. He wondered who. It seemed like an odd time to do it, given that Quintillan and Maupertuis were dead, the Baron's thugs were presumably in custody, and Mr Kyte was here, with Sherlock. Who else was there?

He gazed up in wonder, to where the folly was still dropping out of a perfectly circular hole in the ceiling of the cavern with only inches to spare around its circumference. How that hole had been created he would probably never know. It was a miracle of engineering. The whole thing was a miracle – an unseen, unsung wonder of the world hidden beneath the soil and rock of Ireland.

Before he could marvel too much at the work that had gone into creating the tower, something fell from a higher window and hit the surface of the lake, entering with an almighty *splash!*

Mr Kyte, it appeared, had given up on trying to get through the holes in the floors of the tower rooms and had dived from one of the windows.

Sherlock backed away from the edge of the platform. He still had the halberd, and he clutched it in both hands now, holding it in front of him like a protective barrier. Not that it was going to be much use against the unstoppable force that was Mr Kyte.

He was tired. No, he was exhausted. He had used up all his reserves of energy, and he knew that he couldn't fight any more. There was nothing left to fight with.

No, he told himself. If you give up, you die. If you want to see Virginia again, if you want to see Matty, and Rufus Stone, and Mr Crowe, and Mycroft, then you *will* fight. Somehow you will find the energy.

He straightened his shoulders, brought the halberd up so that it was parallel to the ground, and waited.

He could hear splashing from the lake as Mr Kyte swam back to the pumice platform.

Pumice. Something in his brain had latched on to the word 'pumice' and wouldn't let go.

Pumice. It was less dense than water, thanks to the minute holes filled with air that ran through it, and so it floated. It was brittle, fragile. He still had shards of it in his pocket.

Brittle. Fragile. *That* was it!

He only had a few seconds to act before Mr Kyte swam to the edge of the platform.

Whirling around, he grabbed the halberd by the axe head and used the spear point at the top of the wooden shaft to jab at a pumice block in the tower – one that was about chest height. The tip of the spear began to gouge out splinters of pumice. He kept at it, hacking away as fast as he could.

He glanced over his shoulder desperately. A large hand appeared on the edge of the platform, and then another. They rested there for a moment, as if gathering their strength.

Sherlock redoubled his efforts. He had carved a hole – a tube – going deep into the pumice-stone block. Fortunately he hadn't gone deep enough to go through to the other side. That would have ruined things.

Glancing over his shoulder again, he saw the top of Mr Kyte's head appear above the edge of the platform.

Sherlock only had a few seconds.

He turned the halberd around and shoved the far end of the wooden staff into the hole. It hung there at chest height, spear end pointed outward, bending slightly with the weight of the axe head.

Sherlock moved in front of the halberd. He stood, facing the place where Mr Kyte was hauling himself out of the underground lake, with the point of the spear pressing into his back.

This was going to require split-second timing, otherwise he was going to run himself through with his own weapon.

Shaking, partly with cold and partly with fear, he waited.

Mr Kyte pulled himself on to the platform and straightened up to his full, bear-like height. His red hair was plastered down over his scalded head and his shoulders. His eyes were like little red sparks in the twisted mask of his face.

He had retracted the remaining blade attached to his arm, but with a quick knocking together of his wrists he activated the spring mechanism and the blade slid out to its full, lethal length.

'There are countries in this world that have caused us less trouble than you,' he said in a deep, rumbling tone. 'But now, finally, there is nowhere else to run. Just accept your death, Sherlock Holmes.'

With that, he began to run at Sherlock, blade extended before him. His mouth opened and he howled a deep, guttural war cry, obviously intending to pin Sherlock against the tower, flattening him and running him through at the same time.

Just before the tip of the blade touched his chest, Sherlock dropped to the ground and rolled beneath the horizontal halberd.

Mr Kyte, with his unstoppable momentum, ran straight on to the point of the spear. It embedded itself deep in his chest. Only the axe head and the two curved horns on the other side stopped him.

Sherlock stood up shakily. Mr Kyte's head turned, and

his eyes stared deep into Sherlock's soul. There was rage in them, but there was also surprise, and there was an increasing sadness.

'The only person who decides when I die is me,' Sherlock said quietly.

Mr Kyte opened his mouth to answer, but all that came out was a thin trickle of blood that mixed with the red of his burned beard. One moment he was alive, a vital force in the world, and the next moment he was dead – nothing but a slab of unresponsive, unfeeling flesh.

It took Sherlock a full half-hour before he felt able to move, and a half-hour more for him to laboriously climb up through the darkened rooms of the folly, floor after floor. Eventually one of the windows in the rooms opened out into fresh air and bright sunshine. He climbed out into the vividly green Irish countryside, almost falling, to find Mycroft, Rufus Stone, Matty, Amyus Crowe and Virginia standing waiting for him. Virginia took a step forward, hand to her mouth, but stopped before she reached him.

'You took your time,' Mycroft said. His tone was acerbic, but Sherlock could see concern and relief in his eyes. 'Do I take it from your leisurely arrival that Mr Kyte has been dealt with?'

'You know the way that some men collect butterflies, pinned to cardboard?' Sherlock asked wearily.

'Yes. Why?'

'Because I think I've just started a collection of my own.'

'Ah.' Mycroft nodded. 'The lesser spotted criminal, I see. There is obviously a whole story behind that, and one which I look forward to hearing – over dinner.'

'Who was responsible for lowering the tower?' Sherlock asked.

'That was Niamh Quintillan. When she knew that you had gone into the caves, and that the ledge had crumbled behind you, she realized that your only way out was for her to move the tower so that a window was aligned with the tunnel along which you were running.' He paused. 'She knew all about the tower, and how to operate it. She was much more a part of her father's plans than perhaps we had thought. She was, by the way, very concerned about your safety.'

'What will happen to her?'

Mycroft shrugged. 'She was party to a rather large act of fraud. It is entirely a matter for the Irish authorities to deal with, although there are three Emperors, an Empress and a President who might wish to influence the result. Her act in saving your life will count in her favour.'

'And what now?' Sherlock asked. He knew that he should feel elated at his survival, but he just felt tired, and sad.

'What do you want to happen now?' Mycroft asked.

340

Instead of answering, Sherlock walked across to where Virginia was standing watching him. She opened her mouth to speak, but he put a finger on her lips to stop her. Taking his finger away, he moved forward, slipped his arms around her, and kissed her.

After what might have been a few seconds or a few minutes – he wasn't sure – he broke off the kiss and moved back. He looked at Matty, who was gazing at him with a distinctly unimpressed look on his face.

'Let's go home,' he said.

AUTHOR'S NOTE

Usually, with these Young Sherlock Holmes books, I write a little afterword going through some of the research material that I gathered while putting them together (it's really just a way of proving that I didn't make it all up). The problem with *Knife Edge*, of course, is that it's not set against a particular set of historical events, it doesn't include any 'real' historical characters and it's not set in a particularly foreign location (well, not if you're British, anyway – if you're living in the Republic of Korea then Ireland is probably as unusual as the surface of Mars). This was a deliberate decision on my part. Having written five books in a row that placed Sherlock against a backdrop of real events, realistically described journeys and (some) real people, I thought it was probably about time to set something in a more 'invented' location and to let him spend some time there rather than keep moving around. So although Galway is real and I spent several very pleasant days there soaking up the atmosphere, I have taken several liberties with its geography. There is no castle with the same name or the same layout as the one in this book, and I may have underestimated slightly the distance between

343

the town and the nearest set of high cliffs. If any of you are reading this in or around Galway (hello, Dubray Books!) then I hope you will forgive me. There is, sadly, no legend of a Dark Beast in or around Galway either. That would belong more properly in my other series of books – Lost Worlds.

A great deal of this book involves spiritualism – the belief that it is possible to contact the dead. Victorian England went through quite a long and intense flirtation with spiritualism during the time that Sherlock Holmes is supposed to have been alive, probably because the period between around 1850 and 1900 marks the time at which the British started to move away from supernatural explanations for things happening and towards scientific ones. Spiritualism is, at its core, a pseudoscientific way of getting in touch with supernatural entities, so it hits both buttons at once. The trouble was that a large number of clever confidence tricksters took advantage of this flirtation, using tricks much like the ones Ambrose Albano and Sir Shadrach Quintillan use in this book, and which are described brilliantly in the book *Servants of the Supernatural: The Night Side of the Victorian Mind* by Antonio Melechi (Random House, 2009). I am not going to tread on anyone's beliefs by saying whether or not I personally believe that the dead can be engaged in conversation, but Sherlock in this book maintains a properly sceptical attitude. In fact, in the short Sherlock Holmes story 'The Sussex Vampire' (which does not include real vampires), Arthur Conan Doyle had Holmes say, 'The world is big enough for us. No ghosts need apply.'

Having said that, Arthur Conan Doyle himself developed a strong interest in spiritualism and communication with the dead in his later life. He even published a book entitled *The History of Spiritualism* in 1926. This belief was probably because he lost a brother and a son in the First World War, and somehow could not let go of their memories. Despite his highly rational upbringing and training as a doctor, he somehow failed to bring his sharply logical mind to bear on some of the obvious frauds and cheats who pretended to be mediums, and who fleeced gullible and grieving members of the public of their money.

The magic tricks and techniques that Sherlock learns from Ambrose Albano in Chapter Twelve are, by the way, all real. The Magic Circle frowns on having these things revealed, but there are books out there that will take you through the basics of close-up magic. The one I have found particularly useful is *The Ultimate Compendium of Magic Tricks* by Nicholas Einhorn (Hermes House, 2009). Do try these tricks at home. They won't make you into an instant magician – you'll need countless hours of practice

345

for that – but the book is fully illustrated with thousands of photographs and it will show you the different ways to pre-prepare your tricks and to misdirect the audience's attention while you are performing them. After that, it's up to you.

And that about wraps it up. I've had a great deal of fun writing this book – probably more than on all the previous ones. Partly that's because, as I said earlier, it's all set in one location, which means the characters (and the author!) can spend time getting to know the place without fear of suddenly being whisked off in a steam-train, a paddle steamer or a horse-drawn carriage to somewhere else, but partly (if I am being honest) because it reminds me of all Enid Blyton's The Famous Five books I used to read as a kid, which were full of caves, castles and smugglers. Alas, real life isn't.

Until next time . . .

Andrew Lane